# Without Paradise

*Kenneth Sean Campbell*

iUniverse, Inc.
New York  Bloomington

# Without Paradise

iUniverse books may be ordered through booksellers or by contacting:

iUniverse
1663 Liberty Drive
Bloomington, IN 47403
www.iuniverse.com
1-800-Authors (1-800-288-4677)

ISBN: 978-0-595-52649-9 (pbk)
ISBN: 978-0-595-62702-8 (ebk)

Printed in the United States of America

iUniverse Rev. 10/23/08

# *Acknowledgments*

There are people who have supported me all my life. Without them, this book would not exist and the world would have been a sadder and lonelier place. So thank you Walter Atkinson, Ken Shields, Ron Templeton and the perfectly named Molly Loving.

And In *Memoriam*: Mother, Daddy and Julia. Daniel Joslin, Ron Sullivan, Fred White and Tom Lilly.

And there were those wonderful people who supported me while I was writing the book. Thank you Mark Drolette, John Schupay, Lee Johnson, Marie Kiene and Kathy Halstead.

And Rick, you inspire me every day.

This is for you, dood
Everything

The paradise of preambivalent harmony...is unattainable. But the experience of one's own truth, and the postambivalent knowledge of it, makes it possible to return to one's own world of feelings at an adult level—without paradise, but with the ability to mourn.

The Drama of the Gifted Child
Alice Miller

# Chapter 1

Charlie Morgan was 59 years old when it all began. Now that's old for a beginning, but this is the fact: Charlie was 59 years old when he fell in love for the first time. That doesn't mean there had not been skirmishes and minor battles with love, but not Pearl Harbor, not Hiroshima. He had had some very pleasant and even passionate relationships and when they were over, there had only been a sense of relief or mild, prodding disappointment.

There had been a five year relationship with Jim. Yet the kind of love he felt for Jim (and still did) is the family kind of love. It's a kind of love that all gay men understand and many heterosexuals don't. We are betrayed by our home towns, our churches and institutions and often our families. So we create a family of choice. It's your college roommate or boyfriends from your youth who become your best friends. They are brothers but more than brothers. They know you better than anyone. You are bonded and it's impossible to say or do anything that would break that bond. Gay men know about betrayal which means that we know about loyalty and the importance of it. Jim was loyalty for Charlie and Charlie loved him and was grateful.

There had been Kevin and John and Barry and Dan. A year here; six months there. They were all good men, but it wasn't love. No one got deeply involved and no one got hurt. It was sex and companionship and a connection of sorts in a world where connections, even shallow ones, are rare. In the end, they had parted without any misery and remained casual friends for a while before drifting away. Charlie didn't ever fall. He just moved on. It wasn't like you see in those Julia Roberts movies. This was more like a Doris Roberts movie.

After Dan, Charlie rested for a few years. He needed it. He needed to be alone and it was a good alone. It was solid and comfortable and quiet. It was filled with books and good films enjoyed in grateful solitude or with a very small group of friends kept at a polite distance. It worked and it didn't hurt. Charlie saw no reason for this to ever change. Love, it seemed to him, was going to pass him by. And it was OK. He had a lot of everything else. He looked back on his life and was not disappointed. There was interesting work, some good memories and enough money to satisfy most of his itches, if not all. The song "But Not For Me" seemed wistfully true for Charlie. Sad, but not tragic. Wistful is the right word.

The reality of Charlie belies this somewhat lonely romantic resume. He was a happy, handsome man and, even at nearly 60, could still claim cute, although in a more fragile way now. He was in good shape, worked out every day and was on a first name basis with a good dermatologist. He was short and slight, which always seemed to give him an added youthfulness even if youth itself was a thing of the past. And his hair, although silver, was shiny and clipped into one of those scruffy, modern cuts.

Then January 29 happened. It was dentist day. Even though he had lived in Sacramento for years, he kept his dentist in San Francisco. It was a good excuse to go into the City and gave him a chance to dress up a little bit for Charlie was a true clothes horse. Today he chose brown suede boots, Levis, a gray cashmere turtleneck and a brown pinstripe blazer from Banana Republic. When he looked in the mirror, he approved and that made him feel good about himself. He grabbed his briefcase, threw in a book for good measure, and headed for the train station. Charlie's routine was to find a small booth in the cafe car where he could spread out, have coffee and a bagel and read or work on the computer during the trip. But mostly he just looked out the window. No matter how many times he had taken this trip, the view seemed always fresh. Was that a new farm house? Had that mountain always been there? It always fascinated him to watch the geography change so quickly as the train moved from the flat farmland of the Central Valley to the gentle mountains and bay shore closer to San Francisco. It cooled off, too, as one got closer to the ocean and the air smelled fresher, crisper. Charlie remembered having to adjust to the Bay Area climate when he moved there from the land-locked, bayou country of Northeast Texas. His skin had itched at first, but soon the itching stopped and the ocean began to soothe him. That had been twenty-five years ago!

But this day in January, he settled in for the trip comfortable in the predictability and sameness of the day. A regular old January 29th in the Central Valley of California, an area used to seismic shifts. This was not going to be his usual trip to the city. It would turn out to be one of the turning points of his life: a seismic shift of the heart.

#

Ben McSwain was not used to this. Going to the train station and the trip to San Francisco rattled him. Ordinarily, he would get up, go to the office, see patients, work hard and go home to take care of the kids, but the hospital needed someone to sign for the deaf and Ben had volunteered. That meant going into San Francisco every Thursday for the next ten weeks for a class in American Sign Language. His concentration was off and his safety zone had been breached.

Many things were changing in his life. Now that the kids were on their own, he found himself forced to spend more time alone. Even though he worked ten to twelve hours a day and was always on call, he was beginning to be more aware of himself. It had been years since Ben had thought about his own life, his own needs. It seemed impossible that Lynette had been gone for five years now. His heart was ready to thaw. He worked hard, he kept his eyes straight ahead and didn't look back. He was a good man, handsome, healthy and serious. His life had not been frivolous. It had been filled with hard work, some tragedy and disappointments and an abiding faith in God that everything would be all right. He didn't think about much else. It was easier not to, but somewhere on the periphery of his vision, there was a huge chasm in his life. He knew if he looked he might fall and never come out. So he looked straight ahead, neither right nor left, those clear, kind blue eyes showing only a hint of fear of the unknown.

Ben dressed quickly and efficiently. He had always enjoyed being neat and clean and well groomed. He hadn't the time or money to spend on himself the last few years of providing for the kids, but he had a natural, easy grace and style. He had on a khaki blazer he had found on sale and clean, freshly pressed jeans. A white button down shirt and driving mocs finished the look. He felt good about himself as he headed for the train station in Davis.

It seemed odd not to be going to the hospital to his job. A whole day to not think about patients and work. What would occupy his thoughts instead? Somewhere in the recesses of his heart he longed for something to happen, an adventure of some kind that would take him out of his ordinary life. Today was his forty-sixth birthday. Perhaps there would be a birthday surprise.

# Chapter 2

The train pulled out of the station on time in Sacramento. Charlie got a cup of coffee, a bagel and the San Francisco Chronicle. He rarely read a paper anymore, except online, but this was part of his ritual, so he settled into his small booth to enjoy the paper and the trip.

It was not long before the train pulled into Davis, the first stop along the corridor. Davis is a college town and usually only a handful of students and teachers get on here. Most of them disembark at Berkeley as the train makes an easy commute between the two universities. Small and somewhat "artistic" in design, the station is fitting for the progressive, energetic reputation of Davis. Charlie enjoyed looking out the window at the people boarding. The sun was out now and it was a crisp California winter day that made one instantly forget how dreary and gray and wet the valley can be this time of year. Charlie noticed a handsome man climbing onto the train and his healthy libido registered admiration. After he muttered "wow" under his breath, he returned to his paper and his plans for the day.

The train started up again and a few of the new passengers queued up for coffee in the cafe car. With pleasure, Charlie noted that one of them was the handsome man he had seen a moment earlier. He was probably younger than Charlie, but about the same size, 5' 8" or so and slim. He had on jeans and a khaki blazer. It suited him for his coloring was vivid and healthy and he didn t need the distraction of bright clothing. He had brown hair with a salt shaker full of gray and a tan that looked like it had been earned honestly. But it was the eyes that made this man special. They were the color of the Sonoma County sky in spring. This was a California boy! There was also something else, something guarded in those eyes. He realized that he was staring and looked away quickly, not wanting to get caught.

As he averted his gaze, something got in his eye. Perhaps a cinder from the tracks or maybe just something in the air, but it felt like shards of glass. The pain was intense and his eye began watering immediately. He reached for a napkin and realizing that he didn't have one, quickly headed to the cafe steward's window. As he stumbled forward, the man he had been watching touched his sleeve.

"Is there something wrong?" the man asked, his voice and face showing genuine concern.

"I've gotten something in my eye and, man, does it hurt. I was going to get a napkin to try to get it out."

The young man reached into his pocket and pulled out a clean handkerchief. "Here, let me help. I'm a nurse. Let's move closer to the light so I can see better."

He led Charlie gently over to a window and cupped his cheek in his hand. He held Charlie's head back, pulled down his eyelid and flicked the handkerchief quickly. Immediately, the irritation in Charlie's eye was gone.

"Oh wow, thanks so much. You have no idea how excruciating that was!"

"Easy problem to fix." The stranger smiled slightly.

"Well, nevertheless I'm grateful for your kindness and I'm lucky that you were here. Will you let me buy you a cup of coffee? " Charlie was flirting a little.

"That's not necessary, really. I was just going to have some juice." The stranger was polite but guarded.

"Then let me buy your juice. It's the least I can do for a good Samaritan." Charlie smiled.

Their eyes met and Ben smiled for the first time. Charlie felt a small explosion in his heart. It was a beautiful smile and somehow familiar. Instantly, he felt a bond with his rescuer.

"Uh, thanks. That would be nice." Ben blushed slightly, unused to this kind of attention from someone else. When he looked this man in the eye something had happened. He had felt a catch in his throat and had to stop himself from uttering a gasp. This had never happened to him before and he didn't know how to react. He felt as if they had known each other for a very long time.

Charlie ordered the juice and when it came, turned and gave it to the handsome man. "I'm Charlie Morgan." He offered his hand.

"Ben McSwain." Charlie took Ben's hand and was surprised how warm it was.

"Uh, would you like to join me? I was just reading the paper but I would prefer some company."

Quickly, Ben recovered his guarded demeanor. That smile vanished and his eyes clouded over. "Well, I've brought some work to do on the train and I should attend to that." He hesitated when he saw the disappointment in Charlie's eyes, "But I'll sit with you for a little while."

The went back to the small booth and sat on opposite sides. Suddenly they just smiled at each other, like there was a secret they shared that no one else knew. Charlie was feeling lust, but something else, too. Ben had no idea what was happening. He felt confused and almost "out of body." Charlie finally broke the spell, "Do you work in the City?"

Ben laughed, "Oh no! In fact, I rarely go to San Francisco. This is very unusual for me. I'm taking a class in ASL once a week for the next ten weeks."

"ASL? I'm sorry, I'm not familiar…"

"Oh, right, American Sign Language. Our hospital needs someone with those skills. I used to do signing at my church, but I need this course to be state certified, which is required by the hospital. You know how bureaucracy works!"

"I do indeed. Living in Sacramento has opened my eyes to the wonderful world of bureaucracy!"

"Oh, do you work in government?"

"Oh Lord, no. I couldn't play that game if I had to. I have a bunny slipper job." Charlie smiled impishly at Ben.

"A bunny slipper job?"

"I'm self employed. I edit books, ghost write and do some writing on my own. I freelance through an agency in Los Angeles. I'm not famous or rich, but I get by." Charlie was being modest. He was really quite successful in his field, "I get to work at home in my bunny slippers. It's a bunny slipper job."

Ben smiled with delight. He looked like a little kid. "I've never heard anyone talk like that before. I've also never known anyone who was a writer or did anything like that."

"Well, Mr. McSwain, in the long run, it's no different from any other job. You get up and you go to work and you do whatever they are paying you to do. I'm lucky. I love what they pay me to do. That may be the only difference from most people."

"I do too… love what I do, I mean."

"You mentioned you were a nurse. So I work in bunny slippers and you get to work in pajamas. How different is your job from mine really?" Charlie's eyes twinkled.

Ben McSwain laughed out loud. It was a sharp, deep bark and very genuine. No one would fake a laugh like that. "Well, I guess you're right. My scrubs are like pajamas, aren't they? And truthfully? The shoes I wear are as close to slippers as they will allow. So, guilty as charged."

Charlie held up his coffee cup, "A toast to bunny slippers and pajamas!" Ben tipped his cup to Charlie and they both sipped at their drinks, their eyes on each other and never wavering. It was the second time this morning that that feeling passed between them. It was the seismic shift again.

Ben averted his eyes. He looked at his watch. "I left my stuff in the next car. I hope it's OK."

"This is a pretty relaxed place. I don't think there are many robberies on here, but you might want to go get them, just to be on the safe side." Charlie was making more room in the booth for Ben's things.

"I really think I should probably go, Mr. Morgan. I've still got some work to do before we get to San Francisco. It's been a real pleasure talking with you. I haven't enjoyed myself like this in a long time. I really mean that."

"Then you have to call me Charlie...Ben, is it?" Charlie reached for his wallet and took out a personal card. "Here's my name, number, etc. I really enjoyed it, too. Let's do it again some time. Maybe next Thursday?"

"Uh, sure, Charlie. That would be fine. I'll be on the train every Thursday for the next ten weeks. I'll look forward to it. Thanks for the card. Have a great day, OK?" They both stood and shook hands again. There was a reluctance about letting go on both sides and Ben seemed embarrassed.

With that, he turned and left the cafe car. He was gone and Charlie was left feeling a bit alone. The other man's presence had brought warmth and comfort. Charlie was definitely attracted to him, but there was something more. Charlie had just felt "right" for that time he was in Ben's presence.

He sat back down in his booth and resumed reading the paper, but it was hard to concentrate for the rest of the trip. His mind wandered back to that smile.

Ben returned to his seat in the car in front of the cafe. He sat down and looked out the window. The scene was changing rapidly as they got closer to San Francisco. The lush, misty mountains in the distance were surprising to Ben who was used to the flat, safe farmland of home. He still felt Charlie's hand in his and it was a warm feeling. He seemed like a good guy. Ben could use a friend. Why didn't he stay? What was he afraid of? This kind of self questioning was unusual for Ben. It made him uncomfortable. He shook off his thoughts and concentrated on the material he had brought with him. He was determined to make good use of the time on the train and the class that he was taking. He burrowed into the books, but Charlie was lurking on the rim of his concentration and was not a totally unpleasant or unwelcome intruder.

With his concentration off, Ben's thoughts eventually found their way to his kids. That usually happened. Pam and Jacen were the center of his life. When Lynette died, they became everything and, unbeknownst to them, the only thing that kept him going. He was completely numb, going through the motions of work and home and school, only able to function because he had to. Everything inside him felt withered and dead. He knew this was not the Christian way to live and he prayed hard for the joy of the Lord to come to him. Yet he was ice inside. After a while, he became so adept at pretending that it seemed like the real thing. The years began to go by and he forgot what it was like to really feel anything and he became grateful for the safety and security he had found in his routine of work and caring for his children, his mother and grandparents. It became enough. It became his life.

He managed to turn his thoughts to the day ahead and the task at hand and before long, the train was in Emeryville and he was on the bus into the City. He didn't see Charlie again and once in the City, he focused on making his way to St. Michael's Hospital for the classes. He had instructions that one of his nurses at the hospital had printed out for him on the computer. It looked simple enough and he found the hospital with no problem. He was surprised how easily he got around the city. It seemed so much smaller than he had remembered.

The classes were interesting and soon he was remembering all of his past instruction. He felt confident that he would be able to pass the state exam. The hospital was paying for this so that Ben could use the certification in his job. He was Patient Care Liaison at the hospital. It was a job that he helped to create from necessity. He had been a registered nurse for twenty-five years and gone back for graduate work fifteen years ago. His Master's degree was in psychology with an emphasis on Christian counseling. He had begun combining the two disciplines and the hospital recognized the value of it. Ben was good at what he did. He practiced his religious faith in his work and he truly wanted to help everyone. Over the years, he had become a valuable asset at the hospital and a close ally and confidante to many of the doctors. It was a county hospital where many of the traditional barriers dropped in the small town atmosphere.

The class was over at two o'clock and the bus didn't take him back to the train station until three-thirty. He decided to walk around the city a bit. It was a beautiful winter afternoon. A chilly breeze was blowing from the ocean, but walking in the sunshine was surprisingly warm and pleasant. From his map, he made his way to Union Square and found a place to sit in the sunshine.

He surveyed the stores, shops, flower vendors and bustle that surrounded Union Square. It was a world that was so foreign to him. Suddenly Ben saw Charlie, the man from the train. He was at a distance crossing through the Square. He had an urge to call out to him, but didn't. He didn't know what he would say. He didn't even know why he thought of doing that. He just seemed to be drawn to him and wanted to know more about him. Charlie was walking quickly and Ben saw him go into Neiman-Marcus. Ben had never been inside Neiman-Marcus in his life!

He knew what it was, of course. He kept up with things and was interested in his appearance, but his resources were limited because the kids came first. He kept himself in good shape at the staff gym in the hospital and he tanned easily, so working in the yard, mowing the lawns for his mother and his grandparents on the weekends kept him bronzed and healthy. On some level, Ben was aware that he was handsome, but it embarrassed him to think about it. Why was he thinking about it now? What about the man from the train had triggered all of this concern about his appearance? Ben was not used to allowing his thoughts to stray so randomly. It was unnerving, but an excited pulse beat in his throat. He didn't know whether he liked it or not. He looked at his watch and it was time to catch the bus. He made his way over to Market Street and wondered if he would see Charlie on the train. If he did, he would try to be friendlier. He didn't know why he was drawn to Charlie and he didn't want to examine it too closely. He just knew he wanted to see him again.

# Chapter 3

Charlie had decided to stay overnight in the city. He had friends there still and one of them had suggested dinner, so he went to the Briarcroft Hotel and got a room for the evening. It was a small hotel just off Union Square, clean, quiet and a great bargain. It was that shabby, Victorian style that comforts San Franciscans and is perfect for someone like Charlie who had lived in San Francisco for so many years. He didn't need a fancy hotel, just a warm one.

He was not prepared to stay, so he had to go to the drugstore for supplies. Those new suede boots had caused a blister and he decided to run into Neiman's and pick up a pair of driving loafers. They had an Italian brand that he had worn for years and he knew they would be comfortable right out of the box. He needed a new pair anyway, so it wasn't that much of an extravagance...OK, it was Neiman's...it was an extravagance, but the shoes would run about $140.00 and would last another 5 years. Charlie always found comfort in his ability to justify shopping!

He just had time to get back to the hotel, shower and change for dinner before his friend, John, showed up. He and John had met over twenty years ago in San Francisco. John was a very talented painter and as artists, they had an immediate bond. They just seemed to be on the same wave length. It was a solid friendship that had weathered the years and the miles. John had moved back to his home town of Philadelphia in the late eighties for a few years and Charlie visited him there on a trip back east. It was Charlie's only visit to Philadelphia and he had fond memories of the time there with his old friend. He had gone back east to end a long distance relationship and was nursing a wounded heart when he got to Philadelphia. John had been kind and gentle and sympathetic. He had been a good friend to lean on and

Charlie had always been grateful for that. The love affair was long forgotten, but his friendship with John was as vital as ever. That seemed to be a pattern for Charlie. He was a great friend, but had a hard time holding on to love.

John suggested an Italian restaurant that was right next door to the hotel. Charlie may not have needed those new shoes after all if they were only going to walk twenty yards! It was not crowded, as it was still early, and they were quickly seated in a plump, comfy booth. It was quiet and private and they settled in for a good, long talk after ordering pasta and salad. Charlie started the conversation by telling John about the cinder in his eye and his handsome rescuer. He was embarrassed by how eager he was to talk about it. He hadn't been able to shake the feeling he had about that man. Their eyes had met and there had been something there...it wasn't just sexual, but promised so much more. It made Charlie a little nervous.

As he related all this to John, he became even more animated. John picked up on that right away and was very curious. Had Charlie gotten his name? Was there some way to get in touch with him? Did he want to see him again?

Charlie realized that he knew nothing about him and only now, voicing it, how that brief meeting had affected him. It had meant something, but he didn't know what. He laughed off John's romanticizing of the incident, fearing the truth of it, and managed to steer the conversation to other things.

John and Charlie had met at an AA meeting. They were both still sober and still attending meetings after more than 20 years. They talked about people they had known who were gone now. Maybe, that too contributed to their closeness. They had shared the horror of the eighties and AIDS as they watched most of their friends die. The two of them remained HIV-, not because of any virtue, certainly, but just plain, dumb luck. As two of the healthy few, they each took their turns caring for sick and dying friends. It was these friends that they spoke of tonight and honored with remembrance. Even though it was a horrible time, it was also a time of great caring and solidarity and love in the gay community. It had changed all who lived through it in very profound ways. Both John and Charlie felt that.

The wistful mood created by all that talk of friendly ghosts was dissipated when the food arrived. It was quite good and they both ate well. After dinner, they decided to walk towards the financial district in search of coffee and/or dessert. The wind had picked up and they dug their hand into their pockets. When they found just such a place on Grant Avenue, the warmth was as welcomed as the coffee and mocha torte. Again the talk turned to the event on the train. John didn't want to leave this alone.

"Tell me more about him. What did he look like? How old was he?"

"Well, he was about my height because I looked him straight in the eye. Probably younger than us, but then most of the world is younger than us. The thing I remember most is his eyes: beautiful, blue, kind and mysterious. There was something behind those eyes and behind that open facade. Something more complex, more serious. And, you know, John? I felt something when I looked into his eyes. I don't know what, but something that feels like it is important. I know that sounds silly and melodramatic, but I can't shake that feeling. I know we are destined to see each other again." If Charlie had been talking to anyone else, he would have been embarrassed to sound like such a school girl. John knew that Charlie did not love quickly or lightly.

"Wow, Charlie...how are you going to find him? All you know is that he is in health care and he got on the train in Davis. That doesn't mean he lives in Davis and you have no idea what hospital. And even if you did, you don't even know his name!"

Just then, Charlie remembered something, "Yes, I do! It's Ben McSwain!" He felt a rush of relief. He could begin to try to find him again.

# Chapter 4

The week following his trip into San Francisco, Ben was busy. He made sure of that. It had become a habit with Ben that when feelings, when awareness of his own life, his own needs, began to surface, he got very, very busy. It worked. It had saved his life when his wife died and he saw no reason to change now.

The kids were no longer at home. There were no more pizzas to bake or nachos to stack for the crowds of kids that always seemed to be at the house. After Lynette died, his mother had helped out a great deal with the children. As time went on, Ben increasingly took on the responsibility for everyday things: cooking, laundry, chauffeuring. He could have hired a housekeeper, but he wanted to do it himself. The children had been deprived of one parent and he wanted to make sure that they were not deprived of the other. It was exhausting with his schedule at the hospital and there were nights when he only got three hours of sleep. It was his life and he knew no other.

Coming home from the hospital was different these days. It was one of the reasons that he was working longer hours and volunteering for extended shifts. They were very short handed at the hospital anyway and no one questioned his willingness to do the extra work. It filled the time and the evenings he would have spent with Pam and Jacen.

They seemed to be gone so quickly! One day, he didn't have enough time to do everything that they required and the next, they were gone...on their own. They were only a year apart and upon graduation from high school, neither had seemed very interested in college. Pam, the older, married only seven months after graduation. Like her father and mother, she married her high school sweetheart. Her husband, Brett was in partnership with his father and owned several gas stations in town. They were successful and he and Pam had a secure future together. They had bought a modest house and were looking forward to a baby. Their life seemed certain and happy. Ben was grateful that Pam was such a good kid. She had been an average student but happy and popular. The small town life was enough for her and the environment in which she was born suited her as an adult.

Jacen had had some trouble early in his teens, but nothing serious, a couple of fights at school, some minor rebellion. Ben thought at the time that it was growing pains and that had turned out to be true. Their strong religious beliefs and their active involvement in the church had been instrumental in setting Jacen straight. Pam had always seemed to have a firm, quiet faith, but Jacen was more volatile. However, he had dedicated his life to Jesus as a sophomore in high school and, since then, seemed to be on the right path. When he finished high school a year after Pam, the Iraq conflict was front page and he had decided to enlist in the Marines. Several McSwain men had been Marines and the whole family was proud of him. He was a good kid with conservative family values taught at home, at school and at church. It was the right direction for him.

Ben thought of his own youth. His parents had divorced when he was a junior in high school. There had been no warning, no signs of trouble. His father had always been quiet and distant and that hadn't changed. One day he just wasn't there anymore. Ben didn't really miss him and he suspected that his mother didn't either, but they did miss the financial support that stopped when he left. Ben had two younger siblings and went to work immediately to help his mother care for them. He worked two part time jobs, delivering pizza on the weekends and working at the cineplex four hours a day after school. It left him with very little time for a social life, but he was a shy kid, unsure of himself and awkward. He had no idea how handsome he was, beautiful even. He had met Lynette at church in the youth group when they were in the seventh grade. He had made her laugh and he liked that. So they started hanging out together and everyone just assumed they were a couple. Neither of them ever thought about it and they didn't talk about it. It was just how things were. Their parents seemed pleased and that was important. It was comfortable and sure.

It was so long ago now. Those simple assumptions, chance meetings and happenings had been what had shaped Ben's entire life. The decisions that he had made without thinking, the choices made that seemed unimportant, those had been the ones that changed his life forever. He had made a young girl laugh and from that event, his whole life had been ordered.

And now, that life had been served. He raised his kids, made a home, was a good father and a good provider. He enjoyed his work and succeeded in his field. He was 46 years old. Was his life over? What happens next? He had never really thought about that before. Of course, there was his mother to care for, and his father's aging parents were dependent upon him. Both of his siblings had left Goldmine when they finished high school and neither had returned. Ben had been the one to stay and provide for the family. He knew his mother was grateful. Ben had made do. He had done what had to be done for his family and had never regretted any of it. His work brought him great joy and he was proud of what he had accomplished. Everyone at the hospital knew how hard he worked and he was liked, indeed well-loved by his coworkers and the doctors associated with the hospital. It was a good life and he was content. Except...

He came home from the hospital on Wednesday evening. Tomorrow was his day in San Francisco for class. He closed the door and the quiet surrounded him. It was something he was not used to. Sometimes he would admit to himself that he was lonely. He claimed very little time for himself and when he did, he did not like to dwell on his loneliness. He called Pam. No one was at home. He left a message. He called Jacen but he was not in the barracks. He checked his email. Nothing but advertising and forwarded jokes from the kids. Since he had all evening to kill he decided to surf the net for a while, something he rarely had time or inclination for.

He didn't even know where to begin. He started by going to the website for ASL. He thought he would catch up before tomorrow's class, but he was restless and not interested in anything related to work. He checked his daughter's FacePage blog. It was a sweet, silly combination of gossip about her wedding last year, enthusiastic musings about the baby and mash notes about her husband. She was a kind, immature young bride. The events of her life would bring her all the maturity she needed. There was advertising at the bottom of the page for services available on the internet. He clicked on the links without giving it any thought.

The first thing to come up was a website for masseurs. Ben had wondered what it would be like to get a massage. He had not been touched by another human being since Lynette's death and the idea of it was appealing. Everyone needs human contact. Ben looked at the pictures and realized they were all men. The idea of a massage from another man sounded right somehow, less intimidating than from a woman. There was something fraternal about it. Yet he also realized that he was getting sexually aroused by the idea. He immediately clicked off the website and shut down the computer. It was not the first time he had had sexual thoughts that involved another man, but it was the first time that it had been so concrete, a picture of another man and an imagined situation. He realized, too that the man in the picture had reminded him of the man on the train last week. Their eyes had met and Ben had felt something there, perhaps it was sexual. It felt like that and more. Ben didn't like to admit it, even to himself, but he had thought about that guy, Charlie, a lot the last week. He was lonely. It was time to let someone in. He admitted finally that he hoped he would see Charlie again. He would look for him tomorrow on the train.

# Chapter 5

It was a busy week after Charlie got home from San Francisco. He thought about Ben more than he should have, but he couldn't help it. He met a lot of men. He liked sex and it was easy to hook up on the internet, but he usually forgot them before they were out the door. It was just sport sex, like going to the gym or going bowling. It was fun, but it had nothing to do with an emotional connection that he had with Ben. That was something Charlie didn't feel very often.

He went on the internet when he got home and Googled Ben's name. He came up with several entries. One was a botanist in Iowa. One was a high school basketball star in North Carolina. Nothing for a Ben McSwain in California. Interesting. So Charlie dug deeper. He went to one of those websites that will do a search for a price. He typed in the information he had and it came up with 16 Ben McSwains and three of them were in California. Only one was in Northern California and it was a town called Goldmine near Davis! Bingo! There was no other information available unless you wanted to pay for it. Charlie just couldn't bring himself to do that. It wasn't the money. It was invading someone's privacy and a sleazy thing to do, but at least he had a town. He wondered if there was a phone number for a Ben McSwain in Goldmine. He called information. Bingo again! He had the phone number, or what he thought was the phone number. What if this was not him? He decided to drop it. If it was meant to be, it would happen.

Charlie enjoyed the life he had created for himself. He worked freelance and hadn't had a "real job" in more than 30 years. In his thirties he was lucky enough to get in on the beginning of the romance novel craze and he made a comfortable living for a decade as "Penelope Pilgrim" the flighty and giddy author of such bodice rippers as <u>Love Slaves of Zanzibar</u> and <u>A Penny for Your Thoughts</u>. It was a good living and a lot better than an office, but the time came when he simply could not write one more purple, pulsing word. He had set his last book in San Francisco and used a gay character as the heroine's best friend. His editor called immediately after she read his manuscript.

"You can't do that, Charlie...you know that. You'll have to change it to a girl friend. You know the rules." Claire used her editor voice.

"Oh for god's sake, Claire, it's 1994. Those women in Des Moines know about gay men. They probably have gay friends. Is it that big a deal?" Charlie was ready for this fight.

"You've been in San Francisco way to long, my dear. You think the whole world is like that. It isn't. And those women in Des Moines don't want her to have a gay friend. Have you never heard about the religious right? The evangelical movement? Cross the Bay sometime, Charlie. See how the world really is. You can't do it. The bottom line is that it wouldn't sell. Period."

"I'm not changing it Claire." Show down time!

"Then we're not publishing it, Charlie." She was not going to budge.

"Well, that's that, then. Thanks Claire. I've been wanting to end this for a while and this is as good a time as any. You're a good friend and I love you. I'll be in touch later. Maybe someone else will want this thing."

"Nobody's gonna touch that book, I can tell you that, Charlie. I'm sorry, but the world isn't the way you want it to be. Your fans aren't ready for a gay character. Even in 1994. I'll call you next week. Think about it, honey, OK?" Claire was really a good egg. She just had a job to do.

That had been over ten years ago and Charlie never did publish that book, but he went on to do other things. His agent found him work that was consistent if not always of the highest literary quality. And he did some editing. After moving to Sacramento, he found a steady source of work through state agencies that had literally tons of reports and studies and profiles and queries and memos that needed editing and polishing and tidying up. Charlie was a bit of a politics junkie anyway and found it interesting. And he met some great people along the way. It was a hodgepodge of a career, but it worked, it paid the bills and he didn't have to go to an office. That was the best part.

His family in Texas had never really understood his way of life at all. It wasn't just the gay thing, although the gay thing was a big deal to them. It was his whole approach to the concept of work and living. Charlie was a dreamer as a kid. When he was six years old he wrote a short story about pirates and treasure. When he was eight, he saw <u>The Red Shoes</u> for the first time. When he was nine, he saw Stewart Granger in <u>Scaramouche</u>. The sophisticated Mr. Granger in tights was the ultimate to an impressionable youth from Texas. He didn't know whether he wanted to BE Stewart Granger or was in love with Stewart Granger. It would be another couple of years before he knew that it was love.

His parents had wanted him to be a doctor, of course, to follow in his father's footsteps. That was impossible. It was the last thing that Charlie could have been. So they lowered their expectations to dentist or lawyer. Again, Charlie could not cut that particular brand of mustard. He compromised with his family, went to a church school and majored in English literature with the intention of teaching. That lowered expectation satisfied his parents who were just glad that he hadn't run off to join a commune. This career path didn't really thrill Charlie. He had never voiced it before, but he didn't like children very much. He found them selfish and petty and dull. He couldn't imagine having to spend every day with them. He enjoyed school even though he didn't look forward to his career choice.

He never did teach. After graduation, he quickly took a job with a small specialty publishing company to avoid the question of teaching. And that job led to other jobs that led to other jobs. They all blended in to each other... the same office, the same people, the same gossip. Nothing ever changed. Charlie observed that most people stopped growing in the seventh grade. If you could maintain any enthusiasm for that mentality, you did well. If not, you were bored enough to daydream about stapling your boss's mouth shut.

Salvation came at the age of thirty-one when he sold that first romance novel. He was then regional personnel director for a department store. He quit his job the day he learned that the novel had sold. He had no idea whether he would ever sell another one, but he didn't care. All he knew was that this was a way out of all those offices and he took it.

That had been nearly 30 years ago and Charlie had never looked back. He was happy with this life. It was simple now. He worked hard and had a few good friends with whom he could spend a quiet evening. He wasn't much of a partier these days and he liked his own company. He always felt lucky about that.

But the truth is that, when he finished reading in bed every night and reached to turn out the light, he missed having someone there. No just anyone, but someone special. Someone who would get him completely, who would understand his life and his heart. He had not thought that was possible anymore. Now, Ben McSwain's eyes and smile came unbidden to him in the dark. It had been years since he dreamed about the possibility, but he dreamed about it that Wednesday night.

# Chapter 6

There had been a crisis at the hospital and Ben had to swing by there on his way to the station. It made him late for the train and he had to push it to get there on time. He ran from the parking lot and hopped on just as the train was pulling out. The Capitol Corridor train was a commuter and it didn't tarry long in the station. The casual day-trippers were always surprised and sometimes alarmed at how quickly it completed the station stops.

He was out of breath as he climbed the stairs to the upper level of the train. He was looking for Charlie and he realized that his effort to make the train was more about Charlie than about the classes. Charlie had been on his mind all morning, even when he was choosing what to wear. He didn't want to think what it might mean that he was dressing to please another man and one that he hardly knew at all. He just did it.

Charlie was not in the first car, so Ben made his way to the cafe car. That was where he had seen Charlie last week and perhaps he was there again this week. Ben walked the length of the car, looking at all the booths and seats. Charlie wasn't there. He took a deep breath, willing his heart to return to a normal beat. He was disappointed, no question about that. He was curious to know if he would have the same reaction/attraction to him a second time. He took a seat and made himself comfortable. He got a hot tea and nosed into the books he had brought with him. The disappointment, like most feelings, didn't stick to Ben for long. The quiet, chilling indifference seeped into his brain and into his bones. Automatic pilot was engaged. He spent the remainder of his commute time working on his assignment and he didn't think of Charlie again.

The work he had done on the train paid off and he breezed through the morning classes. Ben's aptitude for ASL was apparent and he was confident that he would have no problem with the state exam when it was time for that. It was another way to be of service to the hospital, to the community and to witness for his religious beliefs. He was an outwardly expressive person, given to gestures and smiles. That was helpful in signing. Sometimes he felt that he was over compensating for the secret coldness he felt in his heart. He was trying to be the person that everyone wanted him to be. It worked, for everyone else seemed to think he was cheerful, ebullient even, and they benefited from it. He had become inured to the numbness inside. It helped him ignore that hole, that loneliness.

Ben was ashamed of himself about his emotional reaction to Charlie's absence earlier in the day. He didn't know what had come over him. He knew that those vague feelings he was having were not normal and certainly not morally acceptable. He and Lynette had been devout members of their church and had brought up the children with those same beliefs. Thinking about people of the same sex in some kind of romantic way was wrong. It was a sin against God. It was that simple. Ben knew that he needed to concentrate on his work and his service. He was just lonely and someone had been nice to him. That's all. No need to make a big deal out of it. Put it in perspective.

He walked along Sutter Street heading down toward the Embarcadero. He stopped in front of a store window and looked at the clothes. It was a fashionable and expensive men's store. He had never even considered shopping in a store like that, but he liked to look and something in the window caught his eye. It was a brown blazer with a gray pinstripe. It was a very cool jacket and he was trying to remember where he had seen it before. Of course, Charlie had been wearing one just like it last week. Again, feelings crept in and he was disappointed that Charlie had not been on the train. He walked on towards the station.

He shivered and dug his hands into his pockets, for the wind had picked up. He couldn't seem to shake his thoughts of Charlie. He entertained the idea, briefly and hesitantly, that the thoughts were like you might have about a woman you were attracted to. He didn't have much experience in that area either so it was hard to pin down what he was feeling, exactly. It was new and strange and frightening. He talked to God about it. Why would God allow these feeling to happen to him? Was this some kind of test? Was God testing his obedience to His will? If so, why in this way? Ben wanted desperately to do the right thing. He knew what the right thing was. Maybe he would never see Charlie again. All of this would pass.

But he did recognize sadness when he felt it. He had really wanted to see Charlie again.

# Chapter 7

Charlie either missed the train on Thursday morning or he decided not to take it. He was not sure which it was. He didn't need to go in to the city that day; he just wanted to see Ben. He knew this was a potentially dangerous sign. That's why he dawdled and waited too long to make it to the station on time. He had been drawn to men in this way before, not after such a brief encounter certainly, but he recognized the feelings. He thought perhaps that the best thing to do was to stop NOW before it got any more complicated. And it was certain to be very complicated.

He went to the gym instead and felt good about his decision. It was the right thing. His life had been calm the last few years without boyfriends or infatuations. He had learned to enjoy concentrating on his work, on the house, on friends and on his garden. But his big fat feline roommate, Emma Thompson, had died last year and left a hole the size of Wyoming in his affections that was hard to fill. He didn't realize how much he would miss her. They had been together for fifteen years after he rescued her from the pound in San Francisco. It had not been love at first sight. Emma was one tough cat and he had to fight for her affection, but she had grown to trust and love him and he had always loved her sad little face and plump, lazy body. That heft was comforting at night. Now that she was gone, he felt her absence and missed her warmth and that familiar weight. It underscored how lonely he was. Perhaps it wasn't too late for all of this. Perhaps he had made a mistake in not going into the city. Perhaps, perhaps, perhaps. He pumped up the incline on the treadmill and dug in. It was really better his way.

Yet he continued to think about Ben all day. He had lunch with his friend Cassie, a very savvy public relations executive he had met at his gym. She was beautiful, fortyish and just married for the first time. She and Charlie had absolutely nothing in common, but there was a connection there that both felt. They were pals and each knew that they could tell the other anything without judgment. Charlie knew that Cassie would love this story, so he couldn't wait to run it by her.

"I met this guy on the train." He started. He teased her and she bit like a great big fish.

"That's it? You met this guy on the train? That's all you're gonna tell me? OK, I have to have details." She looked him straight in the eye and knew she would get what she wanted.

"I got something in my eye and he helped me get it out. It was just a moment. We barely even introduced ourselves. It didn't mean anything really. But I can't stop thinking about him. Our eyes met, there was a connection of some kind. God, I sound like some chick on <u>Party of Five</u>.

"You poor old man. <u>Party of Five</u>? How long has it been since you turned on a television set?" Cassie grinned. She knew that Charlie was the same age as her father and delighted in referencing that in oblique (and not so oblique) ways.

"Sorry, but I leave the culture of mediocrity up to you youngsters. It just sounded like a young and stupid reference point. The real point is that I am emotionally flustered by this and I don't think I like it very much. My life is working just fine right now. This has a very sticky potential."

"Yeah, it sounds like it does. But do you want to stay single forever? Have you given up on the idea of someone to share your life with? It's OK if you have. Nothing says that you have to be paired off with someone. The question is, do you want it? Is it worth pursuing? If you don't, what do you lose? I'm not advocating for either side, Charlie, just pointing out that there ARE two sides here. You do have a choice about what you do."

"I know. I almost took that train this morning. I came very close. But it felt a little desperate or needy or something. It felt uncomfortable."

"Like you were stalking him?" She smiled. She knew that was not the case.

"No, more like a serial killer. Sort of Ted Bundyish." He was not sure if she was old enough to know who Ted Bundy was. The hoot of laughter confirmed that she was old enough, but Charlie turned serious again. "I realized that someone else had the power to effect my emotions. Or the potential for that power at least. That hasn't happened in my life in a long time. And it was scary."

"Oh Charlie, it's all scary. Marrying Jimmy at the age of 40 was scary. He had already been married and had kids, blah, blah, blah. I was scared to death! I still am! I had waited so long for the right guy to come along. He was the right guy...he may have had some of the wrong baggage with him, but I knew he was the one. Those are the cards I was dealt. I decided to play the hand. So far, with a little bluffing, I'm still in the game. But it's always scary, Charlie. The real question you have to ask yourself is: Is it worth it to put yourself out there and grab for something that might make you happy? Or do you play it safe? No right or wrong answer here, honey. Just the options."

"You're a smart girl. And you're pretty. And you wear great shoes. I think I hate you. Could we get the check, please?"

It was a good lunch and Charlie felt better. They parted with the real promise of doing it again soon. They would because they really liked each other's company. This wasn't a mercy lunch. Charlie drove home slowly. It wasn't far and he wanted to have more time in the car to think. He loved being sealed in the car alone. It was his time to cry or get angry or have those feelings he didn't allow himself "out there." Today he allowed himself to feel vulnerable, to feel apprehensive and genuinely confused. He had just downloaded a bunch of Carly Simon to his iPod and he was listening to that. OK, let the goddam river run. He had Ben's phone number. He would give him a call.

But he didn't call. He stared at his phone a lot and even put the number into the phone's address book. It was there at a touch if he wanted it. He couldn't figure out a good reason to call. It just seemed pathetic. So he set his phone aside and went back to work and went back to his life. It was enough. It was a good life and no apple carts needed upsetting right now. He was too old for upsets and bruised apples. He would get along nicely just as things were.

He had a good week. He told himself he was over the mini-obsession with Ben McSwain. How odd. Here was a man that he didn't know at all that had caused a minor shift in his life. He was back on an even keel now, working and laughing and living the life he had created for himself. He was content. The skirmish only reaffirmed his certainty that this was the life for him. On Friday, Dr. Mueller's office called and they wanted him to come back. The doctor had looked at his x-rays and found a cavity. Believe it or not, this was the first cavity Charlie had ever had in his life, so this was a surprise. His appointment was for the following Thursday at his usual time. He always tried to get a mid-morning appointment. That made it easy to get in and out of the city and he was usually home by four in the afternoon. When he hung up the phone he realized that Thursday was the day that Ben went in for his class. He hadn't thought about Ben for several days and just assumed that odd yearning to see him had gone away, but clearly it hadn't. He was curious and excited about taking the train the following Thursday.

# Chapter 8

It was his third week of going into the city for his class and Ben had relaxed into the schedule now and looked forward to the trip. It was February, so he made sure he dressed warmly and had an umbrella, just in case. Winter in Northern California could be raw and nasty or it could be simply beautiful. You never knew, but you dressed for rain. This week, he managed to get to the train station in Davis a few minutes early. It was a cold but sunny day and he waited in the pleasant station for the train to arrive. He didn't think of Charlie Morgan at all. His old life had closed in over those feelings, burying them under its details.

Charlie wasn't quite that organized on Thursday morning and was running late. So late, that he had to drive to the station instead of relying on light rail. He liked to use public transportation when he could, but driving was faster. He managed to walk onto the train just as it was pulling out of the Sacramento station. He went upstairs and all of his usual booths in the cafe car were taken, so he got a coffee and went to one of the other cars and found a quiet seat. He unloaded his briefcase and coat into the seat beside him and set his coffee and roll on the pull-down tray. It was just a few minutes to the Davis station and in no time he recognized the geography leading up to it. Suddenly, there was a little flutter in his stomach. Ben had been in the back of his mind since he knew he would be taking this train. He wondered if he would see him. He was not expecting it and would not be disappointed if he didn't. He just wondered if he might feel that same crazy phenomenon again. The train pulled into the station.

Ben waited his turn to board the train. There seemed to be a lot of people this morning or maybe he was just impatient to get going. And then he thought of Charlie. It was brief and passing, but he wondered about that fellow with the cinder in his eye. He looked around as he came up the stairs of the car. He didn't see Charlie and remembered that he had been in the cafe car before. He walked the length of the car and crossed into the cafe. He had a clear view of half the car and didn't see Charlie. Walking up to the counter, he slowly checked each booth. Not there. Once at the counter, he could see the rest of the car. It was full, but Charlie wasn't there. Ben ordered coffee and put his disappointment out of his mind. Was it really disappointment or just curiosity? Since there was no place to sit in the cafe car, he continued on to the next car forward and that's when he saw him, sitting alone and working on a laptop. Ben stopped short, considering what he should say. He was more nervous that he thought he would be.

"Good morning. How's the eye?" He smiled as Charlie raised his head and prayed that the nervousness didn't show.

Their eyes met again. It was there all right and they both knew it. Perhaps it was better defined for Charlie than for Ben, but there was a knowledge exchanged between them that was ancient, that had always existed.

Charlie stammered a bit, "Hello. Ben? Hello. Yes, I'm fine. The eye is fine, thanks to you."

"I'm glad. It was nothing. Really. It's good that you're OK." He paused awkwardly. "Well, it was nice to see you again."

Charlie rushed in, "Would you like to join me? Let me move all this stuff."

"No really, that's OK. Don't bother. I'll just find a seat further up. I've got some work to do." Ben didn't move, while Charlie continued to stow his briefcase and coat making the seat next to himself available.

"Well, since you've gone to the trouble, thanks a lot." Ben took the aisle seat next to Charlie.

The two men sized each other up a bit. Charlie noticed first that Ben smelled wonderful. He had on some cologne that Charlie would probably not have liked on anyone else, but it was perfect on Ben. Ben's first impression was that Charlie seemed complex. He had some kind of work on a laptop computer; there were papers with red marks all over them. Charlie was dressed just like the mannequins in the store window that Ben had passed last week and he had on interesting bits of jewelry: a ring, a small bracelet, a clever watch and there was a hint of something at his throat that Ben couldn't quite see. Ben noticed that there was chest hair peeking over the top of Charlie's T-shirt. He had never thought of something like that before, but at this moment he found it very attractive.

Charlie loved the color of Ben's skin and how those blue eyes glowed in his tanned face. His eyes were crinkly, like someone who smiles and laughs a lot and that smile was worth the price of a Prada handbag. They settled in and just grinned at each other. Ben's nervousness eased visibly.

"I thought about you after that last time we met. I wondered if I would see you again." He added quickly, "so I could thank you. It really was a very kind thing for you to do."

"It's what I do. You're very welcome. And I thought about you, too. Wondering if you were OK. I even looked for you on the train last Thursday... to see if you were all right."

"How are the classes going?"

"Oh, you remembered. It's going well. The details are coming back to me. I think I told you that I used to do this at my church until they hired a professional."

"ASL, is that right?"

"American Sign Language, right. You've got a really good memory. Are you going in on business? I'm sorry, I didn't mean to pry."

"No, it's OK. I think it's always fair to ask someone about their destination when you are on a train or plane, don't you? It just makes sense. My trip is not so altruistic or interesting as yours. I've got another dental appointment. It seems I have a cavity that needs attention. It's my first."

"Your first cavity? Wow, you're pretty old to be having your first cavity. Gosh, I'm so sorry. That came out completely wrong. I didn't mean it the way it sounded."

Charlie laughed generously. "You're absolutely right. I know exactly what you meant. I was surprised about it, too. I just hope it doesn't hurt."

"Take it from someone who knows, you'll be OK. Fillings aren't that bad. Be grateful it's not a root canal! And you go to San Francisco to the dentist? Must be a special dentist."

"Well, I live in Sacramento now, but I lived in San Francisco for many years and I established this relationship with my dentist so I've just never made the change to someone local. Besides, it gives me an excuse to take a day off, do some shopping, maybe have coffee or lunch with a friend and breathe in the city air for a day."

"You must miss living there. I hadn't been to the City much; I'm a country boy at heart, but I've enjoyed the last two Thursdays. I walked around after my classes. It's really beautiful, isn't it? And I found myself looking forward to it today. The first day, the day I met you, I dreaded it. I know where I'm going now when I get there, so I'm not nervous anymore. I love looking in the shop windows. In fact, I saw the jacket you had on when we first met. The brown one with the pin stripes." Ben blushed furiously. He had let Charlie know more about his interest in him than he had meant to.

Charlie noticed it. "You remembered that jacket? It's my favorite. I have others that are more expensive or perhaps more stylish, but that's the one I always reach for. Seems like you like clothes, too. I couldn't help but notice. It's unusual for this part of the country."

Ben was suddenly self conscious, "Oh, I just wear clothes, you know. My mom has always called me a clothes horse, but I don't think that's true."

Charlie sensed that Ben was nervous again, so he proceeded gently, "And what would make your mother think you were a clothes horse, Ben?"

"Well, there is this family story that gets told all the time about getting me ready to go off to my first day of school. She says, although I don't remember it at all, she says that I came downstairs and told her to re-iron my shirt. That I couldn't go to school dressed like that. I don't think it ever happened, but mom loves to tell the story, so I go along with it. And, well, truthfully, I do like my shirts neat."

"Me, too, Ben. My mom told a similar story about me. As legend has it, she took me shopping for clothes before I began first grade. Apparently, I walked into the store and just started putting outfits together. I never asked for help from anyone in the store and, in about thirty minutes, I had put together an entire wardrobe and was ready to go...everything lined up neatly on the counter. And I know that it happened because I remember it. I was five years old. I still like to do that, truthfully."

Ben and Charlie smiled at each other stupidly. Infatuation makes you stupid and this was turning into infatuation—fast.

# Chapter 9

They talked about ordinary things and they discovered that they were alike in many ways. It was like a secret handshake, an instant shorthand that they intuitively understood. They enjoyed a similar interest in music and reading and they had the same personal style. Just the fact that they cared about personal style and knew what that meant pleased them both.

Charlie learned that Ben was smart, aware and intuitive. He was interested in many of the things that interested Charlie, but where Charlie had studied and worked in fashion and theatre and music, Ben had relied on a keen interests to take advantage of a limited access to those things. He was a small town boy, but avid curiosity had made him aware of things that most small town boys didn't notice. His enthusiasm lit those beautiful blue eyes and the fact that they shared it was exciting to Charlie.

Ben learned that Charlie had lived a very different life from his. He was a small town boy, too, but he got out of Texas early and had lived all over the country and even a while in Paris. He was a freelance editor and Ben wasn't sure exactly what an editor did. Ben was a terrible writer and was always avoiding emails and memos at work because of it. It made him feel self conscious and stupid. Charlie loved books and movies and plays as Ben did, although his life had not afforded him the time to devote to those things that Charlie's had. Charlie was like some exotic window into a world that Ben had thought about but never entered. Ben was aware of something else in Charlie. For all his outward appearance of polish and sophistication, Charlie was just a nice guy at heart. Sweet was the word he thought of, although he was not used to thinking of guys as being sweet. Charlie was a sweet guy.

The train car was cold as it often is that time of year. As they continued to talk, they hunkered down in their seats and drew their coats over them for warmth. They turned their heads toward each other and talked in a way that was increasingly intimate, yet comfortable for them both. At some point, their shoulders touched. Both men were very aware of the moment, yet neither mentioned it nor moved away from it. It was a light touch, but heavy with suggestion and promise.

"Music has always been so important to me. Sometimes, I feel like there is a score to my life playing in the background. Yet I know I don't have very "high brow" taste even though I've been exposed to all the great music. I've been to operas at La Scala and The Met. I heard Maria Callas sing Lucia and went to Caballe's American debut. I love Italian opera because it's so expansive and romantic! The Germans...not so much. And I'm hopeless when it comes to symphonic music. Bach, Beethoven, Brahms and boredom! I walked out of the movie <u>Amadeus</u>. I've never admitted that before! I love Broadway musicals and tearjerkers. Anything romantic. Right now, I'm listening to Dusty Springfield, K.T. Oslin and Il Divo. Hokey, I know, but it's the kind of stuff that gets me in the heart, you know? And now with this iPod technology, accessing all the schmaltz I love is so easy!" Charlie was animated when he talked about music and Ben watched and listened intently. He had never known anyone like Charlie and he caught his enthusiasm.

"The kids have iPods. They listen to all the pop stuff and some of it is OK, but I don't get most of it. I never thought about an iPod for myself. I love Broadway shows, too. I haven't had a chance to see a lot, but I listen to the soundtracks and I really like that kind of music. I've heard of Dusty Springfield, but I don't know K.T. Oslin or the other one you mentioned. I'd like to hear them sometime. I never thought of it like that before, but I guess I like romantic music, too." Ben thought he could feel the ice around his heart begin to thaw.

Charlie smiled at Ben. He was headed into dangerous water and he knew it. Ben struck a chord with him. Something that was primal. They were alike. Charlie just knew that without much evidence.

"I'll make you a CD of some of my favorite tracks. I'll bring it next time I see you. I think you'll like it." Charlie wanted there to be a next time.

It seemed like only minutes had passed when the train pulled into Emeryville, but it had been over an hour and they had to scramble to gather their belongings when they disembarked. They walked directly to the commuter bus that would take them to the City and found two seats. The spell of the conversation on the train was broken. They both felt a little awkward, as if waking from sleep or a dream and the conversation on the short ride to the city was superficial and polite, like two strangers who find themselves seated next to each other.

They both got off the bus at the Embarcadero. It was Charlie's regular stop and Ben got off just because Charlie did and he didn't want to say good-bye quite yet.

The bus pulled away. Charlie extended his hand.

"It was great seeing you again, Ben, and getting to know you a little better. I don't know when I've enjoyed the trip into town more."

"Yeah, I really liked it too. I had a great time talking to you. We seem to have so much in common even though we are so different. I feel like I've known you a long time instead of just a couple of weeks."

Ben didn't let go and Charlie didn't either. They stood looking at each other. It was that ancient connection again and they both felt it.

"Listen, I usually take the 3:00 p.m. train home. I'll look for you. Maybe we can continue the conversation, OK? I'd really like that."

"Yeah, depending on what happens with the doctor, I should probably be on that train, too. Just in case we miss each other, you've got my card, I believe. I gave it to you the day we met."

"Yeah, I do have it. If I don't see you this afternoon, I'll give you a call. Maybe you can suggest some movies or music. You seem to know so much about those things." Ben had completely forgotten about Charlie's card. It must be in the pocket of the jacket he wore that day. He would find it immediately when he got home.

"That would be great. Call anytime. I work at home, remember? Bunny Slippers?" They smiled at each other with delight. "This has been such a pleasure Ben. I don't want to embarrass you, but, in case we don't see each other again, I haven't met anyone in a long time that I enjoyed being with as much as I've enjoyed being with you. You're a very attractive guy."

The implicit intimacy of Charlie's comment made Ben very uncomfortable. He tried to smile, but his eyes dimmed with fear and confusion, "Yeah, dude. You have a good day, OK? Good luck with the dentist, man."

Charlie thought, "He said DUDE. What was that about? Good Lord, Ben had called him DUDE..."

"I can't believe I called him DUDE!" Ben was angry with himself and mortified, but he was also confused by what he was feeling. He was not ready to look at that yet. His old defenses had slammed in to protect him and he had called Charlie DUDE.

What a way for this to end. Ben turned and walked toward the City. Charlie watched him go and thought to himself, "That, as they say, is that." He had seen it before. The panic. Those guys: they aren't out, they aren't in. They don't know where they are and they are terrified of finding out. He knew better than to get involved. He felt sorry for Ben. Hell, he felt even sorrier for himself because it was already too late. He was involved.

# Chapter 10

Charlie deliberately took a later train that Thursday. He was through with his appointment in plenty of time to catch the 3:00 train, but he waited. He didn't want to run into Ben McSwain. He would have liked very much to see him again, but not after the message he had gotten loud and clear from Ben that morning. It was something best left alone. Charlie shook it off when he got back to Sacramento and called his friend Dru in Palm Springs.

"Hey, guy...what's up? It's cold here and I need to warm my toes. Can I come down for a few days?"

"Hi Charlie! I keep saying you should move down here, then your toes would never get cold. Sure, come on anytime. I'm here by myself and would love the company." Dru could tell that something was up with Charlie, but decided to leave it alone and let Charlie tell him when he was ready. They had been friends since they met in San Francisco boiling turnip greens in a church basement working for Project Open Hand in the early days. They got closer and closer as increasingly friends and acquaintances died around them. That happened with the survivors. The two of them decided they could never do any of the "survivor workshops." It just seemed too self indulgent when everyone you cared about was dying. Their friendship had been very important and they loved each other deeply in that family way that gay men understand.

"Great! I'll call the airline today and get a reservation. I'll come as soon as I can. Hang the expense, I just want to get away and I want to see you."

This trip was just what he needed right now. Since Emma Thompson died, he felt the freedom to take shorts trips that he had not been able to do before without spending half the time worrying about her and feeling guilty about leaving her alone. Now he could do things like this without telling a soul. For Charlie really was alone in the world. His parents were gone and his only sister had died just last year. The phrase "abandonment issues" came into his mind. He didn't think he felt abandoned, or that it influenced his life, but perhaps it did on some level that he was not able to recognize. It did seem that he was more aware of being alone lately. He had always liked the phrase "abandonment issues." It was very California. However, he had learned, having lived in California for more than 20 years now, that many things that were considered to be "very California" were things that the rest of the country didn't want to face...yet. Like abandonment issues, environmental issue...or gay issues.

He was able to get on a flight the next afternoon. There was only one nonstop a day from Sacramento to Palm Springs and it was usually very popular, especially this time of year, but he had lucked out. Dru would meet him at the airport looking very pastel and Southern California now. As he packed for the trip, Charlie thought about Dru, a very different Dru from twenty years earlier. He remembered Dru with long, dark hair, a big mustache and dressed in black from head to toe. They had all looked like that back then. Charlie wondered if everyone in San Francisco still dressed in black. It was like an entire city of Greek widows. Dru was happy now in Palm Springs. He had put on about forty pounds, gotten a lot grayer and a lot tanner. It had been an adjustment for him. His partner, Fred, had finally died after an agonizing time trying to balance an AIDS cocktail. And Dru had had enough. He sold their condo in Noe Valley and bought a big house in Palm Springs. Charlie remembered his phone calls the first year. He hated it. He hated the people and the climate and the Southern California mentality. Gradually the calls became more positive. He began to meet people who were not so bad. He got involved in some activities that were fun. Charlie went down to visit and found a very contented, peaceful man.

The truth is that Charlie hoped some of that peace and contentment might rub off on him this time. He enjoyed visiting Palm Springs, but didn't think he would ever live there. It wasn't his style. He didn't get the attraction of the desert. He had grown up inland in a swampy, marshy part of Texas. He didn't miss that, certainly, and he had not been sure that he would like California at all. He was pleasantly surprised to discover a love for the Pacific Ocean and he found a peace and contentment along the beaches of Northern California that he had never known anywhere else. He understood why Californians were so interested in protecting the environment. It was so glaringly, brilliantly THERE and so much a part of everyone's life. Back home, the countryside was not very pretty and the climate was just plain awful: hot and humid in the summer and cold and icy in the winter. Texans spent most of their time protecting themselves from their environment rather than reveling in it as they did here.

The first time he had gone up to the Russian River, he thought he remembered dreaming about it as a child. He felt certain that he had. He knew it already: the mountains and trees and the river. He knew that those Texans would know what environmental issues were all about if they could see Sonoma County. It had become his favorite getaway and it still was, but today he needed something else. He hoped to distance himself from thoughts of Ben McSwain.

He was light hearted as he packed and prepared for the trip. He made sure all the doors were locked, the sprinkler system was engaged and there was nothing out in the kitchen to spoil. He printed out his boarding pass and was ready to go. It was a good decision to call Dru. He couldn't wait to get there. The heck with men on trains.

Just as he was backing out of his driveway his phone rang. It was his college roommate, Lee. They had remained best friends all these years even though Lee had lived in New York since graduation. He was a playwright and they had collaborated several times, once on a television movie that turned out to be a load of fun and made Charlie enough money to live on for a year. Lee had an interesting proposition. He had been asked to do the book for a new musical based on The Last Picture Show and he wanted Charlie to collaborate with him. It sounded like a fun challenge and a good chance for the two of them to spend some time together. He told Lee about his trip and that he would get back to him in a couple of days, but that he was definitely interested in the project. A musical of The Last Picture Show? Charlie thought about it. What a great idea! He wondered why it hadn't been done before now.

It was something to mull over in the heat of Palm Springs. He liked his life.

# Chapter 11

Ben had a busy week and Thursday rolled around quickly. He regretted what had happened last week with Charlie Morgan. It had just seemed too intimate and it made him uncomfortable. This was like nothing he had experienced before and he was out of his safety zone. He had to admit to himself that he really liked Charlie. He hadn't met anyone recently that he liked as much. Charlie seemed to speak his language, to understand him. He wanted them to be friends, but he didn't know how to approach it. He thought that Charlie was probably a homosexual. His church was very clear on that topic. It was a sin. They didn't talk about it much at his church. It just didn't come up and he didn't think he had ever known anyone who was homosexual. Everyone in his world was married and had a family. There were some widows and single women his age in the church and friends had tried to fix him up. He gave the excuse that he wasn't ready to think about another relationship, but the truth is that he really wasn't very interested in any of the women he met. He also had to admit that, on occasion, he noticed a guy at the gym with a good build. And he was fascinated by a hairy chest, but it didn't feel like he was looking at those men in a sexual way. He was just interested. Was that sexual? He knew that it would be wrong and he wouldn't even consider it.

He liked Charlie and wanted to get to know him better. Even before he met Charlie, he had thought that he should branch out and explore new things now that the kids were gone. He had always wanted to go to the theatre more, go to concerts. And he wanted someone to go with. None of the women he met seemed like the type that would enjoy an evening like that, but Ben could easily see himself with Charlie at a play or concert. He would enjoy that and it would just be friendship. They talked so easily and seemed to see things from the same point of view. It wasn't sexual. He could make that clear to Charlie...or maybe he wouldn't have to. He was just guessing about Charlie. He didn't know for sure that he was gay so perhaps he shouldn't be so quick to judge. He hoped Charlie would be on the train today. It would give him a chance to make up for his behavior last week and he could approach the subject of doing something together. That thought made him really look forward to the trip to the city today. When he got on the train, he immediately looked in every car. Charlie wasn't there. He allowed himself to be truly disappointed this time. He had wanted another chance at friendship. He remembered that Charlie had given him his card and he was wearing the jacket that he had been wearing when they met. He reached into his pocket and there it was: "Charlie Morgan, Freelance Editorial Services, 2100 Atwell Way, Sacramento, CA" and a phone number. So Ben could call him. He didn't want to disturb him during the week, but he would do it this weekend.

After his classes, he took his usual stroll in downtown San Francisco. He walked by that store again, the one where he had seen Charlie's brown jacket. He went in. He had never been to this store before, but it was beautiful and it smelled wonderful—like good leather and cashmere and exotic spices from the scent counter. He was a little intimidated, but people seemed friendly and encouraged him to browse. He picked up a shirt that he thought was cool. The price tag said $185.00! For a shirt! Ben had never paid that for a shirt in his life. He didn't pick up anything else. He wandered around and found himself at the fragrance counter. There were several colognes for men with the label of the store on them. Ben liked to smell good. Someone had given him a bottle of Polo when he was in college and he had been a fan of colognes ever since. The first one he picked up was called Slate. He didn't think slate really had a smell unless it might be like wet cement, but this Slate smelled wonderful. It smelled like Charlie! He made that connection almost immediately. Scent was a powerful memory guide for him. He still remembered what Christmas smelled like when he was five. This scent brought back his conversation with Charlie, sitting close to him on the train, looking at his dark eyes. On a whim, he bought the smallest bottle of the fragrance that they made. It was all he felt he should spend. He tried to tell himself that it was OK to do that now that the kids were raised. He could finally take some time and space and money for himself! As the clerk was ringing up his purchase, he spritzed himself liberally with the tester. The origins of the scent were hard to identify. The clerk was a handsome young man of about thirty and he smiled warmly at Ben.

"That's what I wear about ninety percent of the time. I just love it and my boyfriend does, too. Wait until you've had it on a couple of hours; it will change, become more subtle and you'll like it even more. Is this for you or is it a gift for your special guy? I can wrap it for you if it's a present."

"Uh, it's for me. I don't have a boyfriend. That is, I mean I don't date boys, er, or men." Ben was flushed and flustered. He didn't know what to say. He was afraid he had offended the clerk. "I'm sorry. I hope I didn't say the wrong thing."

"Look, I'm the one who should apologize. Please forgive me. It's just that your smile and your friendliness, I just assumed...oh dear, I think I've done it again."

"Hey dude, it's OK. It's just that this has never happened to me before and I didn't know how to react. Actually, I think I'm flattered."

"You're being very generous, sir. Thank you. I've put in some samples for you...other fragrances, other products. Hope you enjoy it and that you'll shop with us again."

The young man was relieved by Ben's kindness and Ben was relieved, too. He wasn't sure how he might have reacted to this event several weeks ago, before he met Charlie. He knew that he was not as offended as perhaps he might have been. The truth was that he really was flattered. Maybe he would tell Charlie about this. It would be something funny to share with him. It occurred to him that Charlie might be the only person in his life that he could share this story with. His mother wouldn't think it was amusing at all and neither would the kids. He realized he wanted to see Charlie again. He barely knew him at all, but he missed him. It didn't seem possible, but it was so.

He would call him on Saturday.

# Chapter 12

The weather in Palm Springs could not have been more beautiful with blue skies and the mountains in the distance. He could see why so many people found this to be heaven on earth, yet he had just never been a Southern California person. It reminded him of West Texas with Mercedes dealerships and golf. But he had to admit that Palm Springs was glorious this time of year.

Dru had taken Charlie to his favorite lunch time cafe. It was a sleek, contemporary, glassy-classy watering hole. They sat outside on this perfect afternoon. Charlie looked around at the restaurant and it's patrons. It was ninety percent gay and Charlie was probably the youngest person there. He noticed something else: these older gay men, his contemporaries, were changing the rules about aging! The patio was full of handsome silver haired men with flat stomachs and healthy, youthful energy.

"Well, I think you did the right thing, honey. It's too bad because he sounds like a good guy, but there is no place for this to go but down. The man's got lots of baggage...and I mean real baggage Charles. Louis Vuitton type baggage." Dru was commenting on Charlie's tale of Ben McSwain. He couldn't help but talk about it and Dru was a wise but blunt man who would not hold back. "It would be best if this were stopped before it ever started."

"I know, I know, I know. You're right of course. I just wish you weren't and that things were different, that's all."

Charlie realized he sounded like a petulant child. That is what he felt like. It was time to remember that not every day could be Doris Day and sometimes you just had to accept the fact that you didn't get what you wanted. He was breathing easier and smiled tentatively. He was having a good time in Palm Springs and Dru had some very engaging friends. He had even begun to wonder if he couldn't do this after all—live in Palm Springs. It's the people that make a place home, not the geography and the people were certainly warm and friendly here. The support system was here; it must be the gayest old folks resort in the world and these days, that was looking like a pretty good thing.

They were having dinner with friends of Dru's tonight and he was going back to Sacramento tomorrow afternoon. It had been a great distraction for a few days and he had gotten some perspective on the Ben thing. The dry, hot, clean air of Palm Springs had provided some clarity. He was sorry to be leaving, but he needed to return Lee's phone call and find out more about the musical job and decide if he wanted to do that. It sounded like just the thing he needed right now.

The flight home was quick and painless and when he reached his house he could barely push the front door open. The mail was piled up in front of the slot: Netflix envelopes, credit card offers and catalogs. That was about it. Everything else came online these days. He closed the door, dropped his suitcase and scooped up the pile from the floor. Junk, junk, junk. A letter. A letter from Goldmine. The return address just said BLM. Well, well. Benjamin L. McSwain. He dropped the rest of the mail on the dining table and went into his office, sat down at the desk and found a letter opener. He took his time and opened it slowly, having no idea what it might be.

Hey Dude (ha ha)

It's Ben from the train. I started to call you but decided that writing might be better. But I'm not a very good writer, so you better be prepared for that. I just wanted to tell you that I was sorry for the way I must have seemed to be acting the last time I saw you. I didn't mean to be rude to you. I guess I'm just not very good at social stuff. I haven't had a lot of experience with people like you, I mean people outside my everyday life here at home.

I just wanted to tell you that it was nice meeting you and I hope we can meet again sometime. I thought maybe I could come to Sacramento and buy you lunch sometime or something like that. I would like to get to know you better. You said that you hadn't enjoyed talking with someone as much as me and I feel the same way.

My job is long hours and I'm on call 24/7, so getting away can be hard for me sometimes, but I would like to see you when we can find the time.

Please take this in the spirit it was written and remember that I'm not a writer like you.

Ben.

ps...here's my phone number if you want to call. 916-555-2125.

Charlie sat and stared at the letter. He had not expected this. Now what was he going to do? He had spent the last week convincing himself that he was better off without this complication. He could ignore the letter. He could write a warm and polite "no thank you." Or he could accept and see what happens. Who was he kidding? Of course, he was going to see Ben again. There was never any doubt. He picked up the phone immediately and dialed Ben's number.

"Hey. This is Ben. I can't take your call right now, but leave your number and I'll call you back when I get a break. Thanks!"

"Uh, Ben. Hi, Charlie Morgan. I got your letter today. I just got home from Palm Springs. I would love to get together sometime. Just give me a call back and let's set something up. May I offer to make dinner? I'm a fair cook and would enjoy doing that. It would give us a chance to have a good visit and get to know each other better. Let me know what you think. Bye for now."

Charlie felt a little giddy and distracted, but he immediately put in a call to Lee in New York. He answered on the second ring.

"Hey. How're you?"

"Hi. I'm good. I'm breathing. How was Palm Springs?"

"Surprising. Wouldn't want to live there, but I had a good time."

"Old queen's burial ground. When I lived in LA, friends always loved going over there, but I couldn't see the attraction. Just a lot of sweaty, wrinkled old people." It was vintage Lee and Charlie realized how much he missed him.

"Well, yes, Lee. There is that. There is also the fact that you don't look at any man over the age of twenty-two. Your definition of "over the hill" is twenty-eight, isn't it? Naturally Palm Springs would give you the willies. But I had a good time. A friend of mine from SF moved there a few years back. He has a big Palm Springs house with a pool. It was very comfortable, but it's not for me. And not for the same reasons you don't like it. It reminds me too much of the flat land of Texas. I have turned into a Northern Californian, I fear. I mentioned to one of Dru's friends that I couldn't live there because I would miss the ocean. He said that Long Beach wasn't that far. I was taken aback. Long Beach isn't the ocean to me! I was thinking Point Reyes, Bodega Bay. That's what I mean when I say ocean. But I'm glad I went. What have you been up to? Are you going to teach next semester?"

"I guess I will. I can't believe I've been doing this for 10 years. I hate it more every year. The kids are great. It's the faculty and administration that drive me crazy. I make enough money from that to pay bills for the next 6 months, so I can't really afford not to at this point." Lee sounded like he was bored with the prospect of going back to Texas to teach, but they paid well to have a Texas-born genuine New York playwright.

"Well, tell me about this 'Picture Show' thing. What's that all about and why did you call me?"

"Oh my agent threw this at me. I always get the Texas stuff before anyone else. Well, you know what it's like to be tagged as a Texas writer. It does sound like a hoot and we've been wanting to work together on something. I immediately thought of you since I know you loved the book so much and are such a McMurtry fan. Since we spoke, I hear they've hired Luke Beecham to do the music and lyrics. That makes it a lot more interesting. He's THE up and coming young country star." The pitch of Lee's voice changed. "You know I don't listen to that kind of music much. But I met him a couple of years ago in Nashville when he was just starting out. He was certainly good looking, but also down-to-earth and warm and..." Lee's voice trailed off and for once he seemed lost for words, suggesting that there might be more than he was telling.

"I love c&w, and I have his first album. I'll check him out on iTunes and see what else I can find. This sounds like fun. Do you know any more about it?"

"Well, Piper Jones is directing. I think this thing needs a woman director and she's southern. It's a great choice. I know her pretty well. She's very easy going and good to work with. I know a couple of the actors. They are all good, solid New York actors. No one famous...yet. This show might be a career maker for someone. They all have great resumes. I suggested to the producers that I wanted to collaborate with you and that wasn't a problem. I told them we were old friends from college and about your background. Do you have an agent still?"

"Just my book agent. I've never really needed any other kind of representation before." Charlie had not even thought about that side of all this.

"I'll have my agent, Barry, send the information to your email address. Talk to him about handling this for you. He's a sharp guy and will do it right. Just take a look at the information and we'll see what kind of contract they are really talking about. Then we can decide in the next week or so. Apparently the money for the project is there already. I don't know if McMurtry is involved or not."

"Well, it comes at a very good time for me. I'm not really doing anything right now and I could use a distracting project. I met someone and it has disaster written all over it."

"Why disaster, honey?"

"Well, we haven't actually gone out yet."

"Oh that's so like you, Charlie. You haven't even had a date with the guy and already your singing the blues about it not working out. Can you say self-fulfilling prophecy? Charlie, give yourself a break."

"Well, he's not out. I'm not even sure he's gay. He's got a kid who is a marine and he's an evangelical Christian."

There was absolute, dead silence on the other end. Charlie thought he had lost the connection. "Hello?"

"I'm here. Honey, in the forty years that I've known you, you've gotten into some peculiar predicaments. There was the Colorado fling and the Michigan thing. And there have been some very odd boyfriends. But this one leaves me speechless."

So Charlie told the Ben story again.

# Chapter 13

An hour later Charlie hung up the phone. Every time he and Lee talked it was as if they were still in college and no time had passed at all since their last conversation. Charlie couldn't imagine what the last forty years would have been like without him. He had just always been there to share life. After he explained the circumstances about Ben, Lee backed off from his original assessment and thought Charlie should give the guy a chance. He was still so uncertain and Lee's support was surprising, but good to have.

He opened his email and he had the information from Lee's agent. He spent the rest of the day reading through everything and jotting down notes and ideas. Barry had suggested a conference call with Lee in a couple of days to discuss details. Charlie was inclined to say yes. He didn't know about Lee. Charlie often just jumped into things without giving much thought to the consequences and then figuring it out as it unfolded. Lee was a lot more cautious. This was far more about Lee's career than Charlie's. After all, if this didn't work, it wouldn't effect Charlie's career at all, but Lee was part of the Broadway community and a wrong move on his part would be noticed and could effect future jobs. Charlie had known Lee to dicker over contracts for months and even then, sometimes back out of a project. He was very careful about his career and his reputation. Charlie understood that and he would abide by whatever decision Lee made, but he hoped Lee would decide to do it. Charlie had already made up his mind to say yes just for the fun and experience it would be.

He emailed Barry back late in the afternoon and told him how he was feeling about everything after looking over the information. He was already roughing out the book for the show in his mind. Capturing the spirit of the novel—the humor and the pathos—would be the most important thing and the music would be vital, of course. Charlie loved the idea of a country/western score. Nothing else would work as well. He was getting revved up about the project and hoped that Lee would feel the same way. He was so wrapped up in his thoughts that he jumped when the phone rang.

"Hey Dude."

"Dude? OK, what's with this dude business? You called me that in San Francisco. I thought about it all day. Dude??" But Charlie was smiling as he said this. He couldn't seem to stop smiling when he thought of Ben McSwain.

"I'm sorry! I've been around kids too long. When Jacen's crowd is at the house, they all call each other dude. Even Pam's girlfriends use it. It's just part of the language when you've got teenagers, I guess. I hadn't really thought about it."

"Well, yeah, Dude." Charlie laughed, too. "I'm not around young people very much. I didn't know that was still popular. I always think of Keanu Reeves in those movies. I think he started the whole 'dude' thing, didn't he?'

"Uh, I don't know, dude... Hey, I was returning your call. You said something about dinner? That's really nice of you, but you don't have to go to that trouble. We could go out somewhere."

"No, really. I would very much enjoy doing it. When are you free?"

"Well, I'm always on call, but I am free anytime after four tomorrow afternoon. Is that too soon?"

"No, tomorrow is good. Why don't you come over about five o'clock. We'll have an early dinner and just make it a simple evening, OK?"

"Yeah, I guess that would work. I've never done anything like this before. Should I bring something? I don't drink, but I could buy a bottle of wine if you tell me what kind."

"Well, I don't drink either, so we don't have to worry about the wine. You don't have to do anything but show up hungry and eat what's put in front of you!"

"OK, I'm sorry that I sound like such a dork. Like I said, I just don't get out much socially."

"Well, relax. We'll just talk, have some food and you can leave whenever you feel like you need to. I want you to be comfortable."

"I'm sure I will be and I'm looking forward to it. I have your address. Where are you exactly?"

Charlie told him the neighborhood and gave him some landmarks that he knew. Ben seemed to know Sacramento well and was familiar with the area. He would find it with no problem. They ended the call with each expressing that they were looking forward to seeing each other again.

Charlie let out a big sigh when he hung up the phone. He wondered if he would have the same reaction when he saw Ben again—that sense of joy and wonderment. Now what was he going to serve? It was winter, so he thought about chili...maybe he would make chili. Was that too spicy, too Texas? Maybe soup.

Ben sighed, too, when he hung up. His hands were sweaty and he had been gripping the phone so tightly that it hurt a little when he let go. This was a huge step for him. He was beginning to acknowledge to himself that his interest in Charlie was not just as a friend. There was something more there. The conversation had been very different from one he would have had with some of his male acquaintances from church or work. This really felt like a date and Ben was going through with it, that he knew for sure. He didn't stop to think of the consequences.

Ben went to his mother's every Saturday morning to check on her and to see if there were things that he needed to do around her house. Since his dad left when he was fifteen, Ben had been the man of the house. It had been a drastic change for the family. The people at the church had really saved their lives. Everyone had been so supportive with love. More tangible support was there, too, like food and baby sitting help and job offers for Ben and his mom. He had never forgotten that love and the feeling of gratitude brought tears to his eyes, even today. It was the same church he and his mom still attended and would be attending tomorrow.

In fact, Ben had choir practice at eleven-thirty this morning. His mom was feeling good and in a good mood. Her health had been off lately and he was worried about her. He kept trying to get her into the hospital for some tests, but she had been evasive. This morning she was in the mood to talk while Ben worked on the garbage disposal.

"What's going on with you these days, son?" She sat at the kitchen table drinking coffee.

"The usual, mom, work, kids, work, church, work. You know." Ben couldn't decide if he wanted to tell her about tonight. She was good at reading him and he was afraid she would read too well.

"Well, I know about the work all right, but what's with those kids of yours? They are pretty much out of your hair by now, aren't they? Jace is still in Iraq and Pammie's got her own family now. Must be lonesome over at your place." She was fishing.

"Not so lonely. I see Pam real often and I get to chat with Jacen online almost every night. They're not rid of me yet. And I'm still working as many hours as ever. We can never keep enough nurses. The minute we get a new hire, it seems someone else leaves. So I keep working extra shifts and stay on call. It's been going on so long, I don't remember anything else."

"You should have a life for yourself, son. You're still a young man. I know you don't like to hear me say this, but you need to start thinking about finding someone. It's not natural to be alone all the time like you are."

Ben blurted out, "Well, I have a date tonight." He wished he had kept his mouth shut, but he was tired of hearing the same thing from her and wanted to shake her up a bit.

"Really? Well, I'll be! Good for you, boy! Who is it? Someone from the church? I'm really proud of you. It's time, you know. Lynette would be saying the same thing to you. Who is it?"

Ben hesitated. He had never lied to his mother before. It just felt wrong to do so now, but he couldn't tell her the truth. "Well, it isn't really a date, but I am going out. I'm going to Sacramento to have dinner with someone I met on the train when I went to San Francisco for those classes. It's a guy I met. We just hit it off. I called him the other day and he invited me over for supper. That's all."

"Well, that sounds nice, Bennie. Sort of a bachelors' party?" She smiled at her own joke.

"Yeah, I guess you could say that. That's what it sounded like to me. He said an early supper, early evening. And we've got church in the morning. So." Ben trailed off. He didn't really know what he was trying to say to her. It seemed awkward to explain why he was having dinner with another guy. Of course, he often went out for meals with people from the hospital or from church and never thought anything about it, but he already knew them. This seemed hard to explain because there was no reason to know Charlie except that they had met on a train. It sounded odd when he said it, but it had seemed so natural when it happened. He hated lying to his mom. Was it a lie? It felt like one.

He finished repairing the sink and cleaned up. He had to be at choir practice in a few minutes. He wondered if he had time to get a haircut before tonight? Oh yeah, this was a date all right. Regardless of what he had said to his mom. This was a date.

# Chapter 14

It was going to be soup...and bread and salad and ice cream clowns for dessert. It was Charlie's fail safe menu. He was nervous enough about the evening and he didn't want to worry about the food, too. He went to the grocery early on Saturday morning, got the soup on the stove, the salad things washed up and started cleaning the house. He did the bathroom, changed the linens (a deadly thing to do) dusted a bit and ran the Dyson and it was only ten-thirty! He did the bathroom again and wished he had not changed the sheets. It was too prophetic...or was that pathetic? What was he going to do the rest of the day? He picked up his jacket and went out for a walk. He might see the one o'clock feature at the Tower. He didn't even care what it was. It would pass the time. Jeez, he was nervous about this.

He went to the movies and he was glad he did. They were showing a restored print of <u>Strangers on a Train</u>. Charlie thought the irony of that was too good to pass up. He enjoyed seeing it again. He had forgotten the homoerotic overtones in the film. It was really quite sexy for its day. By the time he walked home it was nearly four. The soup was done, a simple vegetable soup with very light seasoning. He didn't know anything about Ben's tastes and had forgotten to ask. He hoped it would be all right. He had gotten a hearty, dense peasant bread with garlic and asiago cheese and he bought additional cheese to go with the bread. There would be a tray of pickled veggies and olives and a simple version of a Caesar salad. He had gone to Here's The Scoop! across the street for his favorite dessert trick. They did these funny ice cream clowns for children's parties, but when he told the owner he liked to serve them for adult parties, she started doing little X-rated clowns for him. Nothing really vulgar, but clowns that looked drunk or stoned or angry. But for tonight, he chose regular clowns with dopey faces. Charlie instinctively knew that Ben would get the joke.

He set the table, gave the living room the once over and was satisfied. Charlie loved his house, but it had never felt exactly right. The furnishings were fine and everything worked, but something was missing. It seemed disconnected somehow, but it looked as good as it was going to today, so Charlie let it go. It was time to jump in the shower and get ready. He had already decided what he would wear: Levis, soft loafers and his favorite Banana Republic shirt. He always had a favorite shirt and just now, it was a red and olive green checked dress shirt. He always pulled it out when it seemed like a special occasion. This was a special occasion. He was brushing his teeth for the third time when he heard a car in the driveway. He spit, rinsed and took one long last look in the mirror. There was fear in his eyes, but he smiled at himself and felt better.

He opened the front door. Ben was still in his car. The car was a surprise. Not at all what Charlie would have expected. It was a sexy/sleek, rust-red Jaguar convertible. Very classy and beautifully maintained. It looked spotless, as if it had just been driven off a showroom floor. Ben got out of the car, closed the door and paused, obviously checking the car for flaws. He looked up and saw Charlie standing on the front porch of his house. He smiled. Charlie smiled. It was quite a moment.

"Hey dude." Ben said as he walked up the path to Charlie's house.

"Hey, yourself, dude." Charlie couldn't stop smiling. "Come on in. Welcome. It's not fancy, but it's home." Charlie's house was great, really. Small, cozy, softly lit and softly furnished. The sofas and chairs were all big, overstuffed things with warm throws draped everywhere. You could curl up anywhere in the house, tuck your feet under you and snuggle down. Since Charlie loved to read, this was deliberate. He liked to be able to perch and dig into a good book. There was a fire in the fireplace and it added to the warmth of the room. And it smelled like soup.

"This is great. And something smells good!" Ben looked around the room with admiration.

"Please, have a seat. Can I get you something? I've got tea or coffee, of course and Diet Coke if you like. Bottled water?" Charlie continued to stand and indicated that Ben should take the sofa.

"I'm a Diet Pepsi guy, myself, but I'll take a Diet Coke if you have it." Ben rested his arm on the back of the sofa and crossed his legs at the knee. He looked comfortable and at home.

Something struck Charlie. Whatever had been wrong with that room was right with Ben McSwain sitting in it. He was the missing piece. The room finally made sense. Charlie had not consciously set up his house with the idea of sharing it, but that room needed Ben to be complete. Charlie turned quickly to the kitchen. He didn't want Ben to see the emotion on his face. It was a silly thought, really. It was way too early to be having those thoughts.

"Diet Coke coming up. I thought we would eat in about thirty minutes, if that's OK with you. Is that too early for you? I'm an early person, I fear. I get up early, eat early, go to bed early." Charlie was glad he was talking from the kitchen so Ben couldn't see him blush.

"I get up at 3:00 a.m. every day. I have to be at the hospital at 4:00. I usually work a ten-to-twelve-hour shift, so it's a long day for me, too. When the kids were at home, I couldn't get to bed until ten o'clock or so, but now I can crawl in a lot earlier if I want. And I'm doing that more often." Ben couldn't seem to stop talking. He was nervous.

"Wow. You get up earlier than I do. I just function better in the mornings. It suits me." Charlie came back to the living room with their drinks. He was having hot tea and he handed the Coke to Ben. He sat down next to him on the sofa. Ben looked a little startled and Charlie wondered if he shouldn't have taken one of the chairs instead, but Ben's body language softened and he turned to face Charlie.

With a reassuring smile he said, "Thanks. Well, here we are. This is great. It's the first time I've stopped today. It feels good to just sit down." He relaxed into the sofa.

Charlie asked about Ben's day and he talked with ease about his mom, choir practice, the small events of his life. Charlie told him about the movie. Ben seemed to be interested. They continued to talk and the minutes flew by. It was small talk, but there was a subtext in their eyes. Each was avidly interested in the other and they moved closer on the sofa until their legs touched. They were both aware of this but neither moved away. Ben nudged Charlie's knee affectionately and without any self-consciousness. There developed between them that short-hand that couples usually only have after a very long time together. It was easy companionship and seemed like an old relationship rather than two people who had just met.

# Chapter 15

"You must be starved!" Charlie sat up and looked at his watch. "It's seven o'clock. We've been talking for two hours!" They moved to Charlie's small dining room where he had set two places across from each other. He lit the candles and pointed out the place he intended for Ben. He went into the kitchen to serve up the soup. Everything was done except plating and they were able to begin eating with very little fuss.

Ben looked a little apprehensive when he saw what Charlie had prepared, but he was complimentary and seemed to enjoy the food, especially the cheese and bread.

"It's a Wensleydale. Like <u>Wallace and Gromit</u>." Charlie said with a smile.

"What's <u>Wallace and Gromit</u>?"

You are a country boy, thought Charlie, but a damned cute one! "It's a British cartoon. Claymation to be exact. I've got it on DVD. We can watch it sometime if you want."

"You don't seem like the cartoon type, dude."

"Well, I really love this particular one, but I don't get up on Saturday mornings to watch them, if that's what you mean."

Charlie got up to replenish the cheese tray. Returning to the dining room, he placed his hand on Ben's shoulder as he put the tray on the table. Ben turned and looked at him, their faces very close together. It was another moment, another seismic shift.

The dessert clowns were a big hit. There was a childlike quality in Ben that responded to the silliness of the ice cream confections and it lightened the mood all around. They were laughing about something silly while Charlie cleared the plates. Ben offered to help him wash up as Charlie came behind him to remove the dessert plate.

"There's not much to do and there's plenty of time for that later, after you've gone, but thanks for offering." And without really thinking about it at all, standing behind him, Charlie reached down and lightly kissed Ben on the top of the head. It seemed like such a natural thing to do, as if he had done it a million times before.

Ben froze. He literally didn't move a muscle. Charlie didn't know what to do, so he retreated to the kitchen with the plates. He stood in front of the sink trying to decide what he should say, how he should respond. The urge had come unbidden and suddenly. He would have edited himself if he could have.

"That was way out of line. I'm sorry." Charlie said simply as he sat down at the table. He looked as miserable as Ben.

Ben reached over and put his hand tentatively over Charlie's. "It's OK. I'm just not used to any of this. I don't know what's happening. I'm not angry or upset that you did it, but I'm confused about what it means." He didn't move his hand.

Charlie looked at him for a long time, thinking carefully about what to say. "I'm not sure what all this means, either, Ben. I guess you've figured out by now that I'm gay. I'd be lying if I said that I didn't find you extremely attractive. But it's more than that or it seems to be at this point. I'm feeling something here with you tonight that is new to me, too."

"I felt like this was a date tonight. It's such a weird feeling. I've been trying to tell myself that guys don't have dates with other guys, but I had that excited feeling that you get when you have a date with a girl you really like. I didn't know what to make of those feelings." Ben finally took his hand away.

"Let's move back to the living room, OK? These chairs aren't very comfortable for lengthy sitting."

They resumed the same positions on the sofa. This time, however, they sat closer together than they had before. Charlie began.

"It was certainly a date as far as I'm concerned. I knew from the moment I saw you get on the train that I was interested. Then, when I met you, I knew I wanted to know you better."

Ben reached out and took Charlie's hand. "Is this OK?"

"It's certainly OK with me, Ben. The question would be is it OK with YOU?"

"After Pam married Brett and Jacen enlisted, I realized that, for the first time in my life, I was going to have time to myself. I promised myself that I would try new things, take some chances. I took a trip to Egypt with some of the doctors from the hospital. It was great except for the food! I came down here to Sacramento and went to an opera. I had never been to one before. It was wonderful and very emotional. The only other time I've heard music that moved me like that was in church. I didn't plan on anything like this, but when I realized it was happening, I knew I wanted to experience it. Whatever it was. Does that make sense?"

"Sure it does, but what is happening here isn't a vacation or an opera. Are you sure?" Charlie wasn't really sure himself, now that it was here. He was going to have to proceed very cautiously.

Ben's feelings were even more tumultuous and confusing than Charlie's, for at least Charlie knew what he was feeling. For Ben it was a feeling without comprehension. This attraction he felt was nameless. His desire to touch Charlie had no hands. His desire to kiss him had no mouth. He was powerless in the thrall of something unidentified. He knew from some place deep within himself what Charlie's skin would feel like. He knew he was on the brink of discovering himself in the touch of another man. Ben moved closer to Charlie and took Charlie's hand and put it on his heart. It was drumming in his chest.

"I want you to kiss me."

Charlie looked into those eyes and saw his own soul come back to life in the blue heat. Ben looked into Charlie's brown eyes and saw endless possibilities in the flecks of gold they contained. They were so close that Charlie drew Ben's breath into his own. Each moved forward only slightly, yet it was a move that would change their lives forever. As their lips met, taste and touch and scent surrounded them and became the air in the room. There was space for nothing except their sensation of each other. Ben opened his mouth slightly and Charlie's tongue found its place. Ben was in his arms and they drank deeply of each other. They broke with a gasp and Ben looked scared to death.

"Was that OK? Did I do it right?"

"Oh yeah, my baby boy. You're a natural." Charlie couldn't believe that Ben had never kissed a man before. He remembered the first time he had kissed a man. He was about 13 years old and had been to a couple of parties where they turned off the lights and kissed girls. He didn't get what all the fuss was about. Then his sister's boyfriend had kissed him one night and a lightbulb went on in his brain. He knew what the fuss was about! It was wonderful and he hoped that was happening for Ben right now.

"Wow. That was different. With your whiskers and all. But in a good way, I mean. I liked it. It was different from kissing a woman."

"Uh, yeah. It is different from kissing a woman. Wanna practice some more?"

Ben was still in Charlie's arms. Charlie nuzzled his neck and the chest hair that peeked above his shirt. He breathed deeply of Ben. It was more than just cologne. It was that magical chemistry that happens sometimes. Maybe it's pheromones, but some people just smell wonderful. Ben smelled wonderful.

Ben tentatively took the initiative and moved in toward Charlie. He had his eyes open and looked deeply at Charlie. He was very serious. His lips parted and he kissed Charlie very softly. Charlie kissed him back and undid one of the buttons on Ben's shirt. He reached in and touched the furry skin of Ben's stomach. Ben shuddered in a sexual way. Charlie continued to explore Ben's skin. He reached further down to his abdomen and felt the top of Ben's boxers. Ben sat up abruptly. Charlie thought he had gone too far. Ben stood up and put his hand out to Charlie to join him. Charlie stood and Ben circled his waist with his arms and smiled. For the first time since they had met he didn't seem guarded at all. His eyes were completely clear and shining. Charlie took his hand and led him to the bedroom.

There was only a dim lamp on the bedside table. Charlie began unbuttoning Ben's shirt. He was tan and furry and just as beautiful as Charlie had imagined him to be. Ben followed Charlie's lead and returned the favor. Soon they were standing naked in front of each other. They kissed and their shared sexual tension made their mouths musky in a way that was delicious to them and they tasted with unquenchable thirst. A sweet misting of sweat covered their bodies and seemed to conduct the excitement from their mouths to every pore, every sinew. They drowned in each other's presence, clinging, trying to touch each other everywhere at once. Around them, the atmosphere became heated and moist with the vapor from their bodies now melted into one passion. Their intuitive knowledge of each other was primeval, it's roots reached beyond their present selves. As they stood there, totally lost, alone in some prehistoric need, there came from within them the beginnings of a tremor that grew and fed on its own excitement. They fell to the bed and at once, the coolness of the sheets brought their ardor to a more luxurious pace. Charlie pulled Ben into his arms and held him. They tried to get as close to one another as possible, as if trying to become one person.

"You smell so good."

"So do you." Charlie began kissing Ben's face and neck and shoulders and chest. He nuzzled the hair on Ben's stomach and reach for his cock. It was large and arched at a graceful angle. It was beautiful, like the rest of Ben and Charlie's eager mouth took him quickly. Ben gasped.

"You taste good, too." Charlie muttered.

"Gosh," was all that came out of Ben's mouth, but he whimpered and breathed raggedly. Charlie sensed that it might be over too quickly, so he eased off and kissed Ben's inner thigh. He scooted back up until they were face to face again. They looked each other in the eye and Ben's hand reached down and found Charlie's erection. Ben's face showed wonder and surprise at how another man felt in his hands. He smiled slowly and quickly found the way to make Charlie writhe with pleasure. He seemed to enjoy being in control of that.

"You're really beautiful man, I mean it." Ben seemed to be amazed by what he was saying and that he was even saying it!

It didn't take long and Charlie arched his back as his orgasm exploded across the sheets and across Ben's chest. Ben laughed with surprised delight and fell across Charlie's chest. They held each other until Charlie was breathing normally. Ben had never experienced the texture and rich earthiness of another man. It made him dizzy with desire and Charlie noticed.

"It's your turn, baby." He began to kiss his way to the promised land and took Ben's cock in his mouth again. Charlie knew what he was doing and did it well. Ben put his hands in Charlie's hair and within minutes Charlie could tell he was ready. He seemed to want to pull out of Charlie's mouth, but Charlie held him firmly until he got every drop of Ben's sweetness.

"I'm sorry. I didn't mean to do that. Is it OK?" Ben was very embarrassed about what had just happened.

"Oh yeah, that was OK."

"That was my first blow job." Ben looked so serious and Charlie exploded in howls of laughter. Ben looked startled at this reaction, but then, he, too, started to laugh. They hugged each other and laughed more. Being together was pure joy.

They eased into an intimate silence. Charlie turned on his side and Ben spooned into him as if they had been doing that forever. Charlie put his face to Ben's shoulder and appreciated the glorious aroma that was Ben McSwain. The skin was soft and very, very warm.

"I'll bet you don't use an electric blanket, do you?" Charlie snuggled closer.

"I don't even use a blanket and I usually throw the sheet off before the night is over. I've always been very hot natured. Mom says I was that way as a baby." Ben's voice was soft and quiet, different from what it had been earlier. He seemed so much more relaxed now. Charlie hoped it was more than just the sex.

They were quiet again. Then Ben cleared his throat. "I guess I should start getting ready to go back home. I pick mom up for church on Sunday morning and Pam's family meets us there. We've always devoted Sundays to church and family. Mom will cook dinner and we'll go to her house afterwards."

"Sounds nice." Charlie didn't know what else to say. He didn't know anyone who went to church. While he was not a "believer" he always tried to respect people of faith. One of the things that had driven him away from religion was intolerance, so Charlie wanted every one to be free to believe as they saw fit—whatever that meant.

"Yeah, it's important to me. To all of us." Ben moved away from Charlie and right away, Charlie felt a chill where his body had been. They both stood up and began to untangle their clothes from the pile on the floor. They were about the same size, Ben being a little larger, and they got their jeans mixed up. They talked easily as they dressed.

"Thanks for a very memorable evening. I can say that I've never had one like it before."

"I hope your OK," Charlie stumbled a bit, "I hope I didn't step over any boundaries."

Ben laughed, "You stepped over every boundary I've ever had in my life. But it's OK. I wanted you to."

"It was a wonderful evening, all of it. I enjoyed your company so very much. I hope we can do this again."

"Well, I work a lot, really a lot. The hospital is always short handed. I'm a supervisor which means I'm on call even when I'm not there, so my free time is very limited."

"Hopefully, we can find some time that would work for both of us. You're always welcome here, you know."

"I'll call you or email you and maybe we can set something up in a couple of weeks. I'll have to see what my schedule is like."

Charlie was taken aback. He had really assumed that, after what had just happened between them, that they would be seeing each other more regularly, but apparently Ben didn't see it that way.

And that was OK. They weren't Lesbians. They didn't have to move in together after the first date. Charlie didn't need to get heavily involved with Ben anyway. It was clear that Ben had a lot to work out and was not at all in the same place in his life as Charlie. Charlie needed to put the brakes on and accept Ben on his own terms. It was OK.

Ben headed immediately for the door. Charlie was a little surprised at how much he wanted him to stay, but he didn't show it.

He kissed Ben lightly. They were standing on the front porch and Ben seemed nervous about being "in public." He didn't know that all of Charlie's neighbors knew he was gay; they even knew about this evening. Ben was very new at kissing guys, too. He was new to it all.

"GREAT CAR."

"Yeah, it is, isn't it?" Ben was clearly proud of it. "I bought it from one of the docs at the hospital. Got a really good deal on it. It took some doing, but it's paid off and totally mine now."

"I thought it was brand new. It looks like you bought it today."

"No, this is a 2003 model. I'm just a car nut. I love keeping them running right and cleaned up. Looks like you take care of yours, too."

"Well, I guess I do. Probably not as much as you, but I like for it to look clean." Charlie's chubby, red, VW Beetle convertible smiled at both of them

Charlie followed Ben to his car and stood in the drive as he pulled out into the street. He wondered it he would ever see him again. It had been a perfect evening. It was a great connection, but there were certainly obstacles—many, many obstacles. Charlie waved as Ben drove off and turned back into the house. He looked around. The house seemed empty again, lacking the sparkle that it had when Ben was there. Charlie picked up dirty glasses and left over cheese plates and went into the kitchen, but before he began cleaning up there, he went in the bedroom to straighten the covers and smooth the pillows. The bed would be easier to face later on. There was a loneliness about a bed after great sex that he wanted to avoid. Then he went back to the kitchen and finished the washing up. He turned on his iPod as he worked. DeDe Warwick was singing "All That Love Went to Waste."

How true, how true.

# Chapter 16

Ben tried not to think at all as he pulled onto the freeway heading home. His hands were shaking slightly. He couldn't believe what he had just done. It went against everything he had ever believed in his life. Yet it had seemed so right at the time. So completely natural. Charlie was wonderful. But he was also a homosexual. That was just not something that anyone he knew could or would accept. What he had done was a grave sin. He knew his church's stance on homosexuality. When Jacen was in high school, he and several of the other dads in the church had gone to a special workshop in Santa Cruz on human sexuality and the Bible for teenagers. The church was clear and absolute on the subject. Nowhere in the Bible is homosexuality ever condoned. In every instance, Old Testament and New, it is considered detestable and a sin against God. He also knew that there was help for those who suffered from homosexual lust and desire. The Grace of God could cure it. The sin of committing homosexual acts was forgivable. He had known their pastor, Jim Tillman, for twenty years and they were like family. Could Ben go to him with this? What would he say? Would he be shocked? Did other people in the church have these feelings? Could he even bring himself to talk about it? No one he knew had ever talked about it except in general terms. He had never heard anyone in the church mention knowing anyone who was homosexual. Of course, if they were brought up in the church, that wouldn't be a problem. Yet he had been brought up in the church.

Then there were the kids. What if they found out about this? He and Lynette had brought them up to trust in the word of God, in their church, in their beliefs and in their parents! How could he breach that faith now? They had already lost one parent. He was all they had left. Right is right and there is no gray area where this issue is concerned. There was nothing in his life to support him in what had happened tonight or continuing to see Charlie. He felt remorse, of course, but at the same time he felt infinite sadness.

He couldn't deny that he had wanted Charlie and the intimacy he offered. He had not had sex with anyone since Lynette's death. They were very young when they met and waited until after they married. It was pleasurable for him and he assumed it had been for her also. They were both shy about their physical relationship and never talked about it. It was infrequent, but both seemed OK with that. Ben had relieved himself more often, but his dad had told him that men had stronger urges than women and that's what they did to handle it. Ben admitted to himself now that sometimes images of men would come to mind when he masturbated, but they were vague images. He would sometimes imagine touching another man's chest. Yet he never really thought about having sex with men before. He couldn't remember ever being attracted to another man. But he was attracted to Charlie, that was true enough. He was getting an erection right now thinking about what had happened earlier. And he had wanted to stay! He wanted to sleep in Charlie's arms! He had never been so confused in his life. He knew what he should do. He just didn't know if he could do it...not just yet.

Something inside him said that it was not over yet. It was part of that feeling he had after Lynette's death that he must find his own life and live it. He had never imagined that something like this would be one of the choices that would be offered to him. As far as the church was concerned, it wasn't a choice. He was clearly out of step with his church, his life and everything he had ever known, but Ben was not ready to look at that yet.

Sunday was difficult for him. His feet felt leaden and he wondered if anyone could see a difference in him. Did it show? His mother looked at him long and hard when he picked her up, but he didn't give her a chance to interrogate him. They drove directly over to the church for services. He sang in the choir and had a small solo part. His mouth felt like sawdust and he hoped he could get through it. He prayed for help and felt like a hypocrite for doing so. He made it through the service and several people complimented him on his voice afterward, so he must have been all right. Dinner at his mother's was easier because Pam's family and his grandparents were there. He managed to get home by three and decided to check the computer for any messages from work. What he found was an email from Charlie:

"Hey dude :) Just wanted to say hello and tell you how much I enjoyed last night. You are one of the good guys, that much is obvious. I hope that what happened wasn't too overwhelming. I don't want to cause you pain... just the opposite. If you want or need to talk, I'm always available, please know that. You are very special to me and I hope to see you again soon.

Warm regards,
Charlie"

It was so sweet and not at all sinful or lustful or evil. There was nothing evil about Charlie. It all sounded so right and so normal when he said it. All the good memories of last night came flooding back to him. His breath caught in his chest as he thought about the intimacy he had shared with Charlie. The truth was that it had been profound to connect with someone on that level and Charlie was the one he had chosen to connect with. Good, bad or indifferent, he had to deal with it. Prayer had always brought Ben clarity and peace. He turned now to find solace there, alone in his house with just his God.

He found some peace by staying busy and his week went well. Work was hard but rewarding. He was good/tired, an old familiar feeling for Ben. He ran errands, helped his mother, cooked for his ailing grandparents and checked up on the kids. It was his life. He was content. Yet several times during the week, he would see something that reminded him of Charlie—a card with a clown on it or anything red. The first thing he had noticed when he walked into Charlie's house was a big red chair and ottoman in the living room. His bed linens had been in shades of red. The towels in the bathroom, lamps, flowers, candles, boxes and jars—it was everywhere in Charlie's home. So, of course, this week, when he saw a red coffee maker at Target, he thought of Charlie. He decided to buy a card and send it to him just to say thank you for the meal. He gave himself permission to do that, to go that far. He selected the card with great care, however, choosing one that was sentimental and sweet rather than one that was funny or edgy. It felt right to him. He wrote a personal note on the card.

"Hey, dude...thanks for everything. You're a very special person. I'll never forget the time I spent with you and the unreal connection I felt with you.
B."

It sounded like good-bye and Ben knew that it had to be. He didn't want to hurt Charlie and this seemed like the best way, ending it before it got more complicated. There were a million things that Ben wanted to ask Charlie, to explore in that relationship, but he knew that it was wrong. Everything in his life told him that. He mailed the card with sadness and a heavy heart.

# Chapter 17

Charlie's week was very different from Ben's. He woke up on Sunday morning feeling better than he had in a long time. He was energized by the connection he and Ben had made and was looking forward to seeing where it might lead. It was early, but he called Lee in New York, after all it was three hours later there. Lee answered on the first ring.

"Good morning, how're you? Did you talk to Barry about the project?" Lee had caller ID and was off and running.

"Hey, yeah, I did. I'm in if you decide you want to do it. It just sounds like a lot of fun to me. I know that you have more serious considerations and I'm OK if you decide not to do it. I think it's a great chance for us to spend some time together and do some good work at the same time."

"Well, here's something else for you to consider. They are going to preview the project in Dallas at the Hilltop Theatre. It would mean several weeks there, working on this thing. That might change your mind or at least dampen your enthusiasm. Of course, I have to go to Texas anyway because of that teaching gig, but you certainly don't."

Charlie was stopped cold. This was something he hadn't even considered. He had not been to Texas in four years, since his father's funeral, and he was not thrilled by the idea of going back now.

"Wow. That does give me something else to think about. I'm not sure how I feel about Texas."

"Barry says they are prepared to rent us a house so we can even walk to the theatre. It could be fun, returning to the scene of some of our earliest misdemeanors together. And this project is hot. Lot's of good buzz. If Barry can get me what I'm asking for financially, I'm in, too."

"Well, that settles it for me, then. I wouldn't go back to Texas for anyone else. I think I need some time away from here right now, even if it is Texas." Charlie was thinking of Ben.

"Oh? What's up that you need to get out of town?"

"Well, it's Ben. The guy from the train."

"I figured as much, kiddo. I've known you for forty years, you know. I know that he's very religious, he's in the closet and he's got kids. That's the trifecta for getting your heart busted up. You haven't known him all that long, have you? It can't have gotten that serious yet. Right?"

"You're right, of course. We just met a few weeks ago. Last night was the first time we really spent any time together alone. He came over for dinner and dessert."

"Dessert meaning...?"

"Well, yeah and that, too. We did end up in the bedroom. I didn't plan it, honestly, although he's really cute and sexy and exactly my type. Even before I invited him, I knew he was struggling with himself about seeing me at all. We met on the train going into the City. I told you about it. I got something in my eye, a cinder from the tracks, and he got it out for me."

There was silence on the other end of the phone and then, "You are fucking kidding me, Charles Brookstone Morgan. Please tell me you are making this up." Lee hooted with laughter.

Charlie was puzzled. This was not the reaction he expected. "I told you what happened last week. What's so funny?"

"You told me you met on a train. You didn't tell me about the cinder in the eye, etc. Charlie! BRIEF ENCOUNTER!!!"

"Oh.My.God. I didn't even think about that! Good LORD, you're right. I can't believe I didn't make the connection. It's one of my favorite movies of all time. I guess I was just so taken with Ben that I didn't even think of anything else. Unbelievable!"

"OK, so you're really not making this up? Then tell me all about it again."

"Oh, there's not much more to add, Lee. I really like him and I think he likes me. If we were just two regular gay guys, we would already have plans for a second date, I'm sure of that. But when he left last night, he left everything completely open. I might never see him again, to tell the truth. And I'm dealing with that. It is probably the best thing, really. Nip it in the bud and all of those cliches. I certainly don't want to fall in love with him. That would be a disaster."

"Best keep him in the doorbell category." Charlie and Lee had a language all their own that they had developed since the very beginning of their friendship in college. The "doorbell category" was for the ones that were unavailable for anything but occasional sex. They would call, come over, ring your doorbell, have sex and leave. They were usually married, always closeted and good sex because they were so hungry. Charlie had a number of doorbells in his life. He always liked them a lot and there had been a few that he could have fallen for, if circumstances had been different. Lee had fallen for one of them and been in a relationship with a younger, married publicity director at Court Collier Publishing. It lasted for several years until the young man called it off. Lee had been bruised but not bloody because he had protected his heart. He cautioned Charlie.

"Protect yourself honey. You remember my years with Brad. I'm glad that I stayed at a distance then. It paid off. You must do the same. I hope the producers can give me what I need to take this job. It'll be fun and you do need to get away for a while. Distance makes the heart grow some perspective."

"You're right, of course. I've been telling myself the same thing all day. I can smell him on my sheets, Lee, and it drives me crazy. There is this real connection there. I can't explain it. I haven't felt like this in a very long time. It's powerful stuff."

"I know it is, Charlie, but be careful. Oh God, we're too old for this. We were supposed to be settled down by now, weren't we? I've met someone, too. On the internet, but he's from Spain. He lives in one of the resort towns on the coast. He's 22 years old."

"Jesus, Lee, you've got socks older than that!"

"I know. I shouldn't. It's just a dalliance on the internet. I bought a webcam and we play around. It's fun and doesn't do any harm. In fact, I need to go. We meet online almost every day at the same time and it's nearly time. He gets really angry if I'm late." There was a nervous edge to Lee's voice that Charlie didn't like.

"Well, fuck him, Lee. So you're a few minutes late. Big deal."

"It is a big deal to him. He's got that Mediterranean temperament. It's just easier to do what he wants."

"Or get rid of him completely. This doesn't sound real healthy, either, Lee. I think we could both use some time away, don't you?"

"Oh, I guess you're right. Don't worry. This is really just fun and he's in Spain. What could he do anyway?"

They talked a while longer about other things, friends in common and Lee's family back in Texas. Charlie felt so much better when he finally hung up the phone. He and Lee had always been there for each other. Through everything, Lee was the one person that Charlie could go to without fear of judgment. It was good to know he was a phone call away.

And he was right about Ben. Ben was dear and sweet and beautiful, but Charlie needed to give him some space and let him find his own way. Charlie just hoped he would find his way back to him.

# Chapter 18

Two days later, Charlie's mail fell through the slot and scared the hell out of him as it did every morning. He scooped it up, knowing that most of it would be junk. On top was a real letter in Ben's familiar hand. He opened it with mixed feelings, glad to hear from Ben but afraid of what he might have to say. It was a card with palm trees on it. They had discovered that they both liked palm trees, so this was sweet and thoughtful and not just random. That discovery had been one of those moments for Charlie and Ben. Charlie had a palm tree shower curtain and accessories in his bathroom. He guessed it probably had to do with his love affair with Hawaii. Ben admitted that he had palm tree sheets and prints in his bedroom. They had smiled knowingly at each other like this kind of thing was expected between them.

It was a thank you note for Saturday evening. The note was short, but full of past-tense verbs. Charlie would notice that and he read the subtext. He looked at the sweet card and he knew what it meant. It was Ben's way of saying good-bye without saying it. It was probably best. It could never be any more than a "doorbell" relationship and he didn't want that kind of thing with Ben. He didn't know what Ben was feeling at this point, but he suspected it was guilt and confusion and fear. That's not the way to begin a new relationship. Charlie didn't want to begin it that way either. It's just that Charlie knew the possibilities for joy and regretted that they would never be. Ben would be spared the knowledge of what might have been, but he had an even worse knowledge: he had done something that went against all his beliefs. Charlie tried very hard to understand that. He had faced down those demons so long ago. Being gay and also a member of a Christian denomination took an intellectual disconnect that Charlie eventually found intolerable. He had let go of an uncomfortable religious doctrine and eased into a tentative kind of spirituality. He was now perfectly comfortable with a secular-humanist view of morality and the world.

Also in the mail was the contract from Barry Shanks, making him Charlie's agent for theatrical work. The contract information about the show itself was not included. He needed to call Sharon. She had been his literary agent for over twenty years and they were friends. He wanted to make sure that this was all OK with her and ask her advice about the project. She was on speed dial.

"Hey Charlie. What's going on with you?"

"Hi honey...I'm thinking about doing a project for the stage. They are doing a musical of The Last Picture Show and my friend Lee Horner is involved and wants me in on it with him."

"That sounds great, Charlie, but you're terrible with dialogue. I can't get you to make people talk in your novels. How do you expect to write the book for a musical?" She was only half joking. It was a problem for Charlie. Dialogue was not his strong point.

"Well, Lee is a master at it and he'll be working with me. I'm really good at the structural elements, like setting up scenes, stage directions, etc. We've worked on plays before and worked well together. It'll get me out of town for a while at a time when I need it." Charlie hadn't meant to mention man troubles to Sharon. She was on a pink cloud these days having come home from an Italian vacation with an eye job and a beautiful thirty-eight year old Italian boy friend. We should all be so lucky. Charlie didn't want to bring her down with his problems, which were beginning to sound juvenile and silly to him anyway.

"Oh, I met someone. It was a "brief encounter" to coin a phrase. It didn't work out, end of story. So a diversion would be welcome."

"I'm sorry. You're right...there is nothing like a change of scenery. Could I suggest Italy?" Her voice sounded like cashmere.

"You certainly could suggest it, but can you guarantee that I would come home with the same souvenirs you did?"

"Well, no guarantees. So why are you telling me about the 'Picture Show' deal?"

"Barry Shanks, Lee's agent, wants to represent me on this. I just wanted to make sure that was OK with you and that I wasn't breaking any rules of our contract. You've been wonderful to me and I wouldn't want to do the wrong thing out of ignorance."

"Charlie. We've been friends for twenty years. I want you to be successful and of course sign the contract. It won't step on my toes at all. I still get a pound of your flesh for everything else! Go. Do. Enjoy." Sharon was a good agent, but she was also a bit of an earth mother. It was a good combination for Charlie. Maybe that's why they had stayed together so long.

"Thanks a million, Sharon. The deal isn't completed yet, so it may not happen at all. I just wanted to clear it with you before I did anything. I'll keep you posted."

"Do that, honey. And Charlie? About that guy? I don't know what happened or who he is, but if he turned his back on you, he's an idiot and you're better off without him, OK? Love you sweetie."

"Me, too. Take care."

Charlie hung up the phone and called Barry. He signed the contract and got it ready to post the following morning. Now, he really hoped the job came through, even though it meant a couple of months in Texas. He was thirty-seven years old when he left Texas for good. There were no family ties left and only a few friends. So much of his growing up had happened after he got to California and his memories of Texas were those of a much younger version of himself, one less clearly defined. The Charlie of today would be a stranger in a strange land in the Lone Star State.

He returned to the card from Ben. He opened his file drawer and went to his special personal file. All his valuable papers were there: birth certificate, passport, book reviews, a letter from his first lover, pictures of Emma. It was like the adult version of a child's cigar box, full of his most precious things. He put the card from Ben in the file. Sadly, Ben would become one of those precious memories before he ever got to be anything else. He wished he could file away the physical presence of Ben, too...how his skin felt, that wonderful smell. Those couldn't go in the file. They would fade with time. Only the little card with the palm trees would remain in Charlie's cigar box.

# Chapter 19

Both Charlie and Ben had decided individually that they would not see each other again, but they were to be very, very wrong about that. Fate was not nearly through with them yet.

Three weeks after he filed that card away Charlie got a letter.

"Hey dude...how have you been? I've been real busy with work and all, but I have thought about you and wondered how you are. Listen, I don't know if you are still interested in being friends or not, but I would really like to see you again. I'm going back east to see my son before he ships out to Iraq and my flight back to Sacramento gets in very late. I was wondering if I could stay with you that night. I dread the idea of having to drive home after flying all day. I know this is short notice and maybe you don't want to do it. I'll sleep on the couch and maybe I could buy you breakfast the next morning. If you don't want to do this, I'll understand, I just thought I would ask and see, OK?

Later, dude :)

Ben"

Charlie read the message several times. He couldn't figure out what Ben was trying to say. He must have misinterpreted the card he got earlier. Ben had warned him that he wasn't a writer! Did he want to be "friends?" Did he just need a place to crash? Neither sounded like the Ben he was getting to know. He knew intuitively that Ben wanted to see him as much as he wanted to see Ben...and that was more than anything! Charlie picked up the phone and called him immediately.

Ben answered on the second ring. Charlie was surprised; he had expected to go to voice mail.

"Ben, hi, it's Charlie. I just got your letter."

"Charlie. Wow. It's good to hear your voice."

"You, too. Uh, your note...I'd love to see you. You didn't mention any dates. When are you going back east?"

" I'm in North Carolina right now in a rental car driving to see Jacen this very minute."

"Oh! I didn't realize you were already there. Aren't cell phones amazing? I thought you were in Goldmine. I could tell you that I'm in the south of France! But I'm not, of course. I'm sitting at my desk watching the squirrels ruin my yard."

Ben laughed, "I've missed you, Charlie. I would love to see you again."

"And that's why I'm calling. Of course you can stay here. You are always welcome at my house. I want you to know that. When are you coming home?"

"I get into Sacramento tomorrow night. Is that enough notice? Sorry to do this to you."

"It's fine, Ben, really. I want you to stay here. Driving home after that cross country flight would be dangerous. What time?"

"Well, we're supposed to land around midnight, but you know how the airlines are. It could be later. I'm sorry it's so late."

"Not a problem at all. I'll try to wait up for you, but I'll leave the porch light on and the front door unlocked for you in case I fall asleep and don't hear you. And Ben, you don't have to sleep on the couch unless you would be more comfortable there. Crawl in with me, if you want. I would like that very much." Charlie tried to sound light, but he didn't think he did it very well.

"Thanks, Charlie, I'd like that, too." Ben's didn't do it very well either.

Charlie changed the subject. "How's Jacen?"

"He's fine." Ben cleared his throat. "He's nervous this time. It's his second tour and he knows what to expect. He's a communications officer. He was always good at writing and talking, even as a child. He was valedictorian at his junior high school graduation. He gave a good speech that he wrote by himself. We don't know where he got that talent. Certainly not from my side of the family! I wish he wasn't going back, but we believe in our country and the President's commitment to our security and Jacen believes in doing the right thing."

"Those kids are so brave. We all owe them a great debt of gratitude." He chose his words carefully. Charlie meant every word that he said. He did believe that the kids who were serving in Iraq were brave and wonderful. He just didn't think that they should have been there in the first place. But this was not the time or the arena to get into some political discussion with Ben.

"He certainly has my admiration and thanks for all he's doing. My very best wishes and thoughts go with him."

"Thanks, Charlie. I can't tell him that, of course, but it means a lot to me for you to say it. Thanks for letting me stay over, too. I'll see you tomorrow night...LATE, OK?"

"I'm looking forward to it, Ben. I don't think you know how much."

"I'll bet I'm looking forward to it more! Bye, Charlie."

Ben hung up the phone. He had tears in his eyes. It was an emotional day—saying good-bye to Jacen again. He knew how serious this was and every day that Jacen spent in Iraq was tempting fate. He just wished it could be over. There had been a special prayer service at church for the troops and the president and all those endeavoring to secure the country. Ben had been one of the most fervent petitioners. He was frightened for his child.

Hearing Charlie's voice again made him feel better. He wanted to confide in Charlie, to tell him how scared he was for Jacen, but he didn't know if that was the right thing to do. He had kept his feelings for Charlie separate from the rest of his life up to now. Bringing him into his "normal" life felt dangerous, risky, too close. He wouldn't talk about this part of his life with Charlie. He didn't want to start depending upon him for that kind of support. It was too difficult to sort out in his head.

Charlie sat for a moment. He was excited and wanted to see Ben again more than anything. He realized that a degree of lethargy and depression had weighted his days since the last time he and Ben were together, for now he felt aware and energized. His mind sorted through the things that needed to be done to be ready for Ben. He had also promised to make Ben a CD of his favorite music. Ben liked music, too, and this seemed like a way to share their lives. It didn't really matter what their differences were, did it? The fact was that being with Ben McSwain made him happy in a way that he had not felt in many years. Was he going to throw that away without at least trying to find out if it could work? He knew this was a dangerous game. He could get badly hurt, but like some of his friends had said, it was worth the risk to find out. He sensed that Ben felt the same way.

His whole day changed after that. He had been working on an outline for the musical. He had just finished rereading The Last Picture Show and had watched the DVD of the movie a couple of times. He had forgotten what a good movie it was. Even though he had not done a single line of dialogue, he was getting a good feel for which scenes from the book and movie would work well on stage and what they would look like and how they would play out dramatically. Lee could be counted on to get the words exactly right. And there was the music from Luke Beecham. Barry was sending the first songs Luke had finished for the project and in the meantime, Charlie had downloaded a couple of Luke's newer albums from iTunes. He loved the music. It was old fashioned country, but with a lush romanticism that characterized much of the modern country idiom. Charlie liked Clint Black and George Strait and k.d. Lange and K.T. Oslin and Shelby Lynne. They wrote and sang heartbreakingly beautiful music. k.d. Lange had the most beautiful voice in the world. Her cover of "Crying" simply put everything else in that genre to shame. No one could touch it.

Except Luke Beecham came close as far as Charlie was concerned. It was hard to describe, like a cross between Clint Black and Shelby Lynne. That sounds odd, but it fits. His work was country, but not redneck or honky-tonk. It was country and smart and sensitive and melodic. It was that new country sound that filled the void left when pop music got so ugly and monotonous like the junk on <u>American Idol</u>. Two of the songs that Charlie wanted to share with Ben were Luke's songs, "Home's Just Not Home Without You" and "I Always Want the One That I Can't Have." They were both catchy, twangy ballads that stuck with you long after they were over and you just had to listen to them again. They both reminded Charlie of how he felt about Ben. He would include them on that CD he wanted to make.

Ben took Jacen out to dinner on this last night together. He was going back home the next day and Jacen shipped out the day after that. It was just the two of them. Jacen had a girlfriend, but she had knowingly decided not to go with them and allow Ben some time alone with Jacen. She was a sweet, sensitive girl and Ben liked her. She worked at the base, although she was a civilian. They had met at a Sunday service at the base chapel and had bonded immediately and it looked serious. Ben was happy for Jacen. He had never really had a girlfriend in high school. He was a good looking kid, but very shy and sports had been his life. He was too busy playing every season to think about much else. Ben knew that his first tour of duty had matured him in a way that nothing else could have. He had come back a more thoughtful, less boisterous, but more joyful man. Ben marveled at the interesting and positive transition in his son and felt that it was time for him to find a serious relationship. Catherine was perfect for him.

Father and son enjoyed a good meal and a good talk. Too soon it was time for Ben to say goodbye again. They had been through this once before.

"Well, son. I'm proud of you and I love you very much. You're mother would be so proud, too, you know that don't you?"

"Yeah, dad, I do. Listen, I want to say something to you, OK? I know what you've done for Pam and me. It couldn't have been easy. You gave up your whole life for us. I just want you to know that we are both so grateful to you and I love you very much. I know we don't talk about this stuff, but it's important for you to know that...if something happens." Jacen looked so young and so scared. Ben had to fight not to cry.

"I know, son, I know. I only did what I could after your mother died. You and Pam are my whole life. I would do anything for you. I wish I could take your place right now."

"But, dad, this is my place. I chose it. I'm a grown-up finally. I know you probably thought that would never happen, but it has. And I've also realized that you're a grown up, too. You must be lonely. I didn't realize how lonely I was until I met Catherine. Dad, I hope you can find someone to love, too. I mean that. I really do."

"You have grown up! I understand what you're saying and love you for it. Who knows? Maybe I've already met someone!" Ben teased but there was some truth in it, wasn't there?

"Nah, Pam would've told me....or grandma. Neither one of them can keep a secret. I would know about it."

"Maybe they don't know either!" Ben realized that he had gone too far, perhaps, and backed off. "I'm just teasing you, Jacen. You'll be the first to know when I do, OK? Thanks for your concern. You just keep yourself focused on your task and keep your mind sharp and your eyes open. Come back to us son. We love you." Ben's voice finally cracked. He hugged Jacen just like he did when he was five. He kissed his baby boy on the cheek and saw that he was crying, too. They both turned and walked away. As he was leaving, he heard Jacen call out, "Later, dude."

Ben had never loved anyone more in his life than at that moment.

# Chapter 20

It was Thursday and Charlie had been in hyperdrive all day. It was the day that Ben was coming home. He had cleaned and prepped and scoured and it was still hours until he would get there. He thought he was too distracted to work on the "Picture Show" script, but he decided to give it a try. Lee had sent him some pages of dialogue. They were working well together. Lee liked what Charlie had done with scenes and exposition, story arc and organization and Charlie loved Lee's words. Lee's plays had always had a musicality to them that reminded Charlie a bit of country/western music. It was perfect for this project. Just that morning, he received three songs from Luke Beecham. Two of them were perky, twangy and funny, certainly country-inspired, but guaranteed Broadway crowd-pleasers. It was the third song, however, that showed Luke's talent to it's full extent. It was a ballad, intended for the coach's wife. It was haunting and sad and the melody was fresh, unexpected and beautiful. It had instant hit written all over it. Charlie would include it on the CD he was making for Ben. It was called "Too Old for Love." The gist of it was that just when you thought you were too old to fall in love again, it happened.

And Charlie finally admitted to himself that it was happening to him. He knew he was in love with Ben. Oh, they hadn't known each other very long and they came from vastly different backgrounds, but they had known each other forever. They had an ancient connection that defied all the conventions of falling. He knew for certain that Ben felt it, too, but he couldn't predict how Ben would process all those feelings.

Ben was busy processing something else. Every flight on his itinerary was canceled that day. He was supposed to fly to Atlanta and then nonstop to Sacramento, but he ended up flying to Cleveland and now he was in Minneapolis waiting for a flight to Las Vegas where he would catch the last flight of the evening to Sacramento. He was going to be late so he called Charlie.

"Hey, dude. I'm in Minneapolis."

"Good lord, how did you end up there?"

"Delays all day. Man, I'm tired. But we're taking off in just a few minutes, then I change planes again in Las Vegas and, if all goes well, I'll get in around 1:30. Is it still OK for me to come to your house?" Ben sounded exhausted.

"Of course. Anytime you get here is fine. Just drive carefully when you leave the airport. You're going to be really jet-lagged. I may not be able to stay awake, but I'll leave the lights on and I'll hear your car when you drive up."

"Thanks, Charlie. You've been great about this. I'll see you when I can."

"Be careful, honey. I'll see you in a little while." Charlie was aware that he had just called him honey, but he didn't care.

"Wish me luck. Bye for now."

Ben was just worn out. Emotionally, it had been a hard trip. Saying good-bye to Jacen and knowing what he was headed for was one of the most difficult things he had ever done. And today had been nothing but noisy airports, cramped planes, junk food and too much coffee. He rarely drank anything with caffeine, but felt that he might need it today. Now he was still exhausted, but cranked up which was not a good feeling. He boarded the plane in Minneapolis. With luck, he would be home soon...or at least at Charlie's. He thought of Charlie's wonderful little house and it sounded as good as home.

Charlie realized that it was going to be a long night and there was no use sitting up waiting. So he watched a movie and went to bed at his usual time. He read for an hour or so and that was the last thing he remembered until he heard a car door through the fog of sleep. He woke up immediately and went to the door. He had left lights on in the living room and on the porch. He opened the door and Ben was getting a small carry-on bag out of the trunk. He went out to help. The dazzling smile was nowhere to be seen, but he managed a small one when he saw Charlie. Charlie walked up to him and took his head in his hands and kissed him, sweetly, lightly, but firmly. Ben didn't resist at all. He returned the kiss, right there in the front yard. Even though it was two o'clock in the morning, it was a big step for Ben.

"Let's get inside and get you tucked in bed for some sleep, OK?" Charlie picked up Ben's bag and Ben was too tired to even pretend to resist his help. They went into the house and Charlie closed the door with a shiver. It was still winter and it was cold out. Charlie set Ben's bag down, but he didn't even bother to open it. He eyed the door of the bedroom and started taking his clothes off as he went. By the time he got to the bed, he was naked and crawling in on "his side." Charlie was surprised, but it was OK. He was clearly near collapse. So Charlie took off his robe and slippers and climbed in beside him.

Charlie turned on his side toward Ben. Ben immediately spooned into Charlie's chest and let out a huge sigh. Charlie held him tightly. Even after such a long, dirty day, he had that wonderful Ben smell and Charlie inhaled deeply. He nuzzled his neck and his ear and he heard Ben breathing evenly. He was already asleep. Charlie lay there for a long time without sleeping. He wanted to remember what this felt like, holding him in the dark and warm and quiet safety of his bed, their bed. Charlie was really in love and it scared the hell out of him.

He must have slept, for the next thing he knew he was awake and the clock said 5:00 a.m. There was a little grayish light outside, but the room was still very dim. Charlie got up to turn on the coffee pot. As he returned, he stopped at the bedroom door and stared in. There was enough light in the room for Charlie to see Ben asleep on his side of the bed. The covers were only up to his waist and his head was turned slightly toward the door. The linens on the bed were orange and hot pink and burgundy. Ben's coloring stood out in sharp relief and the grace of his position made it look like a painting. He gasped at the beauty of it.

"I'm not asleep." A gravelly voice spoke from the dim room.

"Hope I didn't wake you. I've turned on the coffee, but go back to sleep. You can sleep all day if you want to. God, you are so beautiful." Charlie couldn't help it.

"The last thing I would think about myself is that I'm beautiful. Gosh, Charlie, what a thing to say."

Charlie crawled back into bed and Ben immediately turned to him and began caressing his chest. Charlie turned and felt Ben's erection, urgent against his leg. He found Ben's lips and kissed him hungrily. Ben opened his mouth and returned the kiss with equal passion. They made love quietly, slowly and simply. Nothing complicated. Ben was still new at this and Charlie didn't like complicated sex anyway. It didn't seem to be about orgasms for them. It was more about being together, celebrating the unexpected joy of the union between them. Charlie kissed Ben's fingers, his neck, his stomach. Ben returned each for each, asking often if it was OK. When they finally lay together, spent and happy, only then did Ben tell him about airport hell. What a nightmare. Charlie was just glad he was safe and at home now.

"Sleep some more if you want. It's still so early." But Charlie and Ben were early risers and both were wide awake. Charlie got up and made coffee for them, loading Ben's with real cream (bought especially for Ben) and real sugar (ditto). He brought the mugs back to bed and they sat up against the headboard together. Charlie thought he had died and gone to heaven. This was a fantasy he had played out many times waiting for Ben to be here in his bed. And he was finally here.

"What are you doing today? I don't have to be back at work until tomorrow and I'm not officially on call until then. I have a whole day to myself." Ben was feeling refreshed. It was either the sex or the coffee, or both.

"I have no plans today at all. Would you like to spend the day together?"

"I have to call Pammie and let her know I'm back, but I don't have to be home for anything until dinner at mom's tonight. I could stay until then." Ben sounded a little uncertain and a little shy.

"Wonderful. Let's go out for breakfast. I know a great place in midtown and then I'll take you shopping downtown. There is a men's store that I want you to see. Then maybe a movie. No! I know. This afternoon I'll make some popcorn and we'll watch a movie I'm dying to show you. I think you'll know why when you see it." Charlie was so excited, but he stopped and looked at Ben, "Is that OK? We don't have to do any of that. It's your day. What would you like to do?"

"That sounds great, Charlie. I don't think I've ever had a day quite like that, where I can just shop and eat and watch movies. I'm looking forward to everything and I am starving."

"Well, the restaurant doesn't open for a while, but I've got toast or cereal or something to tide you over, if you like."

"No, I'm OK, really. I'll wait for breakfast, but I would like to take a shower, and, can I ask you something?"

Charlie stopped and looked at Ben. He looked very serious. "Of course, Ben. I hope you know that you can always asked me anything."

"Well, I have this fantasy about taking a shower with you. Is that weird?"

Charlie laughed with relief. "Weird? Not weird to me! That sounds wonderful. I'll wash your back if you'll wash mine!" and Charlie got up, went to the bathroom and turned on the hot water.

If anything, Charlie thought Ben was more beautiful wet than dry. They soaped and scrubbed and memorized each other. As Charlie was toweling Ben's back, Ben told him about his last conversation with Jacen. Ben had promised himself that he was not going to discuss his real life with Charlie, but it seemed so right to do it and he thought that Charlie might be the only person who would understand how he felt. Listening to the story of a father and son saying good-bye broke Charlie's heart. He kept forgetting that Ben had these very strong, very rich and very powerful relationships in his life: children, parents and grandparents. While, he, Charlie was alone really, except for Jim and Lee and friends like John and Dru. Ben's roots were very deep. Charlie felt like cut flowers. He realized that loving this man would mean difficulties. At this moment, he was willing and capable of accepting whatever might come. It was worth it.

# Chapter 21

He watched Ben as they dressed and observed how much alike they were in their ritual. They did things in unison. In a time when most men left the house looking like they just rolled out of bed, Charlie and Ben were throwbacks to an era when good grooming was the rule rather than the exception. Both of them understood instinctively that it was not about vanity or pretension, but a natural part of being civilized, of being a gentleman.

They went to a popular midtown restaurant and Charlie noticed with pride that several heads turned as they were seated. It wasn't conceit or even concern about how he was perceived that made him aware of the attention. It was his awareness of Ben, of how perfectly they fit together, of how they completed each other that made him sensitive to their place together in the world. Ben was oblivious to the attention and scanned the menu avidly the moment they sat down. He wasn't lying about being hungry and ate ravenously.

Charlie couldn't believe anyone could eat so much and stay as trim as he was. He asked Ben about it.

"It's my metabolism. I burn calories like a marathon runner. You know how hot I was in bed last night."

Charlie shot him a look, "Yes, I do know how hot you were!"

Ben blushed attractively if nervously, "I didn't mean it like that!" He looked around to see if anyone had overheard their conversation.

"Relax. It's OK, really. And I do know what you mean. You're like a little stove, all toasty and warm."

"Well, that's my point. I just burn a lot of calories. That's part of the reason I don't eat very healthy foods, I guess. I can just eat anything and it doesn't seem to affect my weight. Although, I am noticing that it's slowed down as I've gotten older. I guess eventually I'll have to start eating rabbit food, but I dread the day." Ben was more open and relaxed than Charlie had ever seen him and the food seemed to revive him.

"Why is that? You're a nurse, a health care professional. You should know how important it is to eat right. Or maybe you know something the rest of us don't? Maybe hamburgers and nachos are better for us? Is that it, Ben?"

"Did I tell you that I grew up on a farm? Well, part of the time anyway. And my mother's people have been farmers for several generations. When I was just a little boy we lived on a small farm in Napa County. Every afternoon after school, I would have to pick beans or broccoli or tomatoes. It was boring and hot and I hated it. So I was not exactly thrilled to see all that stuff appear on my plate a few hours later. I just never liked vegetables at all after that. I've tried. I guess I'm better than I used to be, but those early years ruined me. When dad left and we moved to Goldmine, one of the best things was no more veggies!"

"How old were you when your dad left? Is it OK to ask about that?"

"Sure, it's OK. It was a long time ago. Truthfully, it wasn't devastating to me. Looking back, I can see how hurt Mom was, but I was relieved that he was gone. It meant a lot of changes for all of us. I had to go to work, but I enjoyed it. I don't remember not working, Charlie. It's so much a part of my life. Work." Charlie suspected that Ben didn't talk about himself very often.

"Oh wow. I just thought. I fed you vegetable soup the first time you came to my house. You must have loved that!"

"I was hoping you wouldn't notice that I didn't eat much of it. I love cheese, though, and that was great! We're a meat and potatoes family. I should have had more veggies for the kids, but I just couldn't force myself. And they seem to be OK. I guess I didn't ruin them for life!" The light in Ben's eyes changed when he talked about his children.

"I'll try to remember that in the future, although, I think you might really like some vegetables now that you're an adult. I hated broccoli and peas when I was a kid and I love them now. It's like buttermilk. I hated buttermilk and now I really like it."

"Ewww! Now you've really hit a nerve. Buttermilk? My grandmother used to drink the stuff. It even looks horrible in the glass!"

They continued to talk easily through breakfast, shifting gears often. They spoke of silly things like buttermilk and serious things like work, ethics and the future. Externally, their lives were so different. Ben had the structure and security of his family, his church, his job. Charlie was more of a wild card, dependent only upon his own motivation to shape his life. But their hearts met at a common point. They were both good, kind men who shared a lot of the same quirky values and saw life and themselves in much the same way. It was the loving recognition of soulmates.

Charlie insisted on paying the check and they headed out to Ben's beautiful car. "Let's go downtown. I want to take you to my favorite store. You'll recognize my whole wardrobe when we get there! I found out that their clothes just fit me really well. Being small can be a problem. Well, I guess you know that. You sure this is OK with you? Most people I know don't like to shop as much as I do."

"No, Charlie, really, that sounds great. I just don't get the chance to do this very often. There are too many other things taking up my time. Just tell me how to get there!"

"Clothes are important to me. I guess you've noticed. But it isn't for the reasons that most people think. I'm not interested in impressing other people or showing off or spending a lot of money. It's not about status or vanity. Clothes are an extension of me. It's a way of expressing myself, like an art form. It's exciting and satisfies something creative in me. I've been that way all my life. It's the only way I can explain it."

"Wow, Charlie. I've never heard it expressed like that before, but I know exactly what you mean. I feel the same way. I just never knew how to say it like you did. One of the things I hate about my job is that I have to wear scrubs all the time. I feel the same way you do when I get dressed to go somewhere." Ben turned and looked at Charlie, really looked at him, for something awakened in him, something new was being acknowledged. They were sitting in the car and Charlie reached up and put his hand lightly on Ben's shoulder as he drove. It was a gesture that couples are familiar with. It was at this moment that Charlie and Ben first became a couple.

#

"I think this is the store I went to in San Francisco. Yeah, this is the cologne I bought. You want to try it?"

"I have it already and it's one of my favorites. It's the only one of their fragrances that I do like." Ben and Charlie were of one mind when it came to scent. They were both acutely attuned to the sense of smell and shared that trait like a secret super power.

They tried on some things. The clothes had a slim and low-cut profile. The slacks fit snugly and the jackets were cut high in the arm. It was a silhouette that was good on small, slender men like Charlie and it fit Ben like a glove. He tried on lots of things at Charlie's insistence. A baby blue cashmere sweater was the perfect color and looked as if it had been made with him in mind. A silk blazer, casual slacks and a beautiful linen shirt all fit perfectly without any alterations. Ben was having fun and Charlie was having fun watching Ben.

He was not the only one who noticed. While Ben was in the fitting room, the sales clerk came up to Charlie and said, "Your boyfriend looks great in those clothes, doesn't he?" It pleased Charlie that Ben had been referred to as his boyfriend, but he didn't know how Ben might feel about it.

"He does indeed. Listen, while he's in the dressing room, here's my credit card. I'm going to ask you to hold some of these things for me, will you? I'll be back later this week to pick them up. Great gifts for later on."

"Oh, I know who you are Mr. Morgan. I've seen you here often. I'll take care of everything for you. No problem." There was a conspiratorial wink. Sometimes, it was good to be gay!

"And don't say anything in front of my boyfriend, OK?" Charlie knew that he didn't have to add that, but he just wanted to say out loud that Ben was his boyfriend.

"You got it. Here he comes." The salesclerk backed off a bit.

Ben came out of the fitting room in his own clothes. "That was fun, but I don't really need anything. Maybe some other time. Beautiful clothes, though." Charlie got the idea that Ben would have enjoyed spending some money, but couldn't break the habit of saving every penny for the kids, so Charlie was supportive.

"No problem. We'll come back some time and do some serious damage. I don't need anything either. I just paid off my credit card last month!"

They stopped on their way out of the shopping center and bought a bag of gummi bears...enough to get their parking validated, so it was like they were free.

"Now let's head back to my house. I want to show you something very special." Charlie was thinking of a movie. It had clouded up while they were shopping and looked like rain. Perfect. A rainy afternoon watching a movie together. It was Charlie's idea of heaven. When they got to the house, Charlie fixed popcorn and surprised Ben with a Diet Pepsi.

"I don't usually allow this crap into my house, but I made an exception for you." Charlie popped a Diet Coke for himself, piled popcorn, gummi bears and drinks on a tray and went into the den. Ben followed him and took the tray from Charlie as he got the DVD ready. The only place to sit in Charlie's den was a big, wide chaise longue. Ben was hesitant about sitting. He didn't quite know how they were supposed to share it. Charlie hopped on first and Ben just slid in beside him and they snuggled down together to get comfortable. It was amazing. They fit like it was custom made.

"This is <u>Brief Encounter</u>, one of my favorite movies of all time. It's British and came out the year I was born and before you make any cracks, yes it does have sound! It's amazing that it is still as poignant and true today as it was when it was made. There is a scene that you won't believe. I won't say anything else. You'll know." Charlie was in his element talking about movies. Ben watched him as he chattered on—that gray haired, slightly loopy, deceptively young-at-heart man was endearing himself to Ben. He didn't really get most of what Charlie was talking about...the screen play, the director....but he was mesmerized by Charlie anyway. He felt truly happy and alarmed and confused. The affection he was feeling was so brand new.

Ben was surprised how quickly he got into the movie. He usually didn't like old movies. He and the kids just went to see whatever was playing at the cineplex. It didn't matter because it was about being with the kids. That was his only exposure to movies. Charlie obviously liked a different kind of movie and this one was very good. Charlie was right. It was hard to believe that this movie was nearly sixty years old. It was in black and white and the cars and clothes looked old. And it was British, so they talked with an accent, but Ben could relate to the story. He got the part that Charlie had told him about. There was a scene in a railway station where the girl got a cinder in her eye from a passing train and the guy, who was a doctor, got it out for her. It was how they met!

Ben looked at Charlie with disbelief. "You did that on purpose, didn't you!"

Charlie laughed, "NO, I swear I didn't at all. Truthfully, I had forgotten about this scene in the movie. I didn't make the connection until my friend Lee pointed it out. I was telling him how we met."

Ben's smile darkened just a bit, "You told someone about us?"

Charlie was found out. "Yes, of course, I did. He's my best friend. We tell each other everything." He didn't mention that he had told everyone he knew about Ben.

"What did you say about me?"

Charlie had paused the movie and was relieved that Ben smiled as he asked the question.

"I told him I met this handsome fella on the train who helped me get something out of my eye. He howled with laughter."

"What else did you tell him?"

"I told him that I might be in serious trouble where you are concerned."

"What did you mean by serious trouble?"

"We'll talk about this another time, OK? Let's just watch the movie." Charlie started the film again. "Have a gummi bear, have two, have some popcorn. Drink you're Pepsi." Charlie wanted to change the subject. It was way to early for this conversation, even though the feelings were there. It would wait for another day.

They both cried at the end of the movie. When the star-crossed lovers realize they must end the relationship, Alex, the doctor, arranges for a job in

Johannesburg, South Africa and plans to take his family away. Laura stays in the life she's always known.

"It was so sad that they couldn't be together, but they did the right thing didn't they?" The intensity of his reaction to the film took Ben by surprise.

"I think that's what makes this a classic and keeps people coming back to this movie. Did they do the right thing? They did what society expected of them, but was that the right thing for them? We don't know what happened to them afterward. Were they ever really happy with their lives again? Was Laura able to just go back to her old life? Did South Africa provide enough distance for Alex to resume his life and forget Laura? It's those ambiguities that make this such a great film and one of the great love stories."

"I didn't think of those questions. I just thought is was so sad that they couldn't be together."

"Oh, me too, of course. That's the saddest thing of all." In the long run, that was at the heart of it all, wasn't it?

Ben had to leave after the movie was over. He had to drive home and be at his mother's by five o'clock. He got his bag packed up and loaded into the car and came back into the living room where Charlie was standing, looking a bit forlorn. Ben, easy now with Charlie, put his arms around him and hugged him tightly. "It was a great day, Charlie. I've never known anyone like you before. I think we have a very special friendship and I'm so glad that I met you. I'll see you again, soon, I hope."

It was not as romantic as Charlie would have liked, but he realized that Ben didn't have the vocabulary to say those things yet. Perhaps he didn't feel it, but Charlie did and decided to keep it to himself for the time being.

They walked out to the car together. Charlie went around to the driver's door with him. Ben opened the door and turned to Charlie. This time he didn't care who was watching. He pulled Charlie to him and kissed him, right there on Atwell Street in front of God and everybody. It was a huge moment for Ben and a moment of sheer joy for Charlie. Seismic shift.

# Chapter 22

Ben and Charlie turned a corner that night Ben arrived so exhausted from his trip to North Carolina. Charlie was ready for this experience and Ben had found in Charlie something he didn't even know he needed or wanted—a friend or companion. He wasn't sure what word to use. He was happy and excited in a way that he hadn't experienced in many years.

They worked hard to carve out some time from Ben's busy life. Charlie was always able to rearrange things if Ben got some time off at the last minute. He didn't mind. He was just grateful for a life that allowed him to do that. They lived in the Central Valley of Northern California and it was just that... central. They were within an hour or two of so many wonderful places: Lake Tahoe, Carmel, Napa Valley, Yosemite. Ben loved to drive and Charlie didn't, so that got settled. On their first outing, they drove to Lake Tahoe. They were in the Jag and Ben was clearly enjoying the drive over the pass. Charlie sat in the passenger seat and watched him. He could watch Ben for hours if he didn't get caught first. They talked eagerly. There was something at their core that was shockingly the same and yet their outward lives were so different. Charlie had long wondered how couples like James Carville and Mary Matalin ever got together, much less stayed together, but he was beginning to understand that love didn't always fit an equation.

Charlie sat sideways in the seat, turned toward Ben. Ben had his eyes on the road, but his hand was on Charlie's knee. Sports cars are great for infatuated people.

Ben cleared his throat, "You never talk about your family, Charlie. Is it OK to ask about them?"

Charlie was a little surprised by the question. "Oh, uh, sure. It's OK. I guess I don't talk about them because they've all been gone for a while now. You know, they just aren't a part of the "every day" of my life. I loved them a lot, but we were different from your family. We didn't do a lot of things together, even when we all lived in the same house. Daddy was busy with his medical practice. You know what kind of hours they keep. Mom had many interests: historical preservation, garden club, Library Board. My sister was seven years older, so I didn't pal around with her much. And I left home for good at seventeen. Oh, I went back for holidays and visits, but I never lived there again."

"I've lived five minutes from my mom my whole adult life. I can't imagine her not being there."

"My mom and I were close in a different way. We talked on the phone a lot before she got sick. Dad always said she was my biggest fan. But after the Alzheimer's...frankly, I don't remember the last time we had a real conversation. She left so gradually. I still miss her every day and, of course, I regret the things not said. I just didn't realize it was too late to say them."

"I'm sorry. I didn't know about the Alzheimer's. I've seen enough of that. It's a nasty business for everyone. Was it a long time?"

"About five years after she was diagnosed. You're right, though. It was awful. When they called to tell me she had died, I was relieved and happy for her...that she didn't have to go through that any more."

"I'm sorry, Charlie. I didn't mean to bring up all this painful stuff. I was just curious about your family." Ben squeezed Charlie's hand.

"It's OK, really. I'm fine talking about it. You know, I would have told my mother about you by now."

"Really? She knew that you were, uh, gay and it was OK?"

"Since I was nineteen. I just told them. I had a boyfriend and I was happy with who I was and it just seemed stupid not to share that with them. I was very naive! I thought it wouldn't be a big deal. They were better than most parents are I suppose, but it was still a big deal. We never worked through it completely, but you get what you get. It was OK. They loved Jim and Lee. Even they could see that these were good and positive relationships in my life. They just weren't prepared to deal with the rest of it—my openness, the politics, my activism. They were private people. They didn't quite know how to respond to me!"

They talked on through the mountain pass, as fascinated with each other as with the scenery. It changed from the flat farmland of the Valley to the foothills, dotted with fawn-colored brush. As the landscape changed, Ben's view of Charlie changed, too. He saw a side of Charlie he had not seen before. Charlie was alone in the world now, but he wasn't lonely. Jim and Lee were his family. Family was so important to Ben; he was glad that Charlie had somebody and he wondered what they thought of him. He found himself hoping that they liked him. He would never know what his family thought of Charlie.

"Oh, I almost forgot! I made a CD for you. I've had it for a while and keep forgetting to give it to you. It's in my bag in the back seat. You know Luke Beecham is doing the score for the show. There is one song in particular that reminded me of you. I think you'll love it. Charlie found the CD and popped it into the player. The men listened in silence for a while, enjoying the music and the quiet of each other's company. The ballad from the show came up. It really was a gorgeous song. Charlie stared out the window and listened. When he turned to look at Ben and there were tears in his eyes. He liked it, too.

"That song is so you, Charlie. The music you play is stuff that I don't think I would ever have listened to before. But since I met you, I listen to it and hear those words and I have to admit I do love it. I really do. I'll always think of you when I hear that kind of music. I think of it as cruise ship music."

Charlie laughed. Cruise ship music? Ouch, his age really was showing!

They continued to listen to the CD. Ben drove on toward the Lake and Charlie continued to hold his hand as they climbed. With each mile the road became steeper, the hills became mountains, the air cooled and crisped and they were in another world. It was the world of Charlie and Ben, as rarified as the air around them.

They had rented a small cabin on the water for one night. Charlie wished it could have been longer, but Ben could rarely be gone more than overnight. He really meant it when he said he was on call 24/7. These days, he had been able to call in favors from some of the other nurses to cover for him for an overnight getaway. He was still tethered to his cell phone and a pager and they knew he could get a call at any time. Charlie grew up in a medical household so this was not foreign to him. Annoying, yes, but not foreign. He thought he knew a little of what his mother must have felt all those years. Charlie understood why she never complained. It was part of the deal. You have a relationship with someone in that profession and you accept the whole package. Charlie felt that way, too. It wasn't what he would have preferred, but it was what he got with Ben and he would rather have that with Ben than all the time in the world with someone else.

Because it was such a short trip, it was easy to unpack the car. The little cabin was freezing cold and the first thing they did was start a fire in the fireplace and turn up the heat. They had stopped at a specialty store on the way out of town and picked up some steaks, baking potatoes and, at Charlie's insistence, some asparagus and salad greens. There was a bag of gummi bears and some carrot cake for dessert. Charlie unloaded everything in the kitchen while Ben made them at home in the bedroom. It was still light out and they decided to take a walk down to the lake before dinner. It would also give the house a chance to warm up a bit.

They closed the door of the cabin and breathed in the mountain air. The trees formed a dark canopy above them and the broken pine cones and needles on the forest floor formed a neat pathway to the lake. The pine tar was redolent and Charlie thought of home in the Piney Woods of East Texas. It had been a long journey from there to here. He experienced one of those sudden awarenesses. How did he get to this place in his life? He supposed he had just followed a path as he was doing now.

It didn't occur to either of them that they would go out that night. Neither of them were gamblers, Ben because of his religious beliefs, of course. Charlie just didn't like gambling. They talked about it as they walked toward the lake and Ben was surprised by Charlie's take on the subject.

"When I give someone money, I expect something in return: a shirt, a stalk of celery, a pack of gum. Something. I don't see the point of handing over money to someone for no reason. Just seems wasteful."

Ben's response surprised Charlie, too, "I always thought gambling was very exciting, watching it in movies and on television. I've been to one of the casinos here in Tahoe before, but I only did that once when Lynette and I were here skiing. I played the nickel slots and quit after I lost ten dollars. I had fun and I can see how people could get addicted to it. Lynette wouldn't even go in the door of the casino. I think it may have been the only time she was ever really mad at me. I never gambled again and never gave it another thought."

The sun was beginning to set and it was getting even colder. They walked closely together and Charlie slipped his hand in Ben's coat pocket where they held hands. They were alone on the little path down to the lake and even Ben didn't seem too worried about someone seeing them together. Charlie had not really thought about things like that in years, but was aware of it now because of Ben's sensitivity to it. Truthfully, it was a little bit exciting for Charlie to feel clandestine. It had been a long time since he felt like he was doing something "on the sly." He pulled Ben closer to him and Ben didn't resist.

The air was so clean it felt like they were breathing pure oxygen and it crackled with a crisp cold energy. As they reached the lake, the sky turned fifty shades of red and pink and orange and purple and maroon. All of Charlie's favorite colors. It was as if nature had decided to create a sky just for him. The colors stacked up in horizontal bars across the sky. They played and shifted and blended in endless combinations of richest reds. It was, quite simply, glorious. Again, Charlie became aware that this was one of those times he needed to stop, absorb it completely and store it away forever. He turned and looked at Ben's face. He looked serious and a little drawn even though the colors of the sky and the air were burnishing his cheeks to a healthy glow. Charlie thought he was working way too hard, but he looked beautiful to Charlie. Ben felt he was being stared at and turned to Charlie and smiled.

"What? What are you lookin' at, dude?"

"You. You look tired. Are you OK?"

"Only you would notice, Charlie. I am tired. I'm not sleeping well. It's what we're doing Charlie—this is hard to talk to you about. I don't want to hurt your feelings, but I don't have anyone else I can talk to."

"It's OK Ben. What is it? You can tell me anything. Talk to me." Charlie huddled in closer.

"When we're together—just the two of us—everything is perfect. It all feels so natural and good. I haven't felt this way since—well I don't know that I've ever felt this way before. But when I get in the car and head home, back to my real life, I'm so filled with shame and guilt. I can barely look Mom in the face—or Pam. Mom senses that something is going on. Charlie, I've never hidden anything from my family in my life. I've never needed to. But this…" Ben stopped to breathe and to check on Charlie, to see if he was OK.

"Oh Ben, I knew it was going to be difficult for you. I wish I could make it better, but I can't. I could give you all kinds of logical reasons and arguments for why we should be together and why you should just tell your family about us, but this isn't about reason or logic, is it? It's about faith. You choose to believe in something based on faith, not fact. Millions of people make the same choice and it isn't my job to undermine your choice or your faith. Yes, I believe differently from you, but not because someone made me. It was my journey, my discovery. Your journey of faith is your own, too. Not mine. It's a struggle that you must make alone. You'll do what is right for you."

Charlie pulled him close and got a hit of that wonderful Ben smell. Ben brushed Charlie's temple with his lips and said softly, "This perfect sunset. I'm at peace for right this minute and I want to enjoy that." Charlie turned to look at the sun setting quickly behind the mountains on the other side of the lake. It was early for sunset, but it was because of those mountains. Ben turned to look, too. They moved even closer to each other, their cheeks almost touching. Charlie could feel the warmth from Ben's face. They turned to each other and kissed briefly, backed away, looked at each other then kissed again.

Suddenly it was almost dark. They turned and quickly headed back to the cabin. It had warmed up a lot when they opened the door and the bright fireplace welcomed them. They took off their coats and set to the business of dinner. Charlie had been surprised at what a proficient cook Ben was. Of course, he had been cooking for his family for a long time. He was certainly not a fancy chef, but he knew his way around the kitchen and seemed to enjoy it. They worked well together preparing meals. They didn't seem to get in each other's way and had fun sharing those times. Charlie had eaten more red meat since meeting Ben than he had in the last ten years. It was OK with him. He wasn't a devoted vegetarian. He just ate a lot of veggies and fish and chicken because they were easy and quick to prepare. Ben liked steaks and hamburgers and baked potatoes and french fries, so that's what they often had. But Charlie usually got a vegetable in there somewhere and Ben was great about at least trying them. There was NO enthusiasm, but he did try. Charlie was going to serve the asparagus with a Bernaise sauce. He thought that would make it palatable for Ben. He might even just like the asparagus with the rich sauce on it.

As it turned out, Ben did like the asparagus, but it was probably the Bernaise that he liked because he ended up cleaning up the sauce on his plate with some of the Italian bread they had brought with them. Charlie made a mental note that he could serve Ben any vegetable hidden under a healthy dollop of Bernaise.

After dinner they cleaned the little kitchen and packed up the leftovers to take home with them the next day. Then they settled on the sofa in front of the fireplace. There was a television set in the corner, but neither of them bothered to turn it on. Charlie was working on the "Picture Show" project and sat on one end of the sofa. Ben was reviewing his notes from the ASL classes. The classes were over, but he was studying for the state certification exam. He lay on the sofa with his head in Charlie's lap and his feet curled up on the other end. He reached over his head put his hand in Charlie's lap and signed "I love you." It was the first time Ben had said that and Charlie missed it! He did like the feeling of Ben's hand in his lap, however. He changed the book to his left hand and caressed Ben's chest with his right, still reading. Ben stretched and squirmed and Charlie knew what that meant. He nuzzled Charlie's lap. So much for reading.

They made love like they always did, softly and simply. Charlie loved the straightforward way he and Ben communicated sexually. There was lots of touching and lots of kissing and orgasms came quickly. Ben always laughed when he had an orgasm and Charlie thought that was great. What better time to laugh? Ben did something else that was dear. You know how, in porno movies, people always say "Oh God! Oh Jesus! Christ I'm coming!" Well,

Ben always said, "Gosh." Charlie thought that was just the coolest thing ever. Just, "Gosh."

Tonight as they lay in bed after sex, Ben cleared his throat and said, "Sex with men is really messy, isn't it?"

"Yeah, I guess it is. Does that bother you?"

"No, not really. I thought it would when I thought about doing this, but it's exciting. I love watching you. It's so intimate."

"Yeah, sex is pretty intimate." Charlie spooned him tightly and kissed his shoulder. Charlie loved that shoulder. He fell asleep kissing that shoulder.

The next morning, they packed quickly and bundled into the car. It was very cold and very clear and very beautiful that morning. They decided to forego getting the kitchen dirty again with breakfast, even though they had brought supplies. They would stop instead on the way home. It would be more fun. You should always have breakfast at a restaurant when you're on a trip.

They stopped at a pancake house and Ben was in his element. Charlie was a good boy and had an omelet, fruit and coffee, while Ben ordered pancakes and sausage and eggs and hash browns. And Charlie knew by now that Ben would burn it off before they got home, just driving the car. He looked around the diner. It was just a standard diner with lots of mint green formica and bad lighting, but the clientele was pure Tahoe. The tables were full of handsome, chic people in expensive ski wear headed back to Bay Area destinations after a week-end of sports. Charlie had forgotten that skiing was the big draw here and Ben hadn't mentioned it either. Tahoe's two biggest attractions, skiing and gambling didn't interest Charlie and Ben as much as just being together.

Ben drove all the way back to Sacramento. Charlie offered to help but he insisted. He really did love to drive. That was fine with Charlie. He enjoyed the ride, looking at the scenery in the pass and how drastically it changed as they got closer to Sacramento. They stopped at Charlie's house and Ben helped him get his things out of the car, including the unused groceries.

"I better get going. I've got to be at the hospital by three." Ben had to work, but he loved his job and never seemed to resent having to go in, even on a week-end. Ben was just a very good egg all around.

"I know. I'm being selfish because I want you to stay. It was wonderful. Thanks for another great memory. We're building quite a few those, aren't we?"

"Yes, we are, Charlie. It's a very special friendship"

There was that word again.

"Charlie went around to the driver's side of the car and put his head in the window and kissed Ben full, hard, deep and long, leaving him gasping for breath.

"See you later, friend." And with that Charlie turned and walked into the house, not turning around. It took all the discipline he could muster not to turn around, but it really would have ruined the moment. Charlie meant to make a point. He walked into the house and closed the door. Of course, he immediately went to the window and peaked through the blinds.

Ben was sitting behind the wheel of his car looking a bit dazed. That was exactly the reaction Charlie wanted.

"Friendship, indeed." Charlie muttered and laughed at the same time. "Let's see him deal with that one."

Ben finally started the car and slowly back out of Charlie's driveway.

"Gosh," he said.

# Chapter 23

As the weeks went by they slipped into a routine. It wasn't the relationship that Charlie always thought he would find, but the rest of his life hadn't turned out according to plan either. You adjust. And he knew that Ben really tried to carve out some time for them. Ben was stealing time from what appeared to be an already complete life. For Charlie, the time Ben stole was what made his life complete. But it should be understood that it was important to Ben, too. The fact that he was willing to go against his family, his religion, indeed, his own morality, was testimony to his feelings for Charlie. Charlie knew this. What they had right now might be all that they could ever have. It was enough for today.

Charlie had his work, too, and it helped him keep his feet on the ground. The show was shaping up well. Lee was very pleased with his contributions and the time was fast approaching when they would leave for Texas and the workshop. Charlie was excited and looking forward to the experience, but regretted leaving Ben. It had been six months since they met on the train and he wanted to do something to celebrate. He was hesitant to call it an "anniversary" because they still tap danced around certain words. They didn't often go out at night. They were so content with each other's company and Ben's job was so physically tiring that quiet evenings at home were always more appealing. He had never taken Ben to Mollie's, his favorite restaurant. It was a tiny hole in the wall in a very unassuming building that Charlie had stumbled upon by accident several years earlier. He later found out that it was the best kept secret in Sacramento! Mollie's reputation is such that they don't advertise at all and reservations must be made well in advance. It isn't fancy or pretentious...just a welcoming atmosphere, a charming host and the best food in town. What more could you want? Charlie made the reservation well in advance to book the time they wanted and for Ben to plan the time off from the hospital. He didn't mention "anniversary" but he told Ben that it was a special night at his favorite restaurant. Ben had sounded curious and amused on the phone. He had such a sweet temperament, he didn't care where they were as long as they were together.

They got to the restaurant a few minutes early, but the host/owner seated them immediately. Charlie didn't come here that often and he certainly wasn't a "somebody" but the owner made him feel as if he were a special guest. It was one of the charming things about the restaurant. They were shown to a lovely table for two set enough away from other tables that they could feel comfortable talking privately. Charlie liked that, too. He hated restaurants where you were elbow to elbow with strangers. It was awkward for everyone. As they sat, Charlie was again aware that some eyes had turned to them. The restaurant was in a neighborhood that had many gay businesses and bars. It was a favorite in the gay community, for it offered a welcoming atmosphere. The owners, though straight, were sensitive to their gay clients and, tonight, seemed to be sensitive to the fact that this was a special evening for Charlie and Ben. The table was beautifully appointed and red roses accented their chargers. Charlie noticed that there were no roses on the other tables. He had said it was a special occasion when he made the reservation and he guessed this was an acknowledgement of that. He was impressed. Ben didn't seem to notice that particularly, for he was busy looking around at the restaurant and the people with a happy smile on his face.

"What a cool place, Charlie. How did you find it? You know, this is exactly the kind of restaurant that I've always wanted to go to. I just never knew where they were. It's like being in San Francisco or New York City, isn't it?" His eyes sparkled with excitement. He picked up the menu and winked at Charlie, "It's not a vegetarian restaurant is it?"

"Not by a long shot, smartass! You can look at the menu and there are some great things on it, but wait until the waiter comes over to describe the specials. I'm not kidding. There will be twenty specials: chicken, beef, fish you name it. You'll be knocked out." This seemed to be the cue for their waiter to approach the table. He was an attractive guy, around thirty and probably gay. Charlie didn't like to jump to conclusions.

"Good evening, gentlemen. Can I tell you about our specials?" He smiled at Charlie and winked at Ben. Yeah, he was gay.

The list of specials was mind boggling. Charlie decided on swordfish which made Ben wince. Ben chose prime rib and Charlie didn't say anything... all those exotic choices passed by. He knew Ben by now and his willingness for adventure didn't extend too far into the culinary world. The prime rib here was excellent, served with some unique and innovative twists. So Ben might yet have some surprises in store.

After ordering house salads for starters, they settled back and looked at each other with that familiar contentment and unabashed joy. It had happened the very first time they met and now it was part of who they were together... as a couple. Ben looked at Charlie with love. Maybe he didn't call it that, but that's what it was. Charlie, gazing at Ben in the candlelight, knew that he would never find anyone else that made him feel this complete, this justified. When he was with Ben, Charlie felt like all the things he had believed in all his life were true. Here was someone else who believed them too. Charlie reached across the table and touched the side of Ben's hand with his knuckle. He had learned not to overtly hold his hand in public, but this nudging acknowledgement was within Ben's comfort zone. So Charlie nudged for all it was worth.

"I love this place. There are many fond memories here. I always bring out-of-towners here to show off what we have to offer in Sacramento. I brought Jim here when he came out for a visit and I had my birthday here one year."

"It suits you, Charlie. It's warm and friendly and beautiful. Just like you." Ben spoke softly, not because he was afraid of being overheard, but from tenderness.

"Why, Ben McSwain. I would hardly think of myself as beautiful. What a thing to say!" Charlie was echoing the words Ben had used when he had said the same thing about him.

They laughed and talked, leaning in often, so that their heads almost touched across the intimate table. Anyone looking at them would see two people very much in love, whether Ben wanted to call it that or not.

"How's Pam? She must be getting close to delivery by now." He couldn't believe that he loved and lusted after someone who was about to become a grandfather!

"Everything's fine with her. It won't be long now. I can't believe it! My baby girl is having a baby of her own. The only thing that concerns me is if they are ready for this. She and Brett seem so young and immature. I guess I'm just getting old."

"Well, having a child will make them grow up in a hurry won't it? That's what I've always heard anyway. I don't have much experience with pregnant ladies."

"I think you're right, but it's hard to see at this point. I just hope that everything goes OK for them. All we have to do now is wait."

Ben was a little uncomfortable with this talk of his family. Charlie suspected that he liked to compartmentalize his life and he respected that.

Ben not only had a lot on his plate, he had a lot of plates and he was juggling them as best he could.

Speaking of plates, they finished their entrees and, at Charlie's insistence, they ordered *creme brulee* for dessert. Ben had never had it before and had to trust Charlie. They continued to talk over fresh cups of coffee.

"The show is going really well. I think Lee and I have done everything we can do until we start rehearsals in Dallas."

"Yeah, Dallas. That's in Texas isn't it?" For the first time, Ben showed signs of regret that Charlie would be leaving soon. And Charlie was pleased.

The desserts came and Ben looked confused. Charlie picked up his spoon and broke the caramelized shell on top and Ben followed his lead. They both dug their spoons into the sinful custard. Ben's face lit up. "Vanilla pudding!"

God, Charlie was in love. He thought that was adorable.

"Texas is a few weeks off yet. And you could come to see me, you know. Texas isn't Qatar. Well, in some ways it is, I guess." Charlie smiled at his own "oil" joke.

"Well, I'm gonna miss you, doggone it." Ben avoided the invitation.

"Feel free to use the house while I'm gone, if you want." Charlie said casually as he reached in his jacket pocket and produced a small gift box.

"Here. Happy six month anniversary." Charlie pushed the little box across the table.

Ben looked up in surprise, big wide eyes all innocence. Then a sly smile began to creep across his face as he reached into his pocket, too.

"Same at ya, dude! Bet you thought I didn't remember!" Ben was grinning ear to ear.

Now it was Charlie's turn to be flummoxed. Just when he thought he had Ben's "boundaries" figured out, he did something like this!

They looked at their gifts hesitantly. Neither knew what to expect. "You open first."

Ben unwrapped the red paper from the small box. It was a jeweler's box and inside was a silver keychain with a little silver tab on it. On one side of the tab were Ben's initial and Charlie's were on the other. There was a key on the ring.

"It's the key to my house. To our house. I hope you know that it will always be your house, too." Charlie was beaming, but tears stood in his eyes.

"Wow, Charlie. I don't know what to say. You're amazing. Thank you for just being you." Ben seemed at a loss. "Open yours. It's not nearly as cool as my present, but hey, it's me, you know?"

Charlie kept his eyes on Ben as he unwrapped the gift. It was larger than Charlie's gift to Ben and he had no idea what it could be. Inside was a red picture frame with a wonderful picture of Ben in it. Charlie had asked Ben for a picture several times and never gotten an answer. This was the answer. Charlie stared at the photograph.

"Oh cool. I'll take this to Texas with me so I won't forget what you look like."

"You devil! You better not forget! I didn't know what to get you. You had said you wanted a picture. I take terrible pictures, but Pam took that one about two months ago and she said it was a good one, so I printed it out on the computer for you. I think the frame speaks for itself. It's red, right?" Ben was making apologies, but it was clear that he was pleased about his gift

"It's wonderful, honey. Thank you so much. Photographs mean so much me and this is perfect."

They gathered up paper and ribbon and stood to leave the restaurant. The waiter was there to assist them and took the used wrapping from them. He commented on the festive paper. The owner of the restaurant came over and walked with them to the door, as easy as an old friend.

"Were you guys celebrating an anniversary or something tonight?" It was an innocent remark intended to be cordial and friendly.

Charlie laughed softly as he responded, "Well, I wasn't sure when it started, but yes, that's exactly what it turned into! Thanks so much for another memorable evening. You've never let me down."

"It was our pleasure. You guys enjoy the rest of your evening. And happy anniversary to you both!"

Ben had said nothing at this point. When they got to the car, he spoke up, "Did he think we were a couple?"

"Well, yeah, I guess he did. Does that bother you?"

'No, I'm not really bothered. Just wondering...we were just two guys having dinner. Why did they think we were gay?"

"Well, I didn't really think about it. Let's see...It's a romantic restaurant. People go there to celebrate special occasions. We were there alone, just the two of us. We didn't have female dates with us. Our conversation was somewhat intimate. We looked like a couple. We were a couple. Is that so bad?"

"Not, it's not bad. I'm just confused. When I go out with, say, one of the docs from the hospital, do the people in the restaurant think we are a couple? Just two guys?"

"I think it probably has to do with context, Ben. Two guys in their work clothes grabbing a pizza is different from two men dressed up going out to dinner together in a gay neighborhood. Can you see how different assumptions might be made?"

"Do you think I look gay?" Ben's tone turned serious.

"I'm not sure I have ever known what 'looking gay' means, Ben. We are as varied, I believe, as the general population. Maybe we'll go to the Gay Pride celebration this fall and you can see for yourself."

"I'm not sure I'm ready for that." He was quiet for a minute before he continued. "I don't think of myself as being gay, Charlie."

"Well, Ben, you're having sex with another man. How do you define that? Or do you?"

"I'm having sex with you, Charlie. I'm not interested in any other men. I don't look at men that way. You're the only one I'm attracted to. I don't know why, but that's how I feel."

"And I can't tell you how glad I am that you feel that way. But it's a statement that I don't really understand. I'm not questioning the truth of what you say. I'm just saying it's not part of my experience. Does that make sense?"

"Sure, it does. It's not a big deal. I was just surprised at the restaurant, that's all. Do you think other people thought we were a couple?"

"Considering all the elements, yeah, if anyone looked at us, they would probably assume that we were a couple."

"It'll take some getting used to. I just don't think of myself that way."

"Look, you are perfectly free to identify yourself anyway you want. It doesn't matter to me. I like you just the way you are. You don't have to be anything other than wonderful Ben."

"I feel the same way about you, Charlie. I like you just the way you are. Everything about you. You are one of the most special things that has ever happened to me."

Charlie felt a catch in his throat and thought he might cry, but he kept it together and kept it light. "You, too, honey." Oops, that slipped out again, but this time, Ben just turned to him and smiled.

"I guess we are a couple, huh, HONEY?"

That made Charlie very, very happy and very, very happy is always a dangerous place to be.

# Chapter 24

A week after the anniversary celebration, Charlie was organizing the play files on his computer when the phone rang. Caller ID said it was Jim in Chicago.

"Jim, are you all right?"

"Well, good morning to you, too! I'm fine. What's with all the concern?"

"Well, it's so early in the morning. I'm not used to hearing from you at this time of day."

"That's true. I get it. I'm up and about to leave the house because I'm going to the airport. I'm on my way to San Francisco, believe it or not."

"Really? When did this happen? I don't remember your telling me about any trips."

"I didn't find out about it until last night. My department chair was supposed to deliver a paper in San Francisco on Wednesday. Her daughter is expecting a baby and has had some complications and she doesn't want to leave town right now. So she asked me to go in her place and, hell, why not? I won't have to teach for a few days and I get to hit the bars in San Francisco. It's a sacrifice I can make for a colleague."

"Where are you staying and how long are you going to be there?"

"The conference is at the Hyatt Embarcadero, so I'm staying there. Seems like a good location, right?" Charlie knew San Francisco a lot better than Jim, for Jim had only lived there about a year and that was a very long time ago.

"Yeah, good location. Cable car and Muni Station just right outside the door of the hotel. You could walk to the South of Market bars. I know those are your speed."

"Indeed they are. Are you going to be able to come in and spend some time? I'd love to see you."

"I think I can do that. I'm getting ready for Texas, but that's not going to take all my time this week. Ben's working all week, so I won't be seeing him."

"That's the 'Brief Encounter' guy from the train, right?" There was a snide edge to Jim's voice.

"Yes, Jim. Ben...you know...the guy I've been seeing for the last six months?" Charlie was a little snide himself.

"OK...I knew who it was. I'm just not as enamored with this guy as you are that's all." Jim was a skeptic and much less romantic in nature than Charlie...and he was protective. Jim wasn't in love, either.

"Look...when do you get in? Why don't I come down today, we'll go out to dinner. I'll spend the night and come home tomorrow. Then you'll have the rest of the week to do what you actually came to do and to whore around to your heart's content. OK?"

"That sounds great. I'll be there around five-thirty or so, I think. I mean I'll be at the hotel by then. I get in a little earlier than that. "

"Cool. I'll come on in to the City. If you haven't checked in yet, I'll just hang out until you do. This is great. I'm so glad you're doing this. I can't wait to see you. Get going, if I know you, you are running late for the airport."

"Of course, I am. I'll go. I'll see you tonight, OK? Pick out some place for us to go for dinner." Jim hung up before Charlie could respond.

Charlie stopped what he was doing at the computer and sent Ben a quick email telling him what was going on. He would probably be down there and back before Ben even knew that he had gone, but he felt better letting him know. Much of what Charlie did and thought as far as Ben was concerned was habit and expectation. He had a tough time remembering that this was not the regular relationship he wanted it to be. But it wasn't and that was that.

Charlie packed expertly and quickly: extra jeans, toiletries, hair dryer and laptop—the gay man's essentials, all in a chic red canvas and brown leather carryon bag. He locked the back door, surveyed the house quickly, secured the front and headed for the light rail station. Out the door in a matter of minutes. Charlie thought of Ben and what it took for him to get away. There were so many details and so many people depending on him. His life had a rich and complex context. With Charlie there was no one to check with and no one would notice that he was out of town and that was really OK with Charlie.

The train was on time and he got into the City around five o'clock. He didn't even try Jim's cell, but did some shopping, bought a French Mac Computer magazine and sat in the sun for a bit. It was a beautiful Sunday afternoon in the City and he was glad to be there. San Francisco had changed a lot since he and Jim moved there in the early 80's It had seemed quaint almost. There were still vestiges of the 60's everywhere and the feel of a village nestled inside a bustling city. A cable car climbing up California Street with the Transamerica Pyramid in the background was the perfect metaphor. The pace seemed faster now and everyone was wired with cell phones and PDA's and laptops. It changed the way people moved about.

It was nearly six when he looked at his watch. He had been distracted just people watching, an official sport in San Francisco. He called Jim's cell and he was already in his room on the seventeenth floor. As he got on the elevator, Charlie wondered if the room would have a Bay view, and, boy, did it—a spectacular one. Jim had the door to the balcony open and a breeze was cooling down the room quickly. Jim embraced him at the door and they stood back to get a good look at one another. They had been in love once and now they just loved each other. They were each other's family. Jim was a redhead. Now there are two kinds of redheads—cute redheads and goofy looking redheads. Think Van Johnson and Red Skelton. Jim was of the cute variety. He had put on some weight with the years and was stocky now, but it suited him. That red hair was clipped short and he was wearing glasses. Charlie was thinking how much he looked like his father, but he knew better than to say that!

"Hey, sweetie. You look great! How was the flight? I'm assuming you didn't miss your original one."

"Har. Har. I got to the airport in plenty of time, smartass. The flight was fine. No glitches on either end. God, I hope I'm not jinxing the trip home. Great room, huh? It's the one that Louise had already booked. I just kept it." They had walked out onto the balcony as Jim was talking.

"I know that's Alcatraz, but what's the other island over there? That isn't Sausalito is it?" Jim had not paid much attention to San Francisco. It was just never his town.

"No. That's Angel Island. It's between here and Sausalito, which isn't an island, Jim. It's in Marin County. You know that. We've been to breakfast there. We DROVE there, remember?"

"It was a long time ago, Charlie. And we were both still drinking then. I'm surprised we got across the bridge without going into the bay."

"Well, that's true enough. You're right. Those days were a little hazy, weren't they?"

"Well, things are certainly better these days, that's for sure. Where are we going for dinner? I'm hungry. They don't feed you on planes anymore."

"Well, I thought about it and you know what? Let's go to The Mediterranean! It is still open and it's the first place we went to after we moved here, remember? It's still great food. After you left, it remained one of my favorite places to go. Is that OK with you?"

"Well, sure, if you want. That sounds fine. Here I am in San Francisco and I thought we would go some place fancy, but that's OK with me. At least we don't have to get dressed up."

"I never went to fancy restaurants when I lived here, you know that. I couldn't afford it! There are so many good neighborhood restaurants, you don't have to spend a lot to have a wonderful meal. In fact, instead of going to The Med in our old neighborhood, let's go to the other location over near the Castro. That way, it'll be some place new for you and I'll get my middle eastern food fix, too. How's that?"

"Sure. That's fine. Isn't the Muni just right down the street? Can we take that?" Jim really had forgotten San Francisco geography.

"Yeah. We can just go out to Castro and walk around a little if you want. See what's happening. I haven't been out there in ages. Come on. Put on some jeans and let's go!" Jim was still "dressed" from the plane. He was one of the dozen people left in the United States who still dressed up to fly.

The Castro had changed a lot since they first moved to San Francisco. Everything changes, of course, but they wondered how different the changes might have been if it hadn't been for AIDS. It set the gay civil rights movement back fifty years and killed most of the people who were fighting the fight. And the Castro reflected that historical reality. It used to be a street full of sexy mustachioed men in 501's and flannel shirts, friendly as Labrador puppies. Today there were straight couples and gay couples with strollers and toddlers. Everyone was on a cell phone and the sexual excitement of the scene had been replaced by something more pedestrian.

As they walked the familiar street, both men reflected on the time they had spent together here. Charlie remembered their first visit to Castro Street. They had held hands and kissed out in the open. He could still feel the freedom of that day.

"Hey, Jim. Remember the first time we were here?"

"We came over to meet Rudy for a drink. That was a Sunday afternoon, too. I'll never forget it. Were we ever really that young?

They continued to walk in silence, comfortable in that way people are after years of rubbing against each other.

"So. Are you waiting for me to ask about what's his name or are you going to tell me over dinner."

"It's crazy, Jim. I don't know what's happening. He's physically very attractive of course, but it's the rest of it that has me reeling. He's everything I said I would never want in a lover. He's conservative, he's religious, he's got kids and all that baggage. Of course, he's not out. He's not even sure he's gay.

I'm sure he is, but that's not the same thing. I keep thinking about James Carville and Mary Matalin. I think I'll email them and see how they do it."

"All that stuff doesn't bother me nearly as much as the fact that you are getting the short end of the stick again. Everything revolves around his schedule, what he wants and you dance attendance. I've seen you do this before and I've never understood why. Why do you put up with it?"

"Wow. I hadn't looked at it like that. I don't see it as putting up with anything. To me, it's just looking at what is possible and trying to figure out how to live with it. If I looked at it the way you do, I would get out of it, I suppose."

"Exactly. That's probably what you should do. You deserve more than what he's giving you. You deserve a real relationship."

"We all do, Jim! You included. But how often does it come along? Why aren't you in a relationship right now? It's fucking hard to find that connection. And when you do, you try to make it work, right? That's all I'm doing here. Back off a little, will you?"

"OK, I'm sorry. I guess I'm a little bit jealous. I see how much in love you are. I've met someone, too and it's a similar situation...he's had a lover for 14 years. The sex is over and they just haven't had the courage to move on and call it friendship. I don't know if they ever will and I don't know if I should wait around. I'm not sure it's worth it."

"When did this happen? Where did you meet him?"

"We met at one of my leather club functions. He's not from Chicago but he's been down to visit me a couple of times. I didn't say anything because there didn't seem to be any place for it to go. There still isn't."

"Well, life's a bitch, isn't it? Here we are...prime catches, both of us...wanting something we can't have. Remember the musical "Promises, Promises?" There was a song called "Wanting Things" that sums this up perfectly."

"Honest to God, Charlie, your life is a fucking musical! You have a song for every occasion, don't you?"

"Well, yeah. I do see my life as a musical. You know, years ago I had this idea of doing my AA pitch as a musical...you know, stopping every few minutes and inserting a song. Wouldn't that be great?"

"Charlie, Charlie. I'm glad you are in my life. It would not have been nearly as much fun if we hadn't met."

"Absolutely. The years have given great value to our relationship, haven't they? I swear my mother loved you more than she loved me."

"Oh, I know Miss Lucille loved me, but she didn't love anyone as much as she loved you, Charlie. You know that."

"Yeah, I guess so. Sometimes I wish she were here. I'd love to tell her about Ben. She would be CRAZY about him. She would want him to get me to go to church and all that stuff. Don't you think?"

"Maybe. But she would just want what I want: for you to be happy. Does he make you happy, Charlie?"

"When we're together, I breathe better. I feel like a whole person. My life makes sense to me. Another song: 'All of My Life Has Led to This.' But when we are separated, I sometimes think it would be better for both of us to just let go of it. I know he's really conflicted. No, that's not exactly right. He's not conflicted at all. He knows that what we are doing is wrong in his world. He's deliberately going against his own values and morality. The only conflict is how he feels about me."

"I asked about your happiness Charlie and you're telling me about Ben. Can you see that?"

"Shut up and let's go eat."

They turned and headed back toward Market Street and the restaurant. Charlie took Jim's hand in his and kissed him lightly on the cheek. For old times' sake. Honoring their past, they continued to hold hands as they walked to the restaurant. They enjoyed a familiar meal and talked quietly of past, present and future. Their long and complex history textured the evening with poignancy, laughter and hope.

The next morning, Charlie caught an early train full of serious looking business types headed to the state Capitol. The cafe car was crowded when he boarded, so he just got a cup of coffee and found a quiet spot in another car. He sat by a window and stared out, alone with his thoughts about his conversations with Jim and as always, the subject that was occupying so much of his brain— Ben. Jim was never one to pull punches and Charlie was glad for that. He had raised some valid and serious points, bless his redheaded heart. Again, Charlie found himself in a situation where he was "making do" with half a relationship. There had been so many times when that seemed to be true in his life. A therapist had once suggested that Charlie was drawn to impossible situations because if it were possible it would be too scary for him. In other words, loving someone he couldn't have let him off the hook for any real commitment.

Charlie had thought about this argument many times in relation to Ben and he wondered if it were true to some extent. But he also knew that, if Ben said yes, he was ready and willing to put everything he had into this relationship. He knew that he and Ben could be happy. The idea of Ben calling him on it didn't frighten him at all. He welcomed it and longed for it.

It had been wonderful to spend some time with Jim, even though it had been brief. They had talked about doing a cruise next winter. The Panama Canal, maybe. Charlie knew that whether Ben worked out or not, Jim would be there for him, his family, his anchor. He was grateful for that as he gathered up his things and left the train, going back into his uncertain future feeling a little more grounded and assured of love.

# Chapter 25

It was a couple of weeks after Charlie got back from San Francisco that Ben had some free time. They were piled up on the couch on a late summer afternoon.

"I've put Dallas off as long as I can. I'm going next week. Tuesday." Charlie just blurted it out. He had been trying to bring it up all weekend. He knew it would be all right with Ben, that wasn't the problem. The problem was him. He didn't want to leave.

"Oh, wow. Already. Time has gone by so fast, hasn't it? It just seems like last week that you found out about this. Aren't you excited?"

"Yeah, I guess I am. The cast gets there tomorrow, I think. The director and Lee are already there. Lee has been in Texas a couple of weeks visiting his family. His two sisters live not far from Dallas, in the town where Lee grew up."

"Is he close to his family?"

"Yeah, he is. In an odd way. This is something you'll find interesting. Lee has never told his family he's gay. You know I told my family when I was still in my teens, but Lee decided to keep it to himself. His family was more conservative than mine. They are Nazarene or something. Anyway, he just decided not to tell them. It's worked out just fine. His mom never questioned him at all and his sisters don't seem to care that much about his personal life."

"Does he still go to church?"

"No. And they don't push it. Although one of his sisters is very devout and always insisting that Lee and I are both going to hell." Charlie didn't know whether to smile or not, but Ben did.

"You know his family well then, I take it."

"Since we were freshmen in college. He knew mine, too, of course. I loved his mother. She was so wonderful and supportive. She thought that whatever Lee did was perfect. Just like a good mom should."

Ben shifted his interest back to the show, "What will your work schedule be like, do you have any idea?"

"Well, I imagine we'll be at the theatre all day watching rehearsals and trying to fix things with the script as they come up. I know from the little bit of work I've done in television that words can sound just fine on paper and be terrible when an actor has to say them. So we'll be busy, I'm sure. I've never done this before, so I don't know exactly." Charlie was beginning to be a little apprehensive.

"Wow, Charlie, it all sounds so glamorous. Like something out of a movie or something. I can't imagine doing what you do."

"A little perspective please. What you do is the stuff of real life heroes. What I do is just nonsense."

"Well, it all sounds very exciting to me. What's Dallas like, anyway?

"It amazes me to say this, but I have no idea. There was a time in my life when Dallas was such a big part of my identity. It's been twenty-five years since I left and I've only been back very rarely and for short periods of time. So I don't know what to expect. One thing I do know is the weather. It will be hotter than the gates of hell and humid."

"Do you still have friends there? Will you see them?"

"I was thinking about that. No, I don't have many friends there. I've just lost touch over the years. Except for an old professor from college and his wife. They have stayed in touch and I love them dearly. I hope to see them and catch up. It will mostly be work. We've got a rental house near the theatre. Lee's already been in the house and says it's spacious. It has a pool. That's a plus, considering the time of year. I hope we have time to use it. We'll probably be working constantly...at least until the preview performances start."

"When will that be, do you know yet?"

"Rehearsals should be about five weeks and then previews. Speaking of that, I would love it if you could come to the opening night preview. It will be a big deal. Lots of people will be there and I would love to have you by my side. You could relax and enjoy it. No one there would know you. I'll know when it is by next week sometime, plenty of time for you to plan the days off. I'll pay for your plane ticket and everything. It would mean a lot to me."

Ben was quiet. He was thinking. It sounded wonderful. He had always loved the theatre and here was a chance to be a part of a play first hand and up close. And to be there with Charlie! It was so tempting, but what would he tell his family? How would he explain a trip to Texas? What excuse could he use? He had lied to them so much lately. It was making him heartsick, but he couldn't give up Charlie. He was a good person, decent and kind and caring of others. Anyone in Ben's church would admire him...if they didn't know he was gay, that is. However, when Ben left Charlie's and went home, he was confronted with his other life, his church and his work and his family. All of those things knew a completely different Ben. He certainly felt hypocritical, but he was also beginning to feel a little bit schizophrenic because of it. He felt like he was living two lives and it was exhausting keeping them separate. He hadn't confided any of this to Charlie. It would only hurt his feelings and there was nothing he could do about it. It was something Ben had to work out for himself. As for trying new things...Ben had no idea what that was going to lead to!

"I'll have to see, Charlie. I'll check the schedule at the hospital this week. I can move things around a little bit with enough notice. I'm sure I can work it out." Ben still had a few weeks to try to come to terms with this. He wanted to go. He wanted to be there for Charlie.

They walked over to the neighborhood movie theatre in the late afternoon to catch a new film, a French romantic comedy with a bit of a gay twist. Ben had gotten more relaxed in the last few months and he was enthusiastic about the film. He was turning into quite a cineaste. They stopped for ice cream on the way back to Charlie's and made love the minute they walked in the door. Ben had to get back to Goldmine tonight, so they were making the most of the time they had.

"Charlie, I just need you to know that I can't say for certain that I'll be able to come to Texas. I'll do my best, but I don't want to disappoint you or mislead you. You know I want to be there. It's just my schedule, you know." They were propped up in bed, cuddled close

"I do know Ben...I probably understand better than you think. And it's OK, really."

"It's just that the last thing I want to do is to hurt you."

Charlie laughed and started to make a joke, "Well then, if you don't want to hurt me, marry me!"

The moment he said it, his eyes brimmed with tears. He realized that this was no joke. He knew that he had never meant anything more in his life. He loved Ben like he had never loved anyone. It hit him in that moment. He wanted to spend the rest of his life with him. This was the man, the person he had waited all his life for.

"Oh Ben, marry me! Live with me and love me back. Don't you know how I feel about you by now? You're my soulmate!" Tears dampened Charlie's cheeks, but he wasn't really crying. He was speaking calmly and surely. It was as if he finally got to say his truth.

Ben looked him in the eye and there were tears in his eyes, too. And sadness. Part of him knew that what Charlie was saying was true for him also, but he knew the obstacles to Charlie's proposal.

"Wow, that's it. Your my soulmate! I never knew what to call it, but that's exactly the right word. We're soulmates. We may not be able to be together the way you want, Charlie, but we will always be soulmates."

"I'm sorry about the outburst Ben. I didn't plan all this. It just came out. I thought I was making a joke, but you must have known I'm in love with you. I was trying to deny it to myself, but seeing you here in my bed, our bed. It just came out."

"I've got to go, Charlie. I'm sorry. I wish I could stay and we could talk this through. I've just never thought about two men being in love with each other like a man and a woman. I'm not sure I had thought about us like that. You said 'marriage.' Two men getting married is something my church and all of my upbringing says is wrong. And I have always believed it is wrong. But marrying you, my soulmate...the idea fills my heart with so much joy. I know it shouldn't, but it does. I just need time, Charlie. Maybe it's good that you're going away for a while. We can both think about things, OK?" Ben got out of bed and started pulling on shorts and a tee shirt.

"Of course, baby. I didn't mean to freak you out. Take all the time you want and do all the soul searching you need to do. This shouldn't be a burden or something you have to deal with. There's no timetable here. Whatever you decide, I'll respect your decision and love you anyway. That won't change no matter what else happens." Charlie had started dressing, also. Summer made that easy and quick.

"Oh, Charlie, what are we gonna do? Is there a solution that will make us both happy?"

Charlie went to him and held him close. "I don't know, baby boy. I really don't know. I hope so. It seems so simple to me. You could move in here tomorrow and everything in my life would be better except for closet space. There is nothing standing in my way. The hard part is yours." They walked arm and arm to the door.

"I know. Gotta go. Charlie," Ben hesitated, but looked him directly in the eyes, "I love you, too, in the only way I know how right now."

"I know that and I thank you for saying it. Go, baby. You need to get home and I've got to fly south."

"Have a safe trip. Email me when you get there? Or call?"

"I will. You, too. Anytime you need to talk."

"You're my best friend, Charlie. I love you."

"Ditto, dude," Charlie was going to lose control completely if Ben didn't leave soon.

And he did leave, pulling slowly down the drive, still looking at Charlie standing at the door. He waved as he pulled away. Charlie closed the door, went back to the living room.

And then he lost it.

# Chapter 26

Charlie wasn't the only one having an emotional melt down at that point. Ben was sad and exhausted and drained. He couldn't keep this up. It was asking too much. He didn't know where to turn for help. He had been able to compartmentalize his relationship with Charlie, to define it as a very special friendship, to think of Charlie as his best friend. It was the only way he could live with it. Charlie had just changed the name of the game. He called it love. Ben knew in his heart that he was right. He loved Charlie, too, completely, just as Charlie loved him. It was so easy for Charlie. For him, the next step was to pick out china patterns. It wasn't like that for Ben. It was foreign terrain and he had to step carefully to avoid land mines of conscience and soul.

Homosexuality was just wrong. It was unnatural and it was a sin. He thought that this might not have happened if he hadn't been so lonely and vulnerable. But in his heart, he knew that wasn't true. He had been lonely for a long time and had women pushed on him from friends and family and coworkers anxious for him to find someone new. None of those women had evoked even a tenth of the feeling that he had for Charlie. He knew that he loved another man. He knew that he felt alive for the first time in years. He was loved and valued and excited about things again. He wanted his kids to meet Charlie. He wanted to tell his mom that he was in love! That it was wonderful!

What was he thinking? He and Lynette had brought the kids up very specifically in the teachings of the church and the church was clear on this subject. There was even a position paper on the topic. It cited chapter and verse in the Old Testament and the New. It was irrefutable that homosexuality was a sin against God and against nature. But he also knew how he felt. How could this be a sin? How could God allow him to feel so loved and happy with Charlie and call it sin? He knew not to trust his feelings or facts. The position paper was specific on that point, too. There were scriptural warnings about trusting reasoning or personal experience to discern the truth. The truth was in the Bible, not in facts.

And there was the question of the kids. Pam and Jacen would never accept his relationship with Charlie. Not in a million years. They had learned the church's lessons well. And they had already lost one parent. Ben couldn't risk their losing another because of this. It was a risk he couldn't take—he wouldn't take. Pam and Jacen had always come first in his life and they always would. That much was not negotiable. If there was an ultimate truth, Ben had just gotten to it. Even if he could overcome his religious misgivings, he couldn't betray the trust of his children.

His eyes were dry by the time he got home. He knew what he had to do. He had to stop seeing Charlie. It was better to do it now, wasn't it? Before it went any further? Should he say something before Charlie left for Texas? No. It could wait and Charlie didn't need this while he was concentrating on the play. Ben would tell him later, at a better time, but he would tell him. He would start letting go now.

He got home and went into his bedroom. It was filled with things from Charlie. They were always giving each other little gifts: a bottle of cologne they both loved or the blue sweater he had tried on that first day they spent together. Charlie had surprised him with it. Ben was always coming home to find a package from Charlie at the front door. He and Charlie both loved palm trees and Charlie had bought him a beautiful framed print that was hanging over his bed. There were CD's and other mementos of their time together in Ben's night stand drawer. There was a tiny silver iPod that Charlie had bought and filled with songs they both liked or that had reminded them of each other. Sometimes after he had gone to bed, he would put on the little earbuds and listen to the sounds of Charlie. Their song was "Everything" by Michael Buble. It was happy and joyous and suited the two of them perfectly. It said exactly who they were to each other in their hearts. When Ben listened to it, it was like having him here next to him. He didn't have to worry about the kids wondering where these things came from. Neither of the kids ever came into his bedroom and they had very little curiosity about him. They didn't seem to think he had any kind of life outside of the one they knew about. But he knew in his heart that Charlie would never see this room, never know that Ben had loved him just as much.

Tonight he went to the garage, got a box and carefully packed away most of the treasures that reminded him of Charlie. He sealed the box and put it in a remote spot on the top shelf of his closet. Out of sight, out of reach... just like Charlie.

Ben allowed himself to cry again. He was alone and no one could hear him or see him, so he cried hard. It made his throat hurt and he couldn't breathe and he cried and cried and cried until he couldn't anymore. He was sweating and breathing hard. It had been a marathon of grief. Ben had to grieve this alone. There was no one for him to turn to except Charlie! The only person who could comfort him was the one person he couldn't call. In that way, this grief was worse than Lynette. At least then, his grief was acknowledged and supported by everyone who knew him. This time, not only did he have to suffer, he had to hide it from everyone. For a moment he envied Charlie's freedom. But he loved God and his children more.

He showered and thought about the days ahead. He would do a ten hour shift tonight. He would do twelve if they needed him. He had missed choir practice today because he was with Charlie, but he would sing in the choir tomorrow anyway. He needed that affirmation. He would work hard, worship God and love his family. That would clear his head and heal his heart. He would look neither left nor right, but straight ahead. He remembered how to do that. He pulled on clean scrubs, grabbed his keys and the old Ben went back to work.

His phone beeped. It was a text message and Ben assumed it was the kids. They were the only people he knew who did the text thing. But it was from Charlie and it was just one word:

"Everything."

# Chapter 27

Charlie got off the plane in Dallas feeling content with the present and excited about the future. He was content because things were going well with Ben. It was a hectic week and they hadn't seen each other again before he left, but stayed in touch by phone. In his work, Charlie was on the computer all day and checking email often was just a part of that business. He considered it a lifeline and the reason he could work at home or anywhere. And everyone he worked with used it the way he did. But Ben didn't even check his personal email on a daily basis. Used to the instant gratification of technology, Charlie was less anxious when he understood that about Ben. They were learning about each other and it felt good.

And Charlie was excited about working on the play and spending time with Lee. There hadn't been enough of that lately. The last time they saw each other was over a year ago. Lee had been in San Francisco to discuss a new play with a local theatre company. At that time Charlie was concerned about Lee's health. He was a little overweight, his skin had a grayish pallor, his eyes were sagging and dull and even his gait seemed hesitant. He needed sun, exercise and vitamins. Frankly, he looked like he needed to get out of New York and come to California for a while. He had spent a few years in Los Angeles in the eighties working on a sitcom and he had been healthy and energetic. Granted, that was fifteen years ago. But, still, Charlie had been alarmed last year.

The Lee that greeted him at the airport was a new man. He was fit, robust and brimming with vitality. The energy was almost visible. What a change! Charlie wondered what had happened to cause such a radical difference. Lee rushed up and gave him an expansive hug. He had never been demonstrative. Charlie was the hugger of the two, so this was a surprise, pleasant, but a surprise.

Charlie stared at his old friend. "You look fucking fabulous."

"I do, don't I? L'amour, Charlie. Well, what passes for l'amour these days at least. OK, maybe just 'la lust.'" For college graduates with degrees in language arts, their own language degenerated horribly when they were around each other.

"Oh, really? You haven't said a word about love to me since Brad and that's been a couple of years. What's going on? Whatever it is, it must have something to do with the Fountain of Youth. You're positively radiant and that ain't easy to pull off at our age."

"Well, I don't think it has anything to do with LOVE, Charlie, but two weeks on the Costa Brava with a twenty-one year old boy will contribute a lot in the radiance department."

"What? When were you in Spain and what twenty-one year old boy?"

"His name is Tadio, he's half Spanish, half German. German mom, Spanish dad."

"Oh, good lord. Let me process this." They were waiting at baggage claim for Charlie's HUGE suitcase. Thank God for wheels. "Where did you meet him and how did you get to Spain?"

"Do you remember last winter when I met that young guy on the internet?"

"Yes, and he was from Spain as I remember...and had a bit of a temper." Charlie was remembering how strange that had seemed at the time and how worried he had been about Lee.

'That's him. We were chatting, you know, just for fun. Well it got to be every day and then longer every day. He invited me over during his break from school. He shares an apartment with two other students who were away on holiday. It's a high rise building right on the ocean. It was fabulous, Charlie, most of the time. But it's more than a bit of a temper, I'm afraid. There were a couple of incidents."

"That sounds a little murky. What kind of incidents?" Charlie was so focused on Lee's tale that he missed his bag and watched the big red monstrosity go around the carousel again. He would grab it next time around.

"Well, with Taddy there are always going to be incidents. He gets insanely jealous. I'm actually afraid of him sometimes. And for some reason he's jealous of you. He's so young. He doesn't understand about a friendship like ours. I hope he'll be better when he meets you.

"One day, while we were out for lunch, he thought I was flirting with someone at another table and flew into a rage. The truth is that I hadn't even noticed the other guy. When we got back to the apartment, Tadio locked me in, took my passport and my money and left me all afternoon. I was terrified. I almost called you to send me a plane ticket."

"Why didn't you! My god." Charlie grabbed the bag before it started around again. It was almost impossible to lift off the carousel. "I can't believe it. Lee, that's crazy. I mean really crazy. Why didn't you just come home?"

"Well, I didn't have a passport. I couldn't even get to the airport. How was I going to get home? It was frightening. But he was terribly apologetic the next day and very sweet the rest of the time I was there, except the night that he hit his mother at dinner. His parents are frightened of him too, I think. They were grateful for my arrival because they got a breather from him. He can be very demanding. Oh Charlie, they are such exotic people. They met when she was on vacation, fell in love and she never went back to Munich. Of course they are younger than we are, but they are perfectly OK with our relationship. His mother told me she would much rather know he was with me than out with people his own age because he would be safer with me."

"Wait a minute, honey, back up here a second. He hit his mother at dinner? Was he jealous of her, too? Does this happen often? Lee, this isn't normal, OK? Are you still seeing him?" Charlie was growing more concerned by the minute and shocked by the fact that Lee didn't seem concerned at all.

"His mother and I had a long talk. She thinks he'll grow out of it. He's very bright and just impatient with other people. Many young people are like that. And you have to understand the European temperament. They are much more volatile and expansive than we are. She said his father was a little like that when the met, although his father doesn't hit. Tadio has been hitting them all his life, but it doesn't happen often. They seem to be used to it by now. It's gotten much better in the last couple of years since he finished high school and has been in college."

It sounded like excuses to Charlie, but the thing about their relationship was that they always accepted each other at face value. They had never judged each other in their lives. It was part of the pact of unconditional love that they had forged for forty years. There was nothing in the world that Lee could do or say that would change Charlie's love, friendship or loyalty. And vice versa.

It took about twenty minutes to get from the airport. Charlie was not surprised by the cute little house they were to occupy. He had been in many houses just like this when he was in college. It was a neighborhood where faculty, graduate students and starter-couples lived. He had no idea what kind of people lived here today, but it looked exactly the same as it had in the sixties.

They schlepped Charlie's gear into the bedroom that Lee had decided would be his. It was a large, sunny room with lots of windows and a private bath. He didn't care much for all that sunlight, but it would suit him just fine. He began unpacking and Lee continued the saga of Tadio, the Teenaged Spanish Sadist.

"It really was a divine trip. Honest. He's smart and charming. Just headstrong. Take a look." Lee produced a photograph of a very young man. He didn't look like anything special at all to Charlie. He and Lee had always had opposite tastes in men. Never once in all those years had they ever found the same man attractive. Lee liked young, thin, smooth boys or boyish men. Charlie tended to go for men his own age or older and he liked hairy guys, even stocky guys. The "bear" thing had been a coming out of sorts for Charlie. He could finally admit that he thought that type was very sexy.

"Well, I'm going to assume that you know what you're doing. Just be careful, for God's sake. I hope this isn't The Roman Spring of Mrs. Stone all over again."

"That's exactly what it feels like, Charlie. Oh let's face it, we're old. I mean really old! It isn't something that is going to happen to us in the future. It has happened! How many more boyfriends are there going to be? This may be my last hurrah. So what if he's forty years younger than me? So what if he's a hotheaded bad boy? At least I feel something! I feel alive and energized like I haven't been in a long time. And if this is the end, so be it. To paraphrase Karen Stone, 'At some point, a cut throat would be a blessing.' It's been a great ride and I have no regrets at all. But I can't go through this again. I just don't have the stamina any more."

"Oh, good God, Lee. We're not that old yet, are we? Are we? I know that some days I wake up and I know that I'm getting there. I wonder what is going to hurt first when my feet hit the floor. There are days when I look in the mirror and I know that I'm not just tired, that it isn't going to change if I get some rest. But lately, I've felt alive and energized, too. I look younger in the mirror and my eyes are bright and clear. My feet don't hurt and there is a rejuvenated spring in my step." Charlie looked Lee in the eye and Lee knew."

"You, too? I'm sorry, honey. I've been so preoccupied with Taddy that I haven't even asked about you. What's going on in the heart department?"

"Remember the guy I told you about on the phone?" Charlie looked at Lee expectantly.

"The one you met on the train?"

"Yeah. He's a nurse and lives in a small town. He's widowed, has a couple of kids. He's not out."

"Oh, Lord. The Brief Encounter guy. He belongs to a fundamentalist church or something? Charlie, I swear. You're as bad as I am in your own way. You're gonna get hurt by this. It just can't end well, do you think?"

"I guess we're both setting ourselves up big time."

By now they were unpacked and had taken seats in the sun room, an air-conditioned room just off the deck. Lee had set up his laptop there and it looked like it was going to be the central nervous system of their working time. Charlie unpacked his computer and files and made a place for himself. It was like college when they were roommates, they just set about quietly living together. They didn't have to discuss things. They just did them and it was compatible. Soon, the room was inhabited by two writers working in tandem. It looked comfortable and felt right for them both. Neither was surprised. Lee went into the kitchen and came back with a couple of Diet Cokes on ice. "Here's to love. I hope it doesn't kill us this time!"

"Here, Here." Charlie raised a glass.

"OK, Let's talk about it, honey. What else do you need to say?"

"Well, you know the facts, where he's from, what he does, who he is in the world. What I haven't told you is the magic and energy that happens when we are together. This is going to sound melodramatic as all get out, but he's the love of my life, Lee. He's the one. The one that I've been waiting for all my life. He's my soulmate. I finally know what that word means! I'm serious. I've never felt this way before. When we are together things make sense. It's the real thing and I wish the same for you. You deserve love, dearest friend, not just a dangerous adrenaline rush."

"I know Charlie. But I've almost given up on that happening and the 'rush' is better than nothing, I guess. So here we are, back in Dallas after all these years talking about boyfriends and life. Some things never change. What do we do now?"

"Well, I guess we could write this fucking play."

"I am so glad that you are finally here. And as for the play, everyone likes what we've done so far: the director, the producers, the cast. They think we're on the right track and I do too, really. You've distilled the book into a nice dramatic arc that works for a musical and the dialogue seems to be writing itself as I go along. The characters are so well defined and their voices are very specific in my head. It feels like I'm just transcribing what they are saying to me. What do you think, so far?"

"Well, what you've sent me is amazing. I'm always in awe of your talent... how you can translate what you hear. I don't know what I am needed for, but I'm glad to be here anyway. It'll be great to spend the time with you, see the show's progress and see what's happened to this town in the last twenty-five years. Here's to us. Yvonne de Carlo isn't the only one who's still here!"

"She's dead, Charlie."

"Oh, well, here's to us anyway!"

They toasted each other with Diet Coke. They were nearly sixty years old, flirting with feelings that are treacherous and, frankly, scared to death.

Thank God for friends.

# Chapter 28

Ben's life settled back to its familiar pulse when he knew that Charlie was in Texas. His resolve had not wavered. As he gained distance on the feelings that he had when he was with Charlie, the reality of his own world came back into focus and it sharpened to 20/20 when he got the call that Pam was having the baby. She had come in to his hospital, of course, so he just took the elevator to the maternity floor. He knew all the doctors and staff and was not as concerned as many of the expectant parents, grandparents and other relatives milling about in the waiting room. He went into the pre-op area to see Pam. She looked a little flushed and frightened, but her face changed completely when she saw her dad. He felt a rush of love so powerful that he nearly rocked back on his heels. He kissed her and held her hand out of affection, of course, but also to check her signs, a professional habit. She was normal for a slightly overdue pregnant lady. Brett was there, too, looking frightened, a little nauseated and earnest. Ben liked Brett. He's not the man he would have chosen for Pam, but then, what father ever really approves of the man who steals his daughter? There was a rivalry for her affections that was as old as our species. Ben knew this and tried to love Brett as a son. Today, he felt especially close to him. He was about to go through a rite of passage that Ben had taken—the one that changed everything in his life forever—becoming a father. It was his compass. It directed his life. He wondered if Brett would feel it as powerfully. He also wondered if becoming a grandfather would be as emotional and life altering. They would both soon find out. Pam's contractions were regular and close now. She and Brett were old-fashioned and shy and had decided in advance that Brett would wait with his parents during the delivery. Ben's mother and other friends had gathered in the waiting area, too.

Ben felt it was up to him to put everyone at ease. "Hi everybody. Gosh, thanks to all of you for coming. I can tell you that Pam is just fine. Everything is normal and we don't expect any complications. It will be a while. I'm sure you all have things to do today so I'll be happy to call you and let you know when we have a baby." Ben had just taken charge here and everyone seemed to expect that. Some of Pam's friends decided to go home to wait it out. Brett's parents and Alvah decided to stay. Brett joined his folks and Ben sat down beside his mother.

"Can I get you something, mom? Coffee? Coke? Valium?"

She laughed. "I'm OK, honey. My grandbaby is having a baby. How did I get so old? When did that happen?"

"Is being a grandparent different from being a parent?"

"Well, yes and no. You don't have the same kind of fear and shock and panic that you do when you become a parent. You will feel exactly the same kind of awe and love when you see that little thing for the first time. That part is the same. Grandchildren are better because you can let the parents do the worrying and you just do the loving. It's a better deal all around!" She was smiling warmly.

"Ah, Mom, that sounds so much like you. I hope you're right. I just want to love that baby. I worry that Pam isn't ready for all this. She seems so young and immature still."

"I felt the same way about you and Lynette. Having the baby is exactly what Pam needs to push her to the next level. She'll grow up a lot in the next few weeks and you'll be surprised at her maturity. She's going to be a good mother. You'll see." Alvah McSwain had a dreamy look on her face, as if she were remembering her own coming of age, when Ben was born. She put her hand on his and squeezed tightly. Ben was her baby and she had done just fine. Look at him!

But Alvah was worried about Bennie. He had not been himself the last few months. He would disappear and not tell anyone where he was or where he had been. He had missed choir practice several times and missed church a couple of times when he had gone "out of town" for the weekend. She always thought he worked too hard and needed more time off, but this wasn't what she meant. It was too mysterious. She knew that another woman was involved, but if it had been someone presentable, he would have presented her, wouldn't he? It must have been someone he didn't want his family to meet. She sensed lately that it was over, or at least cooling off. She knew about men. They can get an itch that comes up real quick and goes away just as fast. Maybe that was it. She hoped so. She wanted to see Ben settled down again, but with the right girl.

They sat and talked small talk while they waited.

"Your grandparents called me last night. They couldn't remember your phone number, or so they said. I think they just forgot where they wrote it down. They were wondering if you could come over this weekend and take a look at their roof. Seems like they heard a flapping noise up there and wondered if some of the shingles were loose."

Ben was used to this. Before he met Charlie he spent every weekend doing for his mom or his grandparents or the kids. It was his life. He worked hard around his house to make it better for the them. He had spent a big part of the early spring and summer last year putting in a swimming pool that he could finally afford, but the kids had barely used it at all. They had other things to do. Now Jacen was half a world away in a hell that Ben could not even imagine and Pam was creating her own home and family. His mom still needed him and relied on him for just about everything. He took care of her car and the house, kept track of her expenses and saw to her taxes. He looked after his father's parents when he left town, too. There was a discomfort between them and Alvah, but Ben bridged the two households with ease. They depended upon Bennie for so much, including meals now. Ben often prepared extra food at home to take to them. He would go by today and give them the news. And he would crawl up on their roof on Saturday. He was happy. His life was back.

About that time, the doctor came through the doors.

"Mr. Cameron?" The doctor was asking for Brett. "Pam and the baby are just fine. She's a robust little thing, eight pounds eleven ounces of healthy baby girl. They both need some rest, of course. We're getting them ready right now and you can go in shortly. The rest of the baby's fan club can go down to the nursery in about 30 minutes and see the little superstar. You should be a very proud man today, Ben. Congratulations. Pam did beautifully."

Ben and the doctor had known each other for years, so he spoke for the family. "Thanks so much Michael. I'm a little overwhelmed right now, but I want you to know I appreciate all you've done for Pam."

"Buy me a beer at our next pizza night, OK, pal? I'm going home. You go introduce yourself to that new grandbaby."

Ben felt like he did when his own children were born, but it seemed to double the joy and love he felt because this baby was from his own baby girl! It was a miraculous moment. His mom had been right. He couldn't wait to see the child, so he went to the O.R where she was waiting to be taken downstairs. He went over and stared at the tiny infant. Somewhere in the back of his mind was an unbidden thought. It was distant and had the ache of a remembered injury. It became more painful as it advanced to the front of his consciousness. He wished that he could share this moment with Charlie. That is what would make it complete. He felt unsure of where his emotions originated. The baby was such a joyful event. Why did he feel sad and alone?

Ben stayed with the baby until they took her downstairs. The rest of the family was already there, but he went back to his office and sent an email to Jacen. He would want to know right away. He would take a picture of the baby today and send that along later. Jacen and Pam were close, only eleven months apart, and had clung to each other when Lynette died. They were always sweet to each other, but tragedy had bonded them even further. Ben was grateful for this technology that allowed him to feel closer to Jacen in his frightening situation. It made it less frightening for Ben.

He kept the message brief and hit SEND on the computer. He noticed while he was in his mail program that there was a message from Charlie. He hesitated. He knew he shouldn't open it, but he wanted and needed to share this joy with him. What was he going to do about Charlie? So he opened the email.

It was just a sweet, happy note telling him about his work on the show and reminding him about opening night. Ben didn't have to answer right now. He could wait and try to decide how he would handle it. He knew he shouldn't go, but he shouldn't have gotten involved with Charlie in the first place and he did. Charlie really seemed to want him to be there. Ben hated disappointing anyone. That's why his life was as busy as it was. He ran around doing for others at work and at home. He was the fixer. The best little boy in the world. But Ben knew that this was more than that. It wasn't that he just didn't want to let Charlie down. He wanted to see Charlie. He missed him. He missed everything about their relationship. And, yes, he missed the sex and the physical closeness. He yearned right now to hold Charlie and share his happiness with him. God help him, but a part of him just knew that a life with Charlie would be happy and would make sense. Why was it such a sin? He knew that it was, of course, but now he was wondering exactly why it was. When he thought about Charlie, nothing made sense anymore.

He answered Charlie's email with the news about Pam. He shared the details and how it felt to be a grandfather, but he didn't tell Charlie how much he had wanted him there and he evaded Charlie's invitation. It would seem OK considering his news, but he would have to address it later. This was enough for today. He was tired and he had to get up early again tomorrow. So, after an appearance in the nursery, he made his excuses to everyone and he called it a day, heading for home.

The house was quiet when he walked in. Sometimes it felt like no one lived there anymore. He still was not used to the solitude. He dropped his things in the living room and went immediately to his bedroom to take a shower. He stripped off his scrubs and turned on the hottest water he could stand. He grabbed the bar of Irish Spring and soaped vigorously. He remembered his showers with Charlie. Having sex in the shower had long been a secret and shameful fantasy. But Charlie didn't seem to think it was shameful at all and to have played out that fantasy with Charlie had been the sexual high point of his life. He felt his body responding to his thoughts of Charlie and he began to fondle himself. His arousal was quick, amazingly strong and it didn't take long to reach a climax that left him leaning against the shower wall gasping for breath. He also realized that there were tears mixed with the water trickling down is face. Here in the privacy of his own bath, where no one else was watching, he admitted to himself that he missed Charlie so much. He ached to be with him. He could do the right thing. He could go through all the motions, but it didn't change his emotional truth. He had to be honest about that. Charlie had been right. They were soulmates. That doesn't change or go away because of external circumstances. It would always be true. It would be another loss that Ben would have to live with. He knew loss well.

# Chapter 29

Charlie was in the sunroom. He was beginning to love this room. Lee had one part of it set up with his computer, papers and files and Charlie had another. Usually Charlie couldn't work with someone else in the room, but it had always been different with Lee. In college, they had an apartment together their junior year. It was the first apartment for both of them and it took no adjustment time at all. They just moved in and settled into a routine that suited them both. Lee made the kitchen table his headquarters and spent many hours there drinking coffee, studying and being the creative person he had always been. Charlie commandeered the living room for his study place. There was a small desk with his Royal Safari typewriter when he needed it, but mostly he studied on the sofa. This room was a modern day version of that arrangement. Lee was at his desk now, with a cup of coffee, a legal pad, his laptop and an iPod with the score on it.

Charlie was sprawled on a big chair near his desk with his laptop on a pillow. His iPod was on, too, but he was cheating and listening to all the songs that reminded him of Ben. He had created a special playlist and could be transported to "BenLand" any time. He received Ben's email while he was listening to this music and thinking of him. He opened it eagerly.

He was thrilled for Ben. He knew how much he loved his children and how much this must mean to him. Charlie had always been indifferent to the idea of parenthood. He had no rapport with children at all and no interest in parenting, either. Yet here was another piece of the thing about Ben. He felt himself caring deeply about his kids. He would really have liked to share in Ben's joy, be with him today. That he felt that way amazed him. As for Jacen, Charlie had never even met him and had only seen one picture of him, but he cared so deeply about his welfare! It terrified him that the boy was in Iraq. Charlie wasn't much for prayer, but he knew that Jacen was, so he asked Jacen's God to keep him safe from harm and to bring him home to his father. It was the same with Pam and the baby. He knew that those feeling about Ben's children had everything to do with his feelings for Ben. He suspected that many stepparents around the country would understand completely what he was feeling.

"Lee, guess what? Ben's daughter had a baby. Ben's a grandfather! God, I'm in love with someone's grandfather!"

"Well, that sounds really sexy. I've always wanted to have sex with a grandfather." Lee didn't want to have sex with anyone old enough to drive.

Charlie punched back. "To make matters worse, this grandfather is fifteen years younger than we are. So be nice. You know, we are old enough be the baby's great-grandfather."

"Oh, now there's a charming thought. Thanks so much for doing the math on that one. I can't tell you what that does for my day. Not to mention my fragile ego. Jesus."

Lee continued to stare at his computer screen and didn't even bother to look over at Charlie. Lee hated getting old. Charlie knew that. Charlie didn't exactly love it, but he wasn't quite as angry about it as Lee was. Of course, Lee hung out with younger people all the time. He was more aware of his age. Charlie's friends were mostly contemporaries. Cassie was his youngest friend and she was forty. Lee's friends were generally in their twenties and thirties. Brad had been twenty-nine when he met Lee. No wonder he felt old.

"Ben must be thrilled. He adores those kids. They're everything to him. If there is an obstacle to our relationship, that is it. The problem is that they would never accept our relationship. I know what that means if it came down to a choice. So long Charlie."

"It's always that way when you try to date someone with children. They will always come before you, no matter how old they get. I only did that once. Couldn't stand it. Pissed me off." Charlie couldn't imagine Lee ever dating someone old enough to have kids but he didn't say that.

"The problem really isn't that he has children. It's what they believe and what that represents in Ben's life. If I'm angry at all it is at a culture that has demonized the relationship that we have. If I were a woman, we wouldn't even be having this conversation. I would have met them, met his mother and everything would be fine."

"Except that their father would be dating a woman who is fifteen years older than he is. What does the culture say about that?" Lee made a good point.

"Well, yes, you're right about that, too. Not only is America homophobic but it's ageist, too. I know that Ben's parents married young. I haven't had the nerve to ask how old his mother is. I'm afraid that she is almost our contemporary. Ye Gods!"

"Can we change the subject? I'm really glad that you are getting off on being a step-gramma, but we have work to do. There is a LOT of buzz on the internet about the show. Have you seen any of it?"

Charlie was the internet junkie of this duo and yet he hadn't gotten into the habit of checking the Broadway blogs. Apparently, there are a host of people out there who dedicated themselves to tracking the shows that are in the works or headed into Broadway from the road. Over the last few years these have become very powerful. They are beginning to rival the critics in their sway over the destiny of a show. Lee read the entries every day. He knew what they were saying.

"Everyone seems to agree that it is a good premise for a musical. People seem to be content with those of us working on it. Luke is getting good buzz and there isn't any negative stuff about us or about Piper directing. So far, we're OK. But those guys have a way of getting insider information. I don't know how they do it...like a piece of music or pages of dialogue and they take a show apart. I just hope they don't get anything of ours yet." Lee wasn't worried about the show. He just knew from experience that the book would undergo many changes. It is different when you get it onstage with actors saying the words in context. Lee had been doing this for years and had no ego about his words. Charlie felt the same. The only important words are those that work. The others can be discarded without any hard feelings.

"I like what is happening in rehearsals. It sounds good so far. When do we start rehearsing with the music?"

"Tomorrow. We start with the musicians tomorrow. Luke gets to town today, I think. I have his cell phone. I'll call him later. I made reservations at the Poinciana for breakfast early tomorrow morning. I thought it would be helpful for just the three of us to have a meeting before we went to the theatre." Lee was jittery and looked nervous.

"That's good thinking. I wonder what he'll be like. He looks kind of mean on his album covers and Nashville isn't the most liberal place...hey, Lee...why do you have his cell phone number?" Charlie noticed the tension level rise.

"He's not mean at all, Charlie. He's one of the sweetest guys I've ever... well, he's great. You'll like him. Just because he's country doesn't mean he's a hick. There are some pretty hip people in that part of the world. And I've got his cell phone because he gave it to me. End of discussion, OK?" Lee was blushing and avoided eye contact. Charlie knew there was more to this than he was getting, but let it go for the time being.

"Are we finished with the scene at the Dairy Queen? I like it as it is now." Charlie was reading a hard copy.

"We can't do any more with it until we see a run through on stage. I think we are as caught up as we can get until the next rehearsal." Lee was ready to call it a day. It was time for him to get on the webcam with the *enfant terrible* from Spain.

It gave Charlie the creeps to see how edgy Lee got when that time rolled around. He seemed terrified NOT to be online when Tadio expected him to be. Charlie made excuses.

"I'm going over to the shops. Do you want or need anything while I'm there?"

"I'm OK for now, I think. Are you going for anything in particular?" This was Lee's way of trying to find out how long Charlie would be out.

"I think I'll catch a movie. There is that new French film at the Beaux Arts. I need a distraction." Charlie really wanted to call Ben, so he would probably find a quiet coffee shop somewhere and do that. He would take his laptop with him, too. At least he let Lee know that he would be out for several hours.

"OK honey, well, have fun. I'm off to Espana. Ole!" Lee made light of it, but there was something really serious going on here that Charlie didn't like at all. He just wished Lee would get rid of the kid. Charlie didn't object to the kid's age, but this one was not quite right somehow. This one was dangerous.

# Chapter 30

Charlie drove to the shopping center because nobody in Dallas walks anywhere and he was afraid of being stopped by the police. He parked and got out of the car. It was hot and very humid and Charlie was taken back to his time as a student at the university nearby. This center had been the hangout. It was still the same layout, but there were changes. The parking lot was full of pick-ups and SUV's. In his day, it had been filled with Mustangs and GTO's. It had been nearly forty years! Charlie wished he could tell these kids how quickly that time would pass. He felt old. The five-and-dime was now a Starbuck's. The students who milled around were dressed in clothes that could be described as Goodwill grungy. Charlie missed Weejuns and madras and oxford cloth! And they were all wired with iPods and cell phones. They looked like thrift shop marionettes.

The first thing he wanted to do was to call Ben, but he was having second thoughts about that. Ben would be with his family now and not thinking about him at all. It was one of those times when Charlie was very much aware of his place in Ben's life. He had probably emailed many people about the baby. He wanted Ben to know how happy he was for him, but he didn't want to make things awkward for him. Maybe it would be better to just email him later.

He walked down to the theatre and bought a ticket. He decided to forget about everything else and enjoy the movie. It was the one thing that Charlie could count on. The movies had always been a place to go and escape from the rest of the world. When he was eight, he took a dime from his mother's purse and went to the movies on his own. His parents had been frantic, even calling the sheriff to locate him. Finally, the theater manager noticed that he had been there all day and called his mother. She sent him home, but he had already seen the main feature three times! His parents were more relieved than angry and, later that evening, they all began to see the humor in it and had a laugh about it. It became one of those family stories that got repeated at the Thanksgiving table and it started a lifelong love affair with the movies for him. And Charlie's family never picked up on the fact that the movie that so captivated him that day was Taza-Son of Cochise, starring a buff, bare-chested Rock Hudson!

Even now, Charlie loved to go to the movies alone, sitting on the back row by himself with a large tub of popcorn and a small Diet Coke. When the lights went down and the credits began to roll, it was the perfect moment. He was lost in someone else's magic for a couple of hours. Bliss.

Tonight was that same experience and he came out of the theatre a little before eleven, bleary and dazed. The movie was wonderful. It was about a little French boy who wanted to be a girl. It was sweet and touching and homophobic and sad and funny. Just like a good French film should be. Charlie realized that a film like that couldn't get made here. Americans can't admit that children are sexual beings. Even though there was homophobia in the film, and the French are not immune to that, at least they dealt realistically with childhood sexual issues. He stopped at a coffee shop and got an iced decaf latte to take home with him. It allowed him to stall a bit about getting back to the house. He knew that Lee was online with the kid about two hours every night. He didn't want to go back until they were through. Charlie was really concerned for Lee. He didn't see how potentially dangerous it all was. Lee had lived in New York for over thirty years and had a different idea of danger than Charlie did. He even admitted to Charlie that the idea of a little danger with a young European lover was glamorous to him. It didn't sound glamorous to Charlie at all. The kid was a whack job.

Charlie killed as much time as he could and finally got back to the house around eleven-thirty. Lee was off the computer and washing up odds and ends of dishes in the kitchen when Charlie came in. Charlie immediately picked up a towel and began to dry. It was a routine from their college years that they just picked right up again.

"How was the movie?" Lee seemed tired, distracted and jumpy.

"It was great. I hope you get over to see it while we're here. Very French, very gay and very sweet/sad." Charlie was more interested in what was going on with the internet love birds. "How was your evening?"

"Taddy was not in a very good mood. He failed a class this semester and was furious. He said the teacher had it in for him because he wouldn't sleep with him."

"And you believed that?"

That remark sounded like an immature kid making excuses for screwing up a course. He either slept through too many classes, didn't do the homework or blew an exam. Lee acted as if everything that Tadio said was the truth. Love is blind as a mole. He wondered how blind he was about Ben.

"The truth is that I was too tired to argue with him. Sometimes it's just easier to let him have the reins. I'm getting tired of all this, Charlie. I realized about an hour into our session tonight that I would rather be at the movies with you! But to be fair, I have no reason not to believe him, you know. After all, he's very beautiful and things are different there."

Beauty is definitely in the eye of the beholder and Tadio's pulchritude could be debated, but Charlie let that go and tried to be a friend.

"It just sounds like the kind of immature excuse kids make for goofing off, Lee. You must see it in your teaching all the time. That's all."

"Well, that's true. I hadn't really thought of comparing him to my students, but you're certainly right on that score. He's also furious that you're here and that we are living in the same house. He's convinced that we are lovers and won't believe anything I say to the contrary. He really seems to hate you."

"Frankly, I don't have a very high opinion of him either, but it isn't jealousy. All my red flags are up. I'm very suspicious of him and fearful for you."

"I know you are, honey, but I'm OK, really. You know how these kids are. He'll move on to some other older man in a couple of months, forgetting about me completely and that'll be it."

Charlie backed off a bit, "OK, I suppose you're right. After all, it is your business and not mine. I'm sorry. I just don't want to see you hurt, emotionally or physically!"

"I know that. Let's just forget about it OK? I've got more news. I talked to Luke tonight. He got in late this afternoon and they've put him in a condo just a couple of blocks from here. He doesn't know Dallas at all and sounded as excited as a little kid. I told him we would come over first thing in the morning to take him out to breakfast before the theatre. You've never met him have you?"

"You know I haven't, but I know his music. I love his voice and his writing and I'm excited about meeting him in person."

"Well, one thing you'll like about him is that he's very much your type with a beautiful chest that even I admired."

"Wait a minute. You said it was a flirtation. Sounds like more than that to me. Would you like to clarify?"

"Perhaps it was a little more than a flirtation. But it was only one time. It was a great one time, but just a beautiful afternoon." The contained emotion in Lee's voice made it sounds like it had been quite a bit more than a flirtation.

"I can't believe you are just now telling me about this!"

"It was so brief. It was a long time ago. It was an impossible situation. Actually, when you started telling me about Ben, it reminded me of the way I felt about Luke back then. He felt like more than an afternoon in a hotel room. Listen, with Tadio's fit and seeing Luke tomorrow, I'm frazzled. I'm going to bed, OK? I told Luke we would be there around seven. Our reservation at the Poinciana is at 7:30. We can fill him in on what's happening and get a sense of how the score is going. I would rather see him in that context than just have him show up at the theatre tomorrow. Things should be OK between us, but I've got to admit to some butterflies." Lee started toward his bedroom, not waiting for Charlie to respond.

"Get some rest, honey. I'm not far behind you." Charlie finished drying the last of the dishes and put everything away. He picked up his laptop and headed down the hall to his room, turning out lights as he went. He undressed quickly, brushed his teeth and washed his face and crawled into bed. Before he turned out the light, he opened the computer and emailed Ben:

"Hey Dude...

I got your note about Pam and the baby. I know what this means to you and I'm so happy for you. I'm glad it was easy for her and I'm sure it helped a lot that you were there. Have they picked out a name yet? I always call new babies Winston because they all look like Winston Churchill to me. Since it's a girl, however, I will refer to her as Winnie! I know that I can't send a baby gift to Pam, but I would like to send something for the baby to you. You can give it to Pam yourself. I won't do it if you think it's weird or awkward. Let me know, OK? It is just my way of acknowledging a part of your life that I can't participate in.

"It's late and I won't make this long. Luke Beecham got in tonight and we're meeting him for breakfast in the morning, so I need to get some sleep. I hope you are not so excited that you are unable to sleep. You need some rest, too, I'm sure. You always do.

"I almost called you when I got your email, but I decided to do this instead. I knew you would be busy with such an important family event. I wish Pam and her family all the best and even though I can't convey it, you will know that it's in my heart....

"As are my deepest feelings for you, my baby boy.

Your Charlie"

Charlie clicked "SEND." He loved Ben. He was so sure of it. He didn't really mind being in a back street relationship for right now. He had his work and his own life. He was just feeling a bit sorry for himself tonight. He wanted to be more of a part of Ben's life. He wanted to be able to send Pam a card, buy the baby a teddy bear, call Ben's mother. If he were the "girlfriend" he could do all of those things. He was well aware of that. The truth was that he wasn't the girlfriend. He wasn't anything except in love.

Charlie turned off the laptop and put it on the nightstand. He picked up the book he was reading and put it back down without opening it. He turned off the light, turned over and cried for a while. Not hopeless tears and not terribly painful ones. Just tears that acknowledged the truth of his situation and the sadness of a world that kept denying him and people like him full access to happiness. Those tears have been shed before and, Charlie knew, would be shed again in bedrooms all over the world. It's possible that the rainbow symbol was created by someone viewing the world through his tears.

# Chapter 31

Ben got Charlie's email at home the next evening. It was so sweet and caring. He could tell that Charlie yearned to be more a part of his life. Deep inside, Ben wanted that, too. Charlie had had his whole life to figure all this out. Ben had only been trying for a few months. When Charlie made the decision to "come out" he was young and single with no responsibilities except to please his parents. That was a difficult obstacle, of course, but Ben faced much more than that. He was a middle-aged man with a family and a career and, most of all, a religious faith that had always sustained him. Finding himself loving another man and wanting some kind of life with him was shocking on so many levels. There were days that he couldn't deal with it all, so he didn't think about it. Yet always, something would remind him of Charlie and he would be right back there in that little house on Atwell Street in Sacramento.

He was sitting at his desk with Charlie's email in front of him, daydreaming, when the phone rang. It was his mother.

"Honey, hi. Listen, I was over at Pam's and something went wrong. It's the baby. We're at the hospital now and Dr. Tierney told me to call you. He wants you to ride in the ambulance with her to a hospital in San Francisco. She's having trouble breathing. They don't know any more than that yet."

"I'm out the door, mom. I'll be there in five minutes." Ben was still in his scrubs. He grabbed his keys and ran out the door without even locking it. He made the familiar drive to the hospital in record time, even for him, parked and was at the ambulance entrance in under ten minutes. They were just bringing the baby down when he got there.

"Good lord, that was quick," Michael Tierney was with the baby.

"What's up, Mike? Mom didn't know anything."

"It seems to be respiratory, Ben. We're taking her to St. Michael's in San Francisco. We've got her on a respirator. She's not breathing too well on her own."

Ben had been a nurse long enough not to let this information panic him, but his mouth went dry and fear surrounded his heart. He had fallen in love with that little girl the moment he saw her."

"Pam and Brett?"

"They are already on the way down in the car with your Mom and Brett's parents. They will probably be there when we get there."

"Well, let's go then. What can I do?"

This was an experience that Ben had had many times in his career. Just last week he took a patient to a hospital in Sacramento. It always seemed routine, but today was different. Every sense was heightened. He never realized how noisy and scary an ambulance is so he sat very close to his precious, new, little relative. She was a part of him and a part of Pam and a part of his mother. She was the continuity of everything he knew and loved. She was so tiny and so very ill, it seemed. They still had no idea what had caused the trauma. Ben knew very well that this happened. It wasn't frequent, but enough that he was familiar with the sequence of events.

They arrived at the hospital in San Francisco where a team was waiting for them. They worked with such efficiency and speed that the next few minutes were a blur and then the baby was gone to a special care unit. Ben looked for his family before heading upstairs. He knew that the baby was getting the best care possible and that there was nothing more he could do. He wanted to see his family and help them if he could.

They were waiting near the hospital admittance desk. They had completed the paperwork and were trying to get information when Ben appeared. He briefed them on the ride down, keeping his voice light and even as if it were a routine event. Pam and Brett wanted to see her immediately, of course, but Ben reminded them of what they already knew, being kids in a medical family. It would be a while before anyone was allowed in to see her. Ben would be on the unit with her and keep them posted.

He found them a comfortable alcove in the waiting area that was empty and private. He warned them to settle in for a wait, perhaps have some food and try to remain calm. He found the elevator bank and located the unit. Just as the elevator doors opened on the floor, he saw Michael Tierney. His face told the story. Something terrible had happened since the baby was brought in.

"Ben. I'm so sorry. By the time we got her up here, she was in convulsions. We did everything we could. She was so tiny. There would probably have been severe brain damage had we been able to save her. What can I say, my dear friend? Is there anything I can do? I'll notify the hospital back home, of course. You take a few days off. Go to your family now. Do you want me to come with you to tell them?" It was always difficult to tell the family something like this. Michael had noticed that Ben seemed troubled lately and hated to add to his burdens.

"No, thanks Michael. You've been great. I'll go down and tell them. Just give me a few minutes. Is it possible to see the baby?"

"I wouldn't recommend it, Ben. You know how it is. You would say the same thing if our roles were reversed."

"Of course. It's probably best. It's just...I wanted to say good-bye to her." With this, Ben began to cry. He leaned on Michael's shoulder and sobbed. All the emotion from the past weeks and months came pouring out.

"Let's get out of this corridor, OK?" Michael was concerned now. He guided Ben into a private office just off the nurses' station. He handed Ben a box of tissues and waited while he pulled himself together.

"Thanks, Mike. I've always been a crier." Ben gave him a weak smile. "I do want to see her."

"Sure. I'll arrange it immediately." Michael left the room and returned within five minutes and led Ben to a curtained area just off the main ICU. There, in a huge hospital bed with Star Wars equipment surrounding her, was Ben's grandchild, quiet, still, pale.

"Oh my little angel. Oh my love. I'm so sorry I couldn't do more. I'm so sorry I won't get to know you and hold you and watch you grow. I'm sorry you won't get to know your parents. They're such good people and were looking forward to knowing you, too. We all love you and we won't forget you. Poor little thing, you don't even have a name yet." Ben whispered. And he remembered something. "Winnie. I'm going to call you Winnie, OK? It's just between you and me. Your mom will come up with something else, but you're my little Winnie." Ben touched her tiny hand and kissed the little head. This must be the worst feeling of loss yet in his life. He was glad that Lynette didn't have to go through this.

Eight hours later Ben was sitting at his house with his family. His daughter and son in law and his mother were all quiet and dry eyed. In shock. He had just kept it simple when he told them. The baby didn't make it. She just stopped breathing. There seemed to be no other answer. God had decided to take her back with Him. When Alvah had suggested that becoming a mother would be the maturing of his daughter, she didn't have this horrific trial in mind. Looking at Pam, Ben could see that she was forever changed. The young girl who had so recently been there was gone forever. Here was a woman, waxen with grief and pain. She had aged ten years in a few hours. Brett still looked boyish, but stricken with grief and focused completely on Pam. Ben's mother was sorrowful, but she would be the strong one during this ordeal. She, too, had lost a baby when Ben was only a year old. She would be able to help Pam get through this. Their faith would see them through. Ben felt that they were so fortunate to be a family of deep faith. Who could understand God's will? They trusted in His love and knew that whatever happened was part of His plan.

Ben looked around at his family. Pam and Brett held on to each other and Pam had a Bible open in her lap. His mother had a far-off look in her eyes, dreamy almost, as if remembering something from long ago. One hand was on her heart. Ben thought she must be praying. Alvah had always had the comfort of her God. She had not needed anyone else when her husband left her. She had been grateful for her children, but the primary relationship of her life was with God. It was clear now that He was bringing her solace in this horrible grief. They had an email from Jacen. He was going to try to get a special leave to come home, but it was just a gesture. They were stretched thin in Iraq and leave was impossible. It was clear from his message that he yearned to be with his family. Ben just hoped this distraction was not a danger for him. He needed to be alert for his job.

But who was to look after Ben? He felt alone, cut off from people and his own feelings. Pam and Brett stood and silently indicated that they were going home. He nodded and told them that he would talk to them tomorrow. His mother left, too, saying that she was going to the church to see about the service. No one objected. It was something that Pam couldn't even bear to think of and Ben just didn't want to handle. Thank God for his mother.

They left and Ben was alone with his grief and his thoughts. He was tired and his mind roamed unedited, "Little Winnie is gone Charlie." He wanted to see Charlie. He wanted to be with him, to bury his head in Charlie's chest and cry until he couldn't cry anymore. He needed to be held. He gasped when he realized what he was thinking. This was not the appropriate time for those thoughts. The baby's death might even be God's way of punishing him for Charlie! He wouldn't allow himself to indulge his emotions in that way. He would get through this with his family. He would grieve alone if he had to. He realized how ironic the situation was. He couldn't risk being with Charlie because of his family, yet here he was needing the support and safety of his family and he was alone, wishing that Charlie were here to comfort him. It didn't make any sense. Sometimes faith isn't supposed to make sense. That's why it is faith and not fact. Ben turned on the computer and emailed Charlie. He just wanted him to know.

"Dear Charlie,

We've had sad news in my family. My daughter's little baby girl died earlier today. It was one of those things that gets called SIDS. No one knows the cause really. She just stopped breathing. I remember thinking as I looked at her that she just didn't want to be here. I have to believe that this is God's will and He has His reasons that I don't question. But to you, and only you, I can say that I have to wonder at a God that would do something like this. I would never say that in front of anyone else I know, but I know you won't judge me. I just have to wonder, that's all. I didn't know whether to tell you about this or not. I feel that it's wrong to for some reason. But it's comforting to me to think that you are with me in this, even so far away.

"I don't know what we have, Charlie, this special, otherworldly friendship. You said once that we were soulmates. That must be true. I feel better now just typing this to you.

"I hope your work is going OK. I just wanted to let you know about this. Don't let it upset you. There is nothing you can do. It just helps to know that you are out there and thinking of me.

B."

# Chapter 32

Luke Beecham was waiting outside when they arrived at his condo on Monday morning. Lee rolled down the window and Luke walked over wearing a slow, sexy smile that gave Lee a pleasant arrhythmia. Luke was low key, low maintenance and low slung, standing only about 5' 9". He was in his early thirties with dark hair that receded in a flattering way and a little soul patch goatee. He was broad shouldered and slim hipped, the perfect body for the Wranglers and boots he was wearing. He leaned his forearms on the car and ducked his head in the window, close to Lee.

His voice was surprisingly soft and southern. "Hey Lee, how's it goin'?" The megawatt smile amped up.

Charlie was amused to see Lee caught off guard, a rare occurrence. "Hi Luke, Uh, I'm fine. You look great. Um, are you ready?"

"Yep" Luke opened the door and slid into the backseat of the rented SUV with vulpine grace.

"Luke this is Charlie Morgan. Charlie, Luke Beecham." Lee was blushing furiously.

"Hey Charlie. Nice to meet you. I hear you're kinda new at all this, too. Let's stick together, OK?" Luke turned that smile on Charlie. Wow.

"Hi, Luke." Charlie reached over the seat and offered his hand "That sounds good to me, but, really, all the people over at the theatre are pretty laid back and fun to work with. You'll be fine." Charlie turned more in the seat to face Luke. "Listen, I love the songs you sent me. You've captured the period and place perfectly. And have you noticed that you and Lee write in the same rhythm? I've always said that the key to Lee's work, particularly to the humor, is understanding the musicality of the language. Your music and his book seem to be from the same source. You know, Lee would be a great lyricist for you."

"Well, I've always written my own words, Charlie, but I read Lee's script and I have to say that I agree with you. I felt a kinship with those words right away and they influenced my music. I think you're right about the rhythm thing. I do see the similarity. Lee, if you have any input about the lyrics, I'm open to just about anything." Luke looked at Lee in the rearview mirror and Lee returned the look, but didn't say anything.

They pulled in front of the Poinciana Hotel and handed off the car to valet parking. This was a new boutique hotel that had opened since they had been Dallasites. It was quite elegant, so Charlie heard. He had never stayed there, but Lee often did when he was in Texas and loved the coffee shop for breakfast. Apparently it was very popular and they had reservations. Lee was pulling out all the stops for Luke.

The restaurant was so Texas! If this was the coffee shop, Charlie would love to see the formal dining room. It was just a little bit grand for breakfast: white linen, heavy silver, carpet so thick you had to be careful not to trip and fall into it. It was only a little after seven and it was nearly full but it had a quiet hushed tone, unusual at breakfast time. He felt like someone was going to sign a treaty at the next table. Charlie, always conscious of how he was dressed, wondered if his jeans, polo shirt and linen jacket combo were appropriate until he looked around and realized that many of the patrons were more casually dressed than he was.

Luke was definitely recognized as they walked to the table and his demeanor changed completely from the car. That relaxed, down-home, almost-sweet quality that seemed so natural to him disappeared completely. It was replaced with this twangy, Western swagger and a pouty, heavy lidded expression that looked like the pictures on his album covers.

Under his breath he said, "Don't worry, Charlie. It's just for the fans. They expect the macho thing. I don't bite!"

Charlie very nearly did trip and fall through the carpet. There was clearly a public Luke Beecham and a private Luke Beecham. Nashville, while a very cool city, was not exactly a bastion of liberalism. Just ask The Dixie Chicks. This public Luke was a projection of what he was expected to be. It was fascinating to watch.

It really was a working breakfast. They discussed the songs that had been finished, their placement, the emotional contribution to the show, etc. Luke was very knowledgeable about music and about the theatre. Apparently he had done some musicals in high school and at Duke University where he earned a degree in history. This handsome young man was more than those album covers. Any fear that Charlie had about working with him vanished. It was going to be a friendly and artistically joyful collaboration. All three men seemed relieved, like a blind date that unexpectedly turns out great.

They accomplished a lot of work that day. The director and producers were thrilled and the actors seemed to come alive and add new dimensions to their work when they were inspired by Luke's haunting, evocative music. It was a very long day but everyone was naturally high as they left the theatre around nine-thirty. They all agreed to meet at a local watering hole to unwind a bit. The place was very hip, but noisy and Charlie, who didn't drink anyway, got bored quickly and decided to walk home. It was only a few blocks and the heat had abated enough that he thought he could make it without a canteen.

The streets were familiar to him and as he walked, memories of his years here came back to him, but it seemed like it had happened to someone else. He had been in California for so long that it was hard to remember life in Dallas. It was a little as if he had moved to a foreign country and learned a second language that gradually became his first language. He hadn't spoken "Texan" in many years and it felt strange. "Californian" felt like his native language. He wondered when and how the transition had happened. He didn't just wake up one morning and feel like a Californian, but he certainly was one now.

He got home to a dark house so he flipped on lights as he headed to the sunroom/office. He thought he would check email before heading off to bed. The message from Ben jumped off the page. He immediately sat down and sadness filled his heart as he read. Poor little thing. He didn't know Pam yet his heart ached for her. But darling Ben! He must be devastated. Charlie called the airline immediately. He couldn't get a flight to Sacramento until the following morning at six o'clock, so he booked it. He went into his bedroom and began to pack a small bag. He didn't need to take much because, after all, he was going home. He sat down to write Lee a note. He didn't know when he would be back. He just knew he had to be there for Ben.

It was already after midnight and he would have to leave for the airport by four. It seemed pointless to even pretend to sleep. He wanted to call Ben, but he didn't. He might be with his family and it would be awkward to talk. He would send a text message in the morning. He went out to the kitchen and opened a Diet Coke and took it out to the table by the pool.

He wondered about the funeral. When would it be? His friend Cassie knew everybody. If anyone could find out the details, she could. It was still early enough to call, so Charlie picked up his cell phone.

"Cassie? Hi, it's Charlie. I didn't wake you did I?"

"Hey, Charlie. No, we're up. How are things in Texas?"

Well, things are fine here and with the show, but I'm coming home tomorrow." Charlie explained everything to her and asked if she knew of some way to find out the details about the funeral.

"One of my best friends from Sac State works for the newspaper. If it's not in the obituary columns, she can find out through other sources. I'll give her a call and get the information to you ASAP. Should I just email it?"

"You're a saint in Jimmy Choo shoes and I love you. Yeah, email me the details. I'll be leaving for the airport in just a few hours and I'll have my laptop with me. I'll probably be home by seven, your time. I'll call you tomorrow. Thanks again honey."

"I'm glad to do it for you. Charlie. I'm so sorry. It's a devastating kind of loss. Take care of yourself and Ben, OK?"

"Bye-bye." Charlie clicked off his cell phone. Suddenly he needed exercise. He was used to going to the gym and hadn't been since getting to Texas. He stood up, stripped off his clothes and dived into the pool. He began to swim laps, not furiously, but methodically with long, slow, strong, steady strokes. It felt good. He swam until he began to ache and that felt even better. After forty-five minutes, he paused, gasping, for the Texas air was so thick and humid that it was hard to breathe. As he clung to the side of the pool, he thought about that poor little baby. He wondered how people who believed in God managed to explain things like that. Why would a God kill a baby? It infuriated him to hear things like "It's not our job to understand God's will in the world." Why isn't it? It seemed to Charlie that God had some explaining to do! But he loved Ben and he respected his right to believe as he chose. All he wanted to do was to support him right now and make it a little easier for him if he could. He would keep his opinions to himself.

He heard the front door open. Lee and Luke were laughing conspiratorially. Everyone was getting along and that was a good thing. They came out to the patio as Charlie was getting out of the pool. He had forgotten that he didn't have a swimsuit, but there was a terry robe of Lee's over a chair and he reached for it. They were a little surprised to see him still up and out at the pool. The three men sat at the table as Charlie explained about Ben's email and his decision to go back to California.

Lee said to him, gently, "Honey, has he asked you to come back?"

"Well, no, and I won't go running to his house or anything. I'll go home and just let him know that I'm there if he needs me for anything. I just have to be there. I can't bear the idea that he would reach out to me and I wouldn't be available."

Charlie got Lee's point and knew that it was a valid one. Nowhere in his note did Ben ask Charlie to come home. He knew that he couldn't go to Goldmine to see him and the idea that Ben would come to Sacramento seemed remote. Was he really helping at all? Charlie didn't have any answers for this. He just knew that he had to be there if Ben wanted him. He had not even thought about it. He never considered anything else. His immediate instinct had been to get the first plane home and he was going to follow it.

"I called my friend Cassie. She's going to get me information about the funeral. Even if I don't hear from Ben, I'll go to the funeral. No one will notice and I probably won't even see Ben. I can just be there. I'll sign the book. He'll know that I was there. That's enough." Charlie didn't know who he was trying to convince.

"I'll drive you to the airport." Lee, always the best friend, simply accepted Charlie's decision without another word. That had always been their place in each other's lives. It had made all the hardships of the last forty years bearable.

"Thanks, Lee. You're always my angel...I'm packed already. I don't need much. I'll go shower and get cleaned up. By the time I'm through, we can leave for the airport. You can just drop me off and come back here and get at least a few hours sleep. I'm sorry to do this to you."

"I'll go too. To keep Lee company. I'm really sorry for your troubles, Charlie. You must love this guy a lot. He's a lucky man. Does he know that?"

Charlie was again surprised by the sensitivity of this young man, "Thanks, Luke. It's not necessary for you to come along, but considerate of you to offer. At least Lee won't have to drive back here alone. And, to answer your question, yes, I do love him. He's my soulmate. Truly. I don't know how lucky he is. It's a long story, but this relationship is causing him more pain than happiness, I fear. Lee can fill you in on the way back if you're really interested."

"I am interested. I'll tell you my story sometime when you return. Not as interesting as yours, but it's there if you're inclined to hear it"

"I'll look forward to that, Luke, and to knowing you better. I think we're going to be friends."

"I certainly hope so. Now, go get in the shower and get dressed. We've got to get you to the airport, OK?

# Chapter 33

Ben checked email again just before he went to bed. Nothing from Charlie. Maybe he was out and hadn't gotten the message. It was just as well. He was exhausted, physically and emotionally. He crawled into his familiar bed and stretched out. It felt good to lie down. He reached into his night stand drawer and took out the tiny iPod from Charlie. It was filled with all the songs that he said reminded him of Ben. They were lush and romantic and sentimental and corny...so much like Charlie! They reminded him of the times they had spent together and of Charlie's funny/sad, hopeful face, his ready smile and that mop of silver hair. Dear Charlie. All he wanted was to love Ben and be loved by him in return. It was so simple and so pure. This was the secret time that he could indulge the idea that it was possible. The songs played at random, so he never knew what he was going to hear. It was the best he had felt all day and he allowed himself to feel it for the few minutes before an exhausted sleep overtook him.

He awoke the next morning feeling relaxed and lazy until he remembered what had happened. At first he was praying that it had just been a nightmare. As consciousness increased he knew that it was real and he heard the phone ring.

It was Pam. "Hi Dad. You awake? We decided on a name for the baby." Her voice was steady, but without emotion. "We're going to call her Alvah Evangeline, after Gramma and Brett's mother. The funeral has been set. Gramma did all that. It will be at the church tomorrow morning at eleven. Since we didn't have a plot or anything, we're using Gramma's. She says there is room for the entire family and that's what she got it for. I've been out there before and it's very peaceful. And the baby won't be alone, Daddy, Gramma's baby is there, too." At this, Pam's voice quavered, but she remained calm.

Ben was surprised. He knew about his mother's lost child, but he had never really thought about it having a grave somewhere. He realized that his mother had carried that heartbreak alone all these years. She never spoke of it to her children, but she must have shared a lot with Pam. Ben was glad. He realized how lucky he was to have the kind of family that he did. They were there for each other.

"Thanks, Pammie. Is there anything I can do for you? Please let me help. I'm feeling more than useless this morning."

"I think everything's taken care of, Dad. Brett and Gramma did most of it, but come on over to the house. People are already bringing food and dropping by. I'm not very good at meeting all those people and you could really help me out. You're so good with people."

"Of course. I'll clean up and be right there. Are you sure you're OK, Pam?"

"I have the Lord, Dad. And I love God. That sustains me through anything, even this. And Brett's faith is strong, too. Brett and God and me. We'll get through this together."

"I'm proud of you, Pam. Faith is the thing that makes the difference in your entire life. I know that myself. Thanks for reminding me to take comfort in that today."

"We'll see you in a while, Dad. I love you."

"Me, too."

Ben hung up and thought about his daughter. She had grown up in twenty-four hours. There was none of the sense of playfulness that used to characterize her voice. She had sounded odd, but her professed faith made Ben think that everything would be OK. God didn't give you something you weren't prepared to handle. The strength of his family's faith would get them through this.

Before he got in the shower, he went to the computer to see if there was any word from Jacen. There was a message.

"Dad. No way to get home. Tell Pammie that I'm sorry. I would give anything to be with her today. Tell her that I haven't stopped praying for her and the baby. I don't have long. Got work to do here and can't talk about it. Just know that my heart and spirit are with my family. Jacen."

Ben printed out the message. He would take the copy to Pam, although he knew that Jacen had probably emailed her, too. This was the first war that was being reported so immediately over the internet. It was comforting in a way, but frightening, too. In this instance, he was grateful for the technology that he had trouble embracing most of the time.

There was also a message from Charlie. Ben didn't open it. He wanted to. He stared at the email address sadly. Charlie was something, someone, in his life that just didn't belong. Moments before, he had been inspired by the spiritual character of his children, of his family and then there was Charlie's note. It went against all he was clinging to and seemed to mock his faith. Perhaps it was the shock of what they were going through, but Ben had a moment of clarity. He saw his life and all it's components as whole cloth, not carefully compartmentalized. In that moment, he realized that no matter how much he loved Charlie, it could never be a part of his real life. Why couldn't he just end it? Where was the strength he needed to do that?

He turned off the computer and headed for the shower. He scrubbed and prayed, hoping the water would wash away his confusion for a moment. He concentrated on being present today for Pam and for his mother.

But he saw Charlie's face before him. Charlie was kind and good and decent. Ben knew that. And he knew with certainty that Charlie loved him. Why was that so sinful? He had a hard time understanding that Charlie was bad. It would be a long day and require all his strength. His entire life had been about caring for his family, so this was not a burden, but an honor. Yet thoughts of Charlie continued to pulse in and out of his brain, as they always did.

So it was not surprising that he chose a shirt Charlie had given him and sprayed himself with Charlie's favorite fragrance. He couldn't explain it. He needed Charlie with him in some way. He hoped God would understand.

# Chapter 34

Charlie walked into his house at seven-thirty in the morning. He felt like he had been awake since the dawn of time. He was achy and his eyes itched for sleep, but the first thing he did was to check the computer for a message from Ben. He had emailed him from the airport in Dallas earlier and hoped that he had gotten it by now. It was a simple message, just letting him know that he was coming home and that his soulmate was nearby if he needed a lifeline.

There was no answer from Ben. Perhaps he hadn't read his email. That would be very much like him. Or perhaps he just didn't have time to respond with people at the house, plans to make, all the painful things that must be attended to at a time like this. He was checking other email when the phone rang.

"Hey, where are you?" It was Cassie. "I got the information you wanted."

"Cass, you're brilliant. I can't thank you enough. How did you manage it?"

"My friend Tory...good ole sorority sisters! Anyway, the service is tomorrow morning at 11:00 a.m. at the Legion of God Tabernacle in Goldmine. The baby's name is Alvah Evangeline Cameron and she is to be interred in the family plot in Goldmine immediately following the service at the church. I've got the address of the church, if you need it."

"Thanks, that would be perfect." Charlie wrote down the address and the other information that Cassie had gotten for him. It was amazing, really, to think that it was that easy to do.

"Have you talked to him? How are you?"

"No, I just walked in the door. I checked email and there is nothing from him. I'm not surprised or concerned. I just hope he knows I'm here if he needs anything, that's all."

"I'm sure he does, honey and that he cares in his own way. Don't be too disappointed if you don't hear from him, for a few days at least. Like you said, it's a lot to process."

"Tory also got some interesting material about the Legion of God denomination. I'll email it to you. You should read this stuff. They are really fundamentalist. Big time." Cassie was a product of Catholic school and had spend most of her adult life trying to recover from that. She was a little chilly on the subject and yet could get hot under the collar about specifics.

"Thanks, I have been on their website, but I would be curious to see what a professional journalist could uncover, too. God, I've got to get some sleep now. I'm going to the funeral tomorrow. I'll just sit in the back of the church. I'm sure I won't even see Ben, but I can sign the book and he'll know that I was there. I need to do that."

"I get it, Charlie. I do. Listen, call me if you need anything else. When are you going back to Texas?"

"Thanks, uh, I'm not sure. Possibly Thursday, depending on Ben, but I'll stay here longer if he shows any indication that he needs me to be here."

"OK...just keep me posted. I love you. Sleep. Rest. Talk to you later."

"Yeah, bye. Thanks again. You're a real friend and I love you."

Cassie rang off. He went into the bedroom and crawled under the comforter with his clothes on. He was asleep in just a few minutes.

The phone woke him. It was in his shirt pocket, so there was no fumbling around for it. He was groggy as he answered.

"Hello?"

"Hey Dude."

Charlie was immediately alert. "Hey, how are you?"

"I've been better. I can't believe this is happening. I just read your email. Thanks for the sweet things you said. I just wanted to call and let you know that there is nothing you can do, really. It's all done. The funeral is scheduled. I'm at my daughter's house right now and people are coming by. Mostly people from our church, but some from the hospital and Brett's family and friends."

"You must be so tired. Did you get any sleep last night?" Charlie wondered if Ben's night had been as sleepless as his own. He could hear the exhaustion in his voice.

"Not much, but you know I'm used to operating on not much sleep, so I don't feel that different from the way I usually feel. Physically at least. Emotionally, I feel like I've been in some sort of disaster, like 9/11 or Katrina.

I feel detached in a way. I think it must be shock. Whatever it is, it's helping me to get through this. But I just wanted to say thanks. How's Texas? Is it hot there?"

"It's going well...or was when I left this morning."

"Where are you?"

"I'm at my house in Sacramento. I said in the email to you that I was coming home in case you needed me."

"You're really here? I thought you meant that you would come back if I needed you to. I didn't know that you were really coming home. You did that for me?"

"Of course I did. I love you Ben. I'll be here and I'm available twenty-four hours a day if you need anything. Just say the word. I'll be at the service tomorrow. Don't worry. I'll just slip in and sit at the back. You don't have to acknowledge me in any way. I just want to pay my respects to your family in the only way I can."

"I wish you could sit with me, Charlie. I can't say that to anyone else, but it's true. I wish I could hold your hand through this."

"You can, Ben...in your heart. Just know that I'm always there with you. My hand is always in yours."

"I gotta go Charlie. Wow. You'll never know what this means to me. Bye for now." He was crying.

"Bye, Ben. Everything."

"Ditto, dude."

They hung up at the same time. Charlie's heart ached for Ben and his family. He tried to think of anything he might be able to do to make things easier for Ben. He would find out tomorrow if he could make a donation to a favorite charity. It was something. And he sent flowers to the church.

He was glad he had come home and he had the rest of the day to himself. He needed to do laundry and the house could use a little work. He also needed to take the car out for a spin. It had been parked for too long and needed some exercise. He would put the top down, head south and meander around the Delta. It would be good therapy for him, too. He also needed to get on the internet and get directions to the church in Goldmine. Tomorrow would be stressful. He tried to keep in mind that this was about Ben and doing the right thing. Ah, the right thing. There's an interesting concept.

# Chapter 35

It was Wednesday and the day of the funeral. Ben experienced something that was rare for him. He didn't want to get out of bed. He could admit to himself there in the privacy of his bedroom that he didn't want to face the ordeal that was in front of him. He knew that once he was up and involved, he would gain strength from his family, his pastor, his friends and coworkers. Just right now, he wanted to avoid it all. He missed Charlie. He missed how he smelled so good and how safe it was being held by him. His parents must have held him as a baby, but of course he didn't remember that. As an adult male, he had always been the one to do the holding. It hadn't occurred to him how much he needed to be held until Charlie. It was a moment Ben would never forget. Charlie folded him into his arms and he had experienced a feeling of absolute peace and contentment. He remembered wanting to stay there forever.

He got up and prepared for the day. He showered and groomed himself meticulously. That always made him feel more prepared, somehow. He had a black suit that was not too much out of style and he decided to wear it. He knew he would be more dressed up than anyone else, but he didn't care. It made him feel better. He finished a cup of coffee and a cinnamon roll and drove over to Pam's. Everyone was meeting there to go to the church. A limousine arrived at Pam's house around ten o'clock and they rode to the church in near silence, only making small talk. Ben's mother seemed dreamy and was reminiscing about earlier days in a way that seemed odd and out of place, but Pam didn't seem to notice. They were shown to a section of the church that had been set up especially for the family, so that they could have some privacy during the service, yet have a clear view of the congregation. Ben was comforted by the obscurity. He didn't have to smile and put on a brave face. He could grieve. He looked over at Pam and she was serene, holding Brett's hand. Brett, too, seemed to be doing OK. They were people of strong faith and this test was proof of that. Their faith blocked them from the pain of their loss.

There were flowers everywhere. The tiny casket was nearly lost in the profusion and when the family first saw it, Ben thought that Pam's resolve would waver, but it didn't. He heard her say under her breath, like a mantra, over and over, "She's with God now." Ben was distracted. The pain and grief seemed to be losing out to that familiar numbness that had engulfed him after Lynette's death. If he remembered, it started at her funeral, too. He felt that it was God allowing him to get through this. He looked up and out over the congregation. There on the very back row, he saw someone else in a black suit and sunglasses. His heart pounded as he realized that it was Charlie. He couldn't stop staring and suddenly he felt that Charlie was looking at him, too, even though Charlie couldn't possibly see him. It was one of their moments. One of those things that had convinced them both that they were soulmates and shared such a special bond.

Ben barely paid attention to the rest of the service. It seemed so strange and dangerous, even, for Charlie to be there. Yet, he was glad and he knew that Charlie would never do or say anything that would compromise him. Ben had absolute trust in him and he felt Charlie's hand in his.

In a daze, Ben left the church, got back into the limousine and they proceeded to the cemetery. The graveside service was short and poignant, lasting less than a quarter hour. As the family rose to leave, Ben heard a whimper that sounded like an animal in pain. It was Pam. Her face was the color of spoiled milk, her eyes glassy. She tore herself from Brett's arms and fell onto the tiny coffin in sobs that were agonizing to hear. Ben had wondered when it would hit her. He reacted quickly and with Brett's help pulled her away from the gravesite. He saw one of the doctors from the hospital and caught his eye. The doctor got his message and Ben, almost carrying Pam, followed him to his car where he had his emergency bag and was already preparing a sedative.

"Thanks, Albert. I was wondering when this was going to happen. She seemed much too composed to me. I guess it's good to get it out, huh?"

"It's the only way, Ben. How're you doing? Are you allowing yourself time to grieve or are you, as usual, taking care of everyone else?"

"I'll have time to grieve, Al. Today my family needs me to be strong. I'll take care of them first. I'll find the time for myself later. I'm OK for right now."

"I'm always here, Ben, if you need me. Marge and I both have great affection for you and you're welcome at our house anytime you need to talk or just need to be with friends. Understand?'

"Thanks, Al. More than you know. I'll take you up on the offer real soon." Ben was genuinely touched. He and Al didn't spend much time together, but from a mutual professional respect, a solid friendship had developed over the years.

Pam was quiet now, and they returned to the waiting limousine where a distraught Brett was relieved to see Pam calmer. They all got back into the car and headed for home. The day was only half over.

There was already a crowd at the house when they arrived. Several of the women from the church, friends of Pam's, had taken over duties in the kitchen and were busy putting out the plates and trays and casserole dishes that had been streaming into the house since yesterday. They were methodically listing the names and contents of each dish as it went out, so Pam would have a record of who brought what. Ben watched and was overwhelmed with gratitude to everyone who showed such kindness and compassion to them. The shot had restored Pam to a place where she could handle the rest of the afternoon. But after a couple of hours, Brett insisted that she go upstairs and lie down for a while. Ben's mother took over for her.

Ben stood back and watched from that detached place that he found so comforting. He had done all he knew to do. So he quietly told his mom that he was going home to rest and slipped out the back door. As he pulled out into the street he turned on the radio. It grated on his raw nerves, so he fished out a CD without even looking at the label. When it began, he realized it was one of the CD's that Charlie had made for him. Charlie seemed to be everywhere as the CD filled the car with lush songs about love and loss and how special people can be to each other. Ben knew right then what he had to do. He turned the car and headed toward the freeway. He would go to Sacramento and see Charlie. Albert had reminded him that he needed to take care of himself and what he needed was to be with Charlie. Ben liked to drive fast and as he pulled onto the highway to Sacramento, he applied a little pressure and the Jaguar responded powerfully and smoothly. He would be there in forty minutes if he didn't get stopped. He prayed about that.

It was getting dark as he got into Sacramento. The traffic was not too bad, as rush hour was over by now. He cruised easily to Charlie's neighborhood and made the familiar turn onto his street. There was that sweet little house with the squatty little car in the drive. A welcoming lamp was on in the front window. It seemed to be lit just for him. He pulled in behind the Beetle and cut the engine on the Jag. The roar of the cat stopped. At that moment, the front door opened and Charlie came out on the porch. Ben got out of the car and hurried to where he stood. Charlie's arms were open and Ben walked into them. He buried his head in Charlie's shoulder and wept. Finally, he could grieve in peace. They stood quietly together on the porch, the light from the living room shining through the door and casting them in silhouette. A passerby would have been touched by the obvious feeling that was being shared on that porch. Two soulmates connecting. A seismic shift of the heart.

# Chapter 36

"Come inside. You look terrible. I mean, you look exhausted and heartbroken and all those things you should be looking. Come inside." Charlie took his hand and led Ben into the living room.

Ben looked around. He loved this room and always felt so at home here. He squeezed Charlie's hand. And Charlie had that feeling again: every time Ben was in this room it seemed to "make sense." When Ben was here, it was as if this was what the room had been waiting for to be complete, to feel right.

Ben pulled Charlie to him and kissed him deeply, as if he didn't he would die. He didn't stop in the living room. He walked toward the hallway to the bedroom. Charlie got the idea and they hurried. In Charlie's bedroom, they both started to undress. Charlie's heart broke at how beautiful Ben was. He looked at Ben's face and Ben was watching him, obviously feeling the same way. They quickly climbed under the patchwork quilt and moved together in a tight embrace. Ben's body, usually warmer than Charlie, seemed feverish today. When Charlie touched him, he ached with longing and desire. Charlie was trying to use all his senses to capture Ben. He wanted to be able to hold those tastes and touches and smells and sounds forever. They made love quickly and simply. Ben had become comfortable with Charlie's body and returned Charlie's lovemaking with energy and passion. When they were spent, they continued to hold each other tightly, not wanting the intimacy to end. They relaxed into a nestled position that allowed them to touch and caress each other at will. And they talked.

"This was one of the worst days of my life. Pam lost it at the cemetery. Fortunately one of the doctors was there and he gave her a sedative. I wonder how she is going to be tomorrow. I can't talk to anyone but you about this.

I don't think Pam's prayers and faith are going to be enough. I'm a man of faith, but I'm also a man of science, Charlie. I think she's going to need some therapy and I don't know how to approach her about it." Ben was absently stroking the back of Charlie's hand as he spoke.

"Ah, sweet Ben. Just listen to her with you heart. You're good at that. You'll know when the time is right to approach it." They held hands lightly, playfully.

"I hope so. I'm not as good as you think. You know, this afternoon, I just left. The house was full of people. I started feeling, I don't know, invisible, shaky and lonely and when I got in the car, one of your CD's was playing. I had promised myself that I wasn't going to see you again—but here I am in your bed. I had to see you to not feel invisible. It's so confusing Charlie. What is the bond between us, this incredible friendship?"

"Ben, you keep calling this a friendship. No wonder you feel confused. Perhaps you just can't bring yourself to call it what it is. I'm in love with you. Romantic love, Ben. The kind people feel when they want to get married and love each other forever and live together and fold each other's underwear. That kind of love. And, if I may presume, I think this 'special friendship' that you feel for me is love. You are in love with me, too. You just can't say it or acknowledge it because it isn't supposed to exist in your world. But that is what this is, my darling boy. This is love. The real thing. This is what it feels like. To tell you the truth, it took me a while to recognize it myself, because I don't think I've felt it before. I've felt infatuation and I've felt fondness, but I've never been in love until you came into my life." Charlie was speaking low, almost a whisper, but his words had the power of his conviction that they were true.

Ben looked pale and shocked. "Of course, that had crossed my mind before, Charlie but I just couldn't bring myself to admit it or say it. Do you know what that would mean in my church? It just isn't possible, Charlie. I don't want to hurt you."

"Do you remember what I said to you the first time you said you didn't want to hurt me? I asked you to marry me. The offer is still on the table and I think I mean it even more now." Charlie smiled a strange smile. He really did want to marry Ben...to commit on that level for a lifetime.

Ben could see what was happening to Charlie on his face. He knew the depth of Charlie's feelings for him and he also knew somewhere deep inside that those feelings were returned. "Do you think we can find a way, Charlie? Is there a way this could work? I can never tell my family about you or this. We raised the kids to know that this is sin. I can't do that to them. They've already lost one parent and this would be like losing another one. All we could ever have is something like we have now. Could we both find a way to live with the limitations and conflicts? I'm not sure it's possible."

"If we both want it badly enough, Ben, we can make anything work. If I know that what we have is real and you feel it, too, I can live with a corner of your life. There is a song from a Broadway show. OK, don't laugh! A woman is having an affair with a married man and the gist of the song is that she would rather have fifty percent of him than one hundred percent of anyone else. And that's how I feel, too. I know I can't even have fifty percent, but I would rather have a small part of you than all of someone I don't love. So, yes, let's find a way to make this work."

"Let's just play it by ear, OK? You know what my schedule is like. I work long hours and even then, I'm on call when I'm not working. Pam is going to need me a lot in the next few months. And mom and the grandparents. I have a full life, Charlie. And there is the moral conflict... I don't know how much I have to give."

"I have a full life, too, Ben. I've got another five weeks in Texas. We've got some time to think about all this and what we are willing to do. The main thing is that we've decided not to give up on each other. That's enough for today. It's enough for me."

"I feel better than I have since this whole tragedy began. When I was hurting so much, I couldn't get any relief. I wanted you by my side. It was not until I walked onto your front porch tonight that I realized that. I guess I do love you Charlie. I know that I shouldn't. God help me that I do. But I do love you."

They held each other quietly for a while nearly drifting off to sleep together. Ben stirred, "I need to head back home. They will be wondering where I am. They need me."

"I know. Do you want something to eat before you go? Or some coffee? I have some of your Diet Pepsi."

"I'll take a Pepsi with me in the car. I'm not really hungry. There was so much food at Pam's."

They got up and embraced again as they dressed. Charlie was about to put on his shirt when Ben stopped him. He stared at Charlie's chest and touched it lightly. "I love your chest. I don't know why. I've never looked at a guy's chest before, but I love yours."

"I love your whole body, Ben. I love you....but especially your dick." Charlie didn't crack a smile.

Ben jumped. He had never heard Charlie use that word before and it brought to the forefront exactly what they were doing. He looked terrified.

"It was a joke. It was supposed to make you laugh, honey...although it is definitely also true." Charlie's eyes twinkled.

Ben blushed crimson and then smiled, shyly at first and then a broad Ben-smile. It was OK. They would be OK. Ben loved Charlie and Charlie loved Ben. For this moment, that was all that mattered. Seismic shift.

# Chapter 37

Ben didn't know how one person could feel everything at once, but that's how he felt as he drove home from Charlie's. He was in exhausted shock over his family's loss. He was worried about Pam. He knew from his own experience with this kind of grief that it wasn't over for her. The episode at the cemetery might have been only the beginning. And he was concerned about his mother. On the surface she seemed the same, but something was going on. Ben's years of experience just put him on the alert to keep an eye on her. Jacen was on his mind every moment, too. Although he agreed with the principles that had sent his son to Iraq, knowing that he was in mortal danger every day was a visceral and constant pain in his heart.

And then there was Charlie. He didn't understand his need for Charlie. No, that wasn't true. He did understand it. Charlie had said it. They were in love. When Ben could admit that, it all made sense and it wasn't confusing at all. Charlie wasn't a special friend. He was the love of Ben's life. He had to admit that he had never felt this way about anyone before. Admitting it didn't make things easier for him, it just made them harder. How could he be in love with another man? It wasn't just forbidden in his church, they didn't even allow that such a thing was possible. There couldn't be love between two men as it is between a man and a woman. His church did talk about sexual contact between two men and that was definitely a sin. There was no gray area about that. But it wasn't possible for two men to love each other. Period.

But he was in love with Charlie. He knew that now. When he saw Charlie standing on his porch and he went to him, it stopped the pain in his heavy, aching heart; it felt like home. Charlie gave him what love gives—a way to transcend your self and become part of someone else. That is what he felt as Charlie held him.

He didn't know what he would do. When he was with Charlie it all seemed so right. But when he left there and went back home it all seemed so wrong. He was forty-six years old. He had asked for new adventures in his life, but he hadn't counted on this. He had made a promise to Charlie to try. He had been honest with him about the lack of time in his life. But it was about more than just the time. It was about the moral conflict that was tearing him apart. He knew he had to keep Charlie a secret and he could do that. He could try to lead two lives and see what happens. But for how long?

He was still going over and over the same argument as he pulled into his driveway. He sat in the car for a while. It seemed easier to face everything, less complicated, sitting in the car. He loved his car. He loved the smell of the leather, the interior lights at night, the luxurious sound system. It was a bubble away from the conflicts of his life. Right now, he wished he could just get back on the highway and drive forever.

He turned off the ignition, opened the door and stepped back into the world. The phone was ringing as he walked into the house and he picked it up just before the voice mail would have kicked in.

"McSwain" he said, forgetting that he was at home and not at the hospital.

"McSwain, this is Mrs. McSwain."

"Hi Mom, I'm a little distracted. Forgot I wasn't at work for a minute."

"I've been trying to reach you all night. Where have you been?" She sounded more worried than usual.

"Why didn't you call me on my cell?"

"I can never remember the number and I don't trust those phones. They don't work half the time."

"Mom, they work fine and you do know the number. It's no harder to remember than this one."

"Yes, it is. You've had this number since you moved into that house after Jacie was born. I've known it for years. That cell phone thing is new. The numbers don't even sound like a phone number."

This kind of complaining was not like his mother at all, yet she had been doing a lot of it lately. It concerned him. He knew that changes in personality in a person her age could be significant. He didn't want to borrow trouble, but he would make an appointment for her with a specialist. He just wanted to rule out possibilities like Alzheimer's. Just a precaution. He would do that tomorrow at the hospital.

"What did you need, Mom? I'm sorry you couldn't get me. I went to Sacramento to see a friend." Ben was too exhausted to think up a lie.

"Bennie, have you got a girlfriend in Sacramento? That's what it seems like. Why won't you bring her home to meet us? It seems awful secretive, like there's something wrong. Is there something wrong?"

Here it was again. She was off the mark somewhat, but her intuition was certainly right on target. She was his mother and she knew him well, but it was unusual for her to confront him with something personal like this. Again this was odd behavior for Alvah.

"No, Mom, nothing like that. I went to see my friend Charlie. You know, the guy I met on the train last winter when I was doing the classes in San Francisco? He's gotten to be a good friend and he's someone I can talk to when I'm troubled. That's all." It wasn't a lie, but it was, perhaps, a sin of omission.

"Well, I wanted to talk to you about Pam. Can you talk now?"

"Of course, Mom. What's wrong?"

"I'm worried about her, Bennie. It isn't just what happened at the cemetery. It was later at the house, after you left. She was upstairs supposed to be resting. I went up to check on her. She wasn't in her bedroom or the bath, so I went looking for her. I found her in the nursery. She was sitting in the nursing rocker holding a stuffed animal and crooning to it. When I walked in the door, she looked up at me with the most beautiful smile on her face and she "shushed" me and told me to be quiet so as not to wake "her" up. I think she thought that toy was the baby, Bennie. Then, she snapped out of it. She stood up, put the toy in the chair and pretended that she was just tidying up. She didn't even seem to remember what had just happened. She went back downstairs and was gracious to everybody. She seemed like herself."

"Thanks for telling me about it Mom. Frankly, I don't know what it means. It might not mean anything. It could be an isolated episode related to grief or to the medication that Al gave her at the cemetery. People have odd reactions to sedatives, so that's not an unlikely explanation. But, just the same, I'll ask some of the docs at the hospital if they think she might benefit from some kind of counseling or therapy...or just talking to a professional. I'll look into it." Ben was a lot more worried than he let his mother know.

"Well, I knew you'd handle it, son. I just thought you should know. And Jacie called after you left. Brett and I both talked to him. Pammie was still asleep. He sounded fine, but far away. My poor grandbabies. Both of them have had to experience the bad things in life way too young. War, the death of a parent, the death of a child. These are things that older people should have to bear, not kids."

"Mom, the people involved in Viet Nam and WWII were kids. They were eighteen and nineteen year olds. They only became 'old' after they were veterans. War and death have always been on the shoulders of young people. They have strong shoulders. They'll be OK. But I love you for caring so much."

"I love you, too Bennie. I've gotten real crotchety lately, haven't I? I guess it's old age. It's made me irritable."

"You're wonderful...and you've earned the right to be a little crotchety. Now, go to bed and get some rest. It's been a long, sad day for us all. Night, Mom."

"Night, Bennie. Sleep tight."

Ben was worried about both of the women in his life. Professionally, he was recognizing behavior in them that needed medical attention. He was a man of faith, but he was also a nurse, a man of science. He didn't see the conflict between the two that so many people did. He knew that faith worked, but he knew that medical science could work "miracles" too. He considered science and technology and the advances in those fields to be a gift of God. It was very simple to him. So he didn't hesitate in making his decision to consult some of his friends in the psychiatric and psychological branches of his profession. He himself had a degree in counseling, but he knew enough to know that another professional opinion was needed here. He would get on it first thing tomorrow at the hospital.

Right now, he desperately needed some sleep. He had almost fallen asleep in Charlie's bed—and oh, how he had wanted to! He decided to sit down and send Charlie an email before going to bed. Just a short note thanking him for being there and to let him know that he was willing to try to find a place in his life to keep his relationship with Charlie. He knew that Charlie would check his email the minute he got to Texas and he wanted him to have something waiting.

He clicked the SEND button turned off the computer and the lights and headed immediately for his bedroom. He washed his face, spritzed himself with that cologne that Charlie liked, put on the tiny iPod and turned off the lights. He listened to the lush music and wept, not for himself, but for his sweet little family: that tiny baby, his children and his mother. Generations of love and caring and pain and loss that just may have become too heavy for some of them to bear. He would have to be strong enough for all of them for a while. In his heart of hearts he was so glad that he had had those few hours with Charlie to renew his own strength, so that he could face tomorrow's challenges.

He turned on his side. Charlie's favorite song was playing. He breathed deeply of the scent that reminded him of their lying together. He could almost feel Charlie's body behind him, the hair on his chest tickling his back. If he closed his eyes, he could feel Charlie's arms fold around him and hear him whisper in his ear, "I love you, baby boy."

Ben slept peacefully for the first time in days, wrapped in the warmth and security of this new, secret and hesitant love.

# Chapter 38

Charlie had to get back to Texas and to work. His heart wanted to stay in California, near Ben if he was needed, but Ben had his family and Charlie knew he would be comforted and supported. He realized he knew very little about Ben's family. That was deliberate on Ben's part and Charlie understood. Even so, he found that he cared about them. He knew they would never understand his place in Ben's life, but he cared anyway, because they were such an inseparable part of Ben. His heart was with that grieving family as the plane took him back to his own destiny in Texas.

Lee met him at the airport with Luke in tow. Charlie was surprised to see Luke. "Hi honey. Are you OK?" Lee's tone was uncharacteristically gentle. Luke remained quiet but there was concern on his handsome features.

"I am OK, amazingly. I'm glad that I did it. It was the right thing. I did go to the funeral. You should see that Tabernacle." Charlie talked as they made their way to baggage claim. "Holy Cow! No pun intended. It's a HUGE church. I'll tell you all about it later. Let's get my bags and get out of here. Enough with airports for a while."

The trip into Dallas was easy. Again it was an off hour flight and traffic from DFW was moving well.

"So, what was the funeral like?" Lee was always curious about how other people did things. He and Charlie had that in common from their earliest years together.

"There was a lot of music and it was that Christian pop kind of stuff. Wonderful, talented musicians, though: a pianist, organist, guitarist and vocalist. And an incredible sound system. Professional. The funeral was held in a space that was more like an auditorium than a sanctuary. There could be an actual "church" somewhere else, but I got the feeling that that was it. There were big screen televisions everywhere even though the altar or podium was easily visible from anywhere in the room. I couldn't figure out what they were for unless they show football games on Sunday morning to keep attendance up. I don't know."

Charlie didn't want to say anything that would sound like he was ridiculing Ben's religion in any way, but it had seemed strange to him and exotic because it was so different from his own experiences. He remembered the memorials that he went to in San Francisco when all of his friends were dying of AIDS. They were joyful and irreverent—more like a cross between a roast and a cocktail party than a funeral. That was what he was used to.

"I had a sense of being back in another time and place. Ben and his family certainly have an abundance of friends and support. There was a huge crowd. Most people were very casually dressed. I hadn't expected that. My parents' funerals were so formal and quiet, but I guess this is the way it's done now. I wore a black suit and felt a little out of place. Some people looked at me, but I think they might have been trying to figure out who I was. I sat in the back and tried to be inconspicuous.

"The service was very emotional, as you can imagine. That tiny coffin. What could be sadder for a family? The minister was not nearly as smarmy as I thought he would be. He was warm and affecting and it was obvious that he knew Ben's family very well. I remember the minister at mother's funeral. He was new and didn't know her at all and it showed in the service. I'm sure this one brought the family much comfort. I didn't see Ben, but I felt his presence, if that doesn't sound too silly. You know funerals creep me out a bit, so I left quickly after the service and didn't go to the cemetery."

Charlie was hesitant to tell them about his meeting with Ben. He felt shy about it for some reason, like telling someone else might diminish their promises to each other, but it carried such joy and he always shared his joy with Lee. Lee would get it out of him!

"Did you get to see Ben at all?"

"Well, yeah, I did. He showed up at my house about seven o'clock last night. He just pulled into the driveway. I had felt all afternoon that he would come to me, so I wasn't surprised. I even left a light in the window for him. He did see me at the funeral so I was right about that. And he was glad I came so it made the whole trip worth while. We made love and promised to try to find some way to make all of it work. I can live with that and be at peace for a while. Now, I'm ready to get back to work on the show. Tell me what's been going on here."

Luke finally said something. "I'm getting the hang of this Broadway *thang.* I've made some changes in the music since I've heard the voices and dialogue on stage. I think it's better. And Lee's words have been really inspirational. The changes are good and important for the show. I think you'll be pleased"

Lee chimed in, "It's going well, Charlie. A little too well. I've never done a show that was this congenial and trouble free. Frankly, it scares the shit out of me. When is the other shoe going to drop?" Lee was never very optimistic, but Charlie did know what he was talking about. There should be some kind of drama going on. Somebody should hate someone or be a pain in the ass by now. That was normal.

"Well, I'm glad everyone is being so cooperative. I feel like a complete beginner and I don't know how I would handle a bunch of bad tempers." Luke surprised them with his admission of insecurity. He was the biggest "star" associated with this show.

Charlie changed the subject, "Do you know what I would like? A chicken fried steak...and mashed potatoes and gravy and black eyed peas. Some iced tea and banana pudding."

"Hmmm. There's that place on Knox Street. We could go there. They will be open."

"Man, that sounds perfect. Let's go. Yee-haw." Luke was obviously on board with the suggestion.

"It just occurred to me that I haven't eaten in over 24 hours! I didn't have dinner last night. I was just about to open some soup when Ben drove up and I went to bed after he left. This morning I was so focused on getting to the airport and all that travel stuff. And of course they didn't feed us on that air-borne cattle car. I am starving." For the first time since this project began, Charlie had a reason to be glad to be in Texas. His love of Texas food was the one thing left from his roots. He was literally salivating for that chicken fried steak.

The restaurant was pure Dallas, Texas. It was done up to look "down home" and rustic, but in a way that made sure the patrons knew that it was intentionally homey. Texans don't mind being "Texan" as long as it appears to be deliberate. Texas is the kind of place where farmers wear starched and ironed overalls with a Ralph Lauren shirt. Shit-kicker chic.

Dinner was great and Charlie began to feel more human. He realized that many of the jagged emotions he had were soothed by the food. It must have been the cream gravy. He relaxed enough to begin to pay attention to his two companions. They seemed to have really bonded while Charlie was gone. They sat easily together on the same side of a booth, while Charlie occupied the other alone. After the last of the banana pudding had been put away, they ordered coffee and sat back with a groan of the overfed. Talk turned back to the show.

"We had this idea about a couple of the scenes, Charlie, that we wanted to run by you. We think the show will run better and make more sense if we put the basketball game before the scene at the church. We need the energy of the basketball scene right there." Charlie noticed that Lee was sitting awfully close to Luke as he talked.

"And musically, it's dragging a little bit the way it is. If we put the basketball scene earlier, it punches up the score earlier, too." Was it Charlie's imagination or were their hands touching on the table? Neither moved. It seemed mutually acceptable.

Charlie was in love and he could recognize the signs of budding infatuation or attraction. He was noticing now that there was definitely something going on between Lee and Luke. He smiled and looked back and forth between the two. They both began to blush sheepishly as they realized they were found out.

"I'll be goddamned. If that doesn't beat all! You guys are doing it, aren't you?"

"Oh that's a charming way of putting it. I hate you Charlie Morgan, I really do." But Lee was smiling warmly at his old friend.

Luke blushed furiously, "Could we have this conversation somewhere else, guys? Who knows where the tabloid trolls might be lurking, you know?"

Lee picked up the tab. It must be love. Lee never picked up a tab.

They drove back to the house in comfortable silence. This time, however, Charlie sat in the back seat and Lee and Luke sat in the front. Charlie looked over the seat and they were holding hands casually, as if they had been doing that for all of their lives.

"Holy *merde*," thought Charlie. This could be the other shoe, the drama that everyone has been waiting for. He hoped that this dalliance wouldn't blow up in everyone's face before they got the show nailed down. He would do all he could to keep things running smoothly. Besides, he was in love and he wanted everyone else to be in love, too. And if Luke made Lee happy, well, that was good enough for Charlie.

The next surprise came as they got back to the house. There was a definite change in the arrangement of things. The living room was filled with Luke's musical equipment: guitars, keyboards, computers and other things that Charlie didn't recognize. As they entered the house, Lee and Luke put their arms around each other and kissed.

"Um, do we have a new roommate, Lee?"

"Luke was in that tiny condo all by himself. Terrible view, nothing to do. We've got the pool and all, so I suggested that he move in here with us. The producers were thrilled. We've saving them a ton of money."

Charlie couldn't resist. "Gee, Lee we only have two bedrooms." Charlie gave him an innocent, clueless shrug.

"Well, yeah, that's right, Charlie." Lee stared him right in the eye.

"Let's see. Three people, two bedrooms. What're we gonna do, hmmm?" Charlie couldn't resist razzing Lee.

"Oh, I don't know, Charlie. You could sleep on the couch, I suppose." It was like old times for the old friends.

"It's OK with you, isn't it Charlie?" Luke really did look concerned about it.

Charlie grinned at him. "Oh of course it is, Luke. Lee and I are just playing. If you guys are happy, I'm thrilled. I want everybody to be in love! I'm just a little surprised is all. I mean, I've only been gone for two days! That's fast work."

Lee cleared his throat and looked over at Luke. "Well, I told you about meeting Luke in Nashville two years ago, right? It seems neither of us really forgot what happened. When we saw each other again, the feelings were still there as strong as ever. Now that Luke's career is established, his managers aren't managing as tightly as they were then." Lee faltered and Luke picked up the conversation.

"My career was so important. I've done what I set out to do and now I want something personal. I've always been clear about my sexuality, Charlie. And I've always been attracted to men older than me. When I met Lee, I thought I had met the guy I was supposed to be with. It reminds me of how you talk about Ben. That's why I was so touched by your love for him. All of us know what we have to give up in order to succeed or even survive in the world and I wanted that career. It was my dream and I couldn't give up just when it seemed about to happen."

"And it did happen. Wasn't your first big hit around that time? I bought the album. It was about two years ago." Charlie was connecting the dots.

"'I Always Want the One That I Can't Have.' That was the big breakout album and song...and it was about Lee."

"Well, I'll be dipped in dogshit and put on the porch." Charlie couldn't believe what just flew out of his mouth.

"Oh, Charlie, you've got to get back to California quickly. IQ points are leaking out of you as we sit here. Where did THAT come from? Was it the chicken fried steak? The Bush administration?" Lee looked as if he smelled something very, very bad.

"I think my uncle used to say it. It just slipped out. Out from where, I have no idea."

"I think it was cute." Luke was the diplomat of the pair, obviously, and well, he did live in the South.

"When I was approached about doing this show, I automatically thought of Luke to do the music, so I suggested it to the producers. They loved the idea and the rest, as they say, is ...."

"When I found out that Lee had suggested my name and that he was going to do the book, I didn't even think about it. I jumped on board, hoping we might have another chance somehow. I'm at a place now that, if handled discreetly, I can have a relationship and this is the one I've always wanted. And we really do work well together." Luke slipped his arms around Lee's waist from behind and peeked over his shoulder.

"This is wonderful and amazing. I just hope you're as happy as Ben and I are right now. Wow, Lee. Who'd a thunk it? I'm glad we hung around, aren't you? I didn't think it could get this good at our age."

They talked for a while longer and everyone was tired, so they headed off to bed. Charlie went out to the sunroom to email Ben while Luke and Lee, hand in hand, headed off to Lee's bedroom at the other end of the house. They looked sleepy and happy.

Charlie sat down at the computer and opened his email. There was a note from Ben.

"Charlie...thanks so much for being there last night. I'll get through this. My faith is strong and my family is a huge comfort to me, but your being there made the hurt go away for a while. I feel better about us, too. I have so little to give you. It seems unfair to ask you to do this, but I want to find a way. Is that selfish of me? Probably. I'm still so confused, Charlie. This is all so NEW to me. You must think I'm a real dope. I'm glad you are there for me and willing to put up with me. I'm glad you're on my side. Let's hope for the best, OK? Take care of yourself.

Love, B"

Charlie read and reread the note. It sounded like Ben: pull me close, push me away, pull me close, push me away. He didn't mean to be that way. It was natural, considering what he must be going through. Charlie just needed to love him unconditionally. After their talk last night, he was reinvigorated to do this. He had to let Ben be who he is, find his own answers in his own time—to love him enough to let him find his own way—and hope that way led to Charlie's door.

Charlie's response was brief, "I love you, baby boy. It's late. I'm exhausted. I've got gossip to tell, but it will keep until tomorrow. Take care of yourself and that precious family of yours. You know that I'm here if you need anything or 'everything.'

Your Charlie" SEND

Charlie turned off the computer and walked into his bedroom. The picture that Ben had given him on the night of their anniversary dinner was on the nightstand. Charlie looked at Ben, really looked at him. That was his guy! His heart still ached for Ben's loss, but already the healing had begun and life would go on. And love would go on. Charlie was a peace when he turned out the light.

# Chapter 39

Everything about the show was charmed. All the creative elements involved seemed to be on the same page: book, music, sets, costumes and cast. And it showed on the stage. It was a beautiful show, so much like the book and evocative of the movie, but magical in it's own right, too. The music and lyrics that Luke created and Lee and Charlie's book transcended the usual fare to become that special Broadway event where one cannot imagine the play without the music or the music without the play. That only happens once in a great while and it was happening to this show.

Even the bloggers were giving it positive buzz. There were "hit of the season" whispers and rumors hitting the internet and the newspaper columns in New York. It certainly felt good to the hardworking cast and crew in Dallas.

Lee and Luke and Charlie had become a real partnership, a united trio at rehearsals and often out and about in Dallas. Because of Luke's celebrity, they were sometimes photographed or made the columns. It was all very positive publicity. They were working on the show together, all from out of town, so it was natural that they would socialize in their off hours, too. Charlie felt like the perfect "beard," for Luke and Lee were definitely a couple. They seemed to grow closer every day and never tired of each other's company. When they were not at work, they were working together at home or talking quietly about personal things. Charlie loved seeing Lee this happy. Lee had become brittle and cynical over the last few years and Luke seemed to be reviving his old friend's joy, energy, sense of humor and creativity.

Strengthened by urging from Luke and Charlie, Lee decided to call Tadio's bluff and end it completely, the devil be damned. Taddy had come online at his usual time and they had a very heated video exchange over the internet. The boy seemed even more volatile than usual. Charlie could hear him screaming through Lee's computer speakers. The anger was crazy and chilling to Charlie, but Lee remained firm and made sure that the youngster understood that the online time had to end. Lee had never officially come out to his family, but now that decision might be ready to bite him in the ass. Tadio had all the information he needed to make trouble for Lee: phone numbers, addresses, names. And Tadio had pictures, apparently. In the dizziness of infatuation, Lee had allowed Tadio to take some digital photographs while he was in Spain that left very little to the imagination. He had threatened Lee with exposure in the past. Not only would his family find out many things they didn't need to know, but the pictures would publicly humiliate him as well. He just had to trust that Tadio would not stoop that low.

He was shaking when he ended the conversation, but relieved, too. It was liberating to finally have it over and done with. He and Luke had decided to go out to dinner to celebrate. They invited Charlie, of course, but he declined because he clearly understood that, sometimes, one really can be in the way.

After they left he put in a call to Ben but he didn't pick up, so Charlie left a short message, just saying hello and that all was OK. He really wanted to know what Ben had done about coming to Texas for the premier that was only a few weeks away, but he didn't mentioned it in his voicemail. He would talk to Ben about it when he got him in person.

He decided to go for a swim and then go to bed early. He had lived alone for many years and he was enjoying his quiet time this evening. He put on a Speedo and dived into the pool. His stamina had improved over the weeks that he had been in Texas and, even though he tried to get to the gym three times a week, the swimming was helping a lot. He knew that this kind of exercise was important for his health and for his appearance. He was very much aware that Ben was fifteen years younger and that was added incentive. Just as he was climbing out of the pool, he heard his phone ring. It was in the bedroom so he made a soggy dash; he knew it was Ben.

"Hey dude, sorry I missed you earlier. I was working. One of the nurses didn't show up in ICU, so I covered half of the shift." Ben's voice was slightly hoarse. He had been up since two-thirty and worked twelve hours straight.

"It's OK, honey, you sound tired. I won't keep you long. You need to go to bed at a decent time tonight." Charlie called Ben honey a lot, Ben never called Charlie that, but Ben didn't seem to mind. He still struggled with how to define their relationship. It wasn't the feelings he had trouble with, it was what those feelings symbolized in his world and how that was perceived. He was getting a glimpse of what gay people go through every day; the hypocrisy and duplicity of a culture that feigns love and charity for all and yet sets about institutionally to criminalize an entire segment of it's population. Ben got it on an intellectual level, but on a spiritual level, it was still a shameful, hidden secret. It had to be that way until he could figure out what to do.

"Just wondered if you had given any more thought to coming out here for the premiere. I've got your ticket and everyone is dying to meet you. It'll be a real event...limos, celebrities, even a red carpet, I think. I wonder if Joan Rivers...hummm"

Ben could hear the excitement in Charlie's voice so his response was careful, "I still don't know, Charlie. When do you have to know for sure? I hate to keep you dangling like this if you want to ask someone else."

"Of course I don't want to ask anyone else. If you can't come, I'll go with Luke and Lee. Take your time deciding. I know this is a big step for you. You make the decision that's right for you and it'll be OK. I don't expect you to do anything that makes you uncomfortable, except in bed." Charlie chuckled. He missed Ben sexually, too. It was tough being around Luke and Lee every day. Their intimacy was palpable, if you were looking for it.

Ben's voice lowered and grew a little huskier, "Oh yeah, what would you do to me in bed to make me uncomfortable."

"Hey, dude, don't start something here you aren't willing to finish, OK? You're the one that gets all weird about the idea of phone sex."

"OK, OK, I'll back off. I admit that I miss you that way. I think of your chest and, well, you know what happens."

"No, Bennie, what happens? Tell me in detail."

"You really are a tease, Charlie Morgan. I'll get you when I see you."

"Not if I don't get you first and I hope that will be HERE in just a few weeks. Did you notice how I got us back to that?"

"Smooth...maybe it'll work Charlie. I'll check the airlines and see what I can get."

"The production will pay for you ticket, I think. They are paying for the conductor's wife to come from New York, so I think I can swing your ticket, too." Charlie wondered if this comparison would get a response from Ben. It didn't.

"Cool! That would help. I've been trying to save to bring Jacen home for a few days after he gets back from Iraq. That will be in a couple of weeks. He met a girl before he left last time and they seem to be serious. He's spending some time with her and her parents in Maryland, but I want him to come home for a few days before he has to go back on duty in North Carolina."

Charlie had only been thinking of the show. He was reminded again that Ben had so many other things going on in his life.

"If there's a financial pinch, babe, you know I'd be happy to lend it to you. Hell, I'll give you his plane fare if you need it. You know that. By the way, How's Pam doing? What about your mom?"

"I know you would Charlie, but I can't take your money. It would just be wrong, you know? Mom seems to be fine, just getting older and slowing down a lot. Pam is seeing a psychiatrist. I'm worried about her. She is definitely not coming back quickly from the tragedy, but that doesn't mean that she won't make it back. Her doctor is a friend of mine. He won't discuss the case with me of course, but he does remind me to be optimistic. She's young and resilient and he seems hopeful. Brett took everything out of the nursery, repainted the room and it's now a guest room/office. I suppose they've decided not to try again for a while. I haven't asked them about it and they haven't volunteered any information. Sometimes I walk a fine line between caring and prying."

"You're a wise man, Ben. Sounds like you've got a lot going on and you're handling it with your usual compassion and grace. I get so wrapped up in my own life that I forget to be considerate. I'll just say this: Please come if you can, but know that I will understand completely if you must stay at home. I know the deal that we struck. We'll make it work when we can and when we can't, we'll make that OK, too. Just be you and do what you have to do."

"I don't deserve you, Charlie."

"No, no you certainly don't, dude, but you have me, so there it is. Good night, Bennie, and Ben? I love you."

There was a silence on the phone and then Ben replied with a clear voice, "Good night, dude. And Charlie? I love you more."

He hung up. Charlie stared at the phone. That was an important moment for them. That had been a "partners" call. Charlie was elated. He knew in his heart that Ben loved him. It was just wonderful to hear him say it.

# Chapter 40

Charlie headed off to bed happy and tired. He slept almost immediately and was deeply asleep when he became aware that someone was shaking him.

"Charlie, wake up. It's Luke. I'm worried about Lee. Charlie?" Luke was sitting on the side of the bed.

Charlie came around, "Luke? What's the matter? What time is it?"

"Charlie, Lee isn't home. It's four in the morning and I'm worried." Luke sounded more than worried.

"Where is he? Didn't you go out to dinner together? This doesn't make any sense." Charlie was still half asleep.

"While we were at the restaurant, that kid from Spain called Lee back. Apparently, he's not in Spain. He has been looking at all of that publicity about us on the internet and flew over here in a fury. He's at the Edgerton Hotel downtown. He was crazy, Charlie, threatening to call Lee's family. I could hear him screaming through the phone from the other side of the table, but Lee didn't seem bothered by any of it. He was so calm! It would have made me nuts. Hell, it did make me nuts!" Lee had obviously not told Luke about his earlier problems with Tadio and his fits of rage and abuse.

"Lee left the restaurant and got a cab. He went downtown to try to talk to Tadio. Although, to tell you the truth, Tadio didn't sound like he was in the mood to listen to anything rational. I wanted to go with him, but he insisted on going alone. Lee was thinking of his sisters. So I drove back here and went to bed. I didn't think it would take more than an hour or so, but he's not home yet. He's not answering his cell phone and I'm worried Charlie."

Charlie was worried, too, more than he let on to Luke, "No use trying to call the hotel. They wouldn't tell us anything over the phone. Let's go down there and find out what's happening. I'm not sure about Tadio's last name. Can we look on Lee's computer and find out? Maybe in his email?"

"I'll look right now." Luke was out of the room and headed for the office. Charlie got up, dressed quickly and followed Luke down the hall.

"Sandal. Tadio Sandal. That's the name. I saw some of the emails, Charlie. I've never read anything like that before. Why didn't Lee tell me about this?"

"I think he was embarrassed, Luke. He got caught up in something that backfired and he was trying to find a way to get out of it when this project came along and you came back into his life. I think he hoped he could just end it last night. Apparently, Tadio has other ideas. Let's go find out what's going on. If he's hurt Lee again, I'll...well, let's go, OK?"

"What do you mean 'again' Charlie?"

"I'll explain on the way. Come on." Charlie had a bad feeling about all of this. The kid was dangerous.

When they explained why they were there, the concierge referred them to the security officer on duty. The Edgerton was a very good hotel and they recognized Luke which helped a lot. They would do everything they could to accommodate him. The security officer was, Charlie surmised after a few minutes, also gay and picked up on what was going on. After a detailed explanation, he agreed to go to Mr. Sandal's room and see if everything was all right. Charlie and Luke were to wait in his office until he returned. It was the best he could do.

He left and Luke and Charlie looked at each other, fear registering strongest in both their faces. It was only a few minutes before the officer was back. His face was ashen, but spots of color burned in his cheeks. "Something terrible has happened up there. I'm not sure exactly what yet. I've called the police and the paramedic team from the hotel is there already. There is blood everywhere. I don't know if anyone is alive. I didn't investigate, I just called for help as quick as I could. You guys stay here, they'll want to talk to you. What's your cell number Mr. Beecham?"

Luke didn't comprehend what the guard was saying to him. He seemed to be in shock. Charlie jumped in, "Let me give you mine. Luke doesn't have his phone with him. Here's a card with my name and number. Was Lee up there? Did you see anyone?"

"I just don't know at this point. Like I said, I didn't stop to investigate, I just wanted to get help up there as soon as I could. I've got to go back. The police will be here. I'll keep you posted on everything that happens, OK?"

He left the office. Charlie reached for Luke's hand and held on for dear life. Neither of them knew what any of this meant. They didn't even know if Lee was in the room, but they feared the worst. If Lee had been OK, he would have been home hours ago. If there was blood...they didn't want to think about what kind of horror that might imply.

It was only a few minutes until the guard called. "Mr. Morgan, this is Randy. I've got some bad news, I'm afraid. There were two people in the room and they are both dead. There appears to have been a struggle, but the police are unclear about the details at this point. I told them how I came to check on the room and they want to meet with you and Mr. Beecham. They would also like to know if you could identify the people in the room. Could you do that?"

Charlie's vision dimmed for a moment. He thought he might pass out. It couldn't be Lee. It couldn't. "I don't know if I can or not. It depends on who they are. I could only identify Mr. Sandal from pictures I've seen of him. I've never met him personally. As for the other person..." Charlie stopped. Could he do this? What if it is Lee?

Luke studied Charlie's face for clues. He knew. He knew what was happening. "Let's go up there, Charlie, come on. I have to go."

"Randy, we're on our way up. Room 1257, right? Tell the police we'll be there in five minutes."

"Luke we need to be calm now. We don't know what we'll find. Are you prepared for this? There will be a lot of people. The press will get this very quickly. Are you sure you want to do this? I can go by myself. The press isn't interested in me."

"I want to go, Charlie. I can handle it. Fuck the press. Fuck the goddam press. They've been ruining my life for years and I just don't care anymore."

"But we both have to care, Luke. For Lee's sake. We have to care. Let's go."

They left the office and went to the bank of elevators. It was the longest elevator ride in history. When they got off on the twelfth floor, there were swarms of people, some in uniform, some not, but they all looked very busy and very grim. It didn't bode well.

An officer immediately approached them and inquired, "May I help you gentlemen? This floor has been closed to the public."

"I'm Charlie Morgan, this is Luke Beecham. We were the ones who asked security to check Mr. Sandal's room. We were told the police wanted to see us."

His demeanor relaxed significantly. "Oh, of course, sorry I didn't recognize you Mr. Beecham. My wife and I are big fans of yours. Right this way, gentlemen." The man turned down the hall and Luke and Charlie followed. He was leading them into 1257. Charlie stopped, as did Luke. They looked at each other for courage and they mustered what they could. They were going to need it.

There was blood everywhere: on the furniture, the floor, the walls. It was so red it didn't look real. It looked like a movie set. That's what Charlie felt like. He was completely disconnected from his feelings. He was playing a part. He looked at Luke and could see a similar thing happening to him. He was becoming the public Luke Beecham.

A young police officer came over. "Thank you for coming up, gentlemen. I know this is hard. We'll try to do this quickly. Would you mind stepping over here? We'd like you to ID the bodies if you can."

Luke and Charlie followed him into a very brightly lit area. Again, there was blood everywhere and it was so red. There was someone on the bed. Charlie forced himself to look. Luke's face was rigid; his eyes hooded and unfocused. Charlie's vision adjusted to the brightness. He saw a dark, small body on the bed. It wasn't Lee, thank God. There was a head wound, but he could see the face clearly enough to know that it was Tadio Sandal. He remembered the pictures of Tadio well. He hadn't thought that the boy was very attractive and he had a strangely shaped head. Charlie recognized that immediately. "That's Mr. Sandal, officer. I'm sure of it."

The officer nodded and moved out of Charlie's line of vision. "And do you recognize this person?"

Charlie looked just beyond where the officer had been standing. There, lying on the floor with his head against the wall at an odd angle, was Charlie's oldest and dearest friend. Charlie felt the world disappear beneath his feet and he fell to his knees. His vision tunneled and his ears began to ring. He whispered, "Oh Lee, oh, Lee. What has he done to you? You'll be OK. It's all right. You can't leave me here by myself. What would I do without you?" But Charlie knew he would not be OK.

The practiced composure that Luke had assumed when they walked in dissolved with a strangled moan. The young security guard realized that he was about to break and befriended them again by leading them quickly out of the room. He said under his breath, "We're going back to my office. I'll take you on the employee elevator where no one will see you. The police can talk to you there and you'll be safe. Don't say anything else right now. Just come with me."

Randy firmly led them to the elevator and down to the main floor. They were in some kind of service hall and never even entered the main lobby, but could hear the commotion. The press was already on this. Randy had probably saved Luke a lot of trouble.

Luke and Charlie were not thinking about the press or anything except the vision of their beloved friend and partner's lifeless body in that hotel room. Luke reached out and clung to Charlie like a child and he wept. It was heartbreaking. Randy had figured out part of the story and now he had the missing pieces. Randy was glad that, for once, being gay had paid off in the world. It felt good to be able to help. The police certainly would not have.

Randy's cooler head and less involved heart prevailed and he took over. "The police will be here in a minute. Mr. Beecham, I'm so sorry for your loss, but you need to hang on for just a while longer, until we can get you through with the necessary questions, OK? How're you doing, Mr. Morgan? Can I get either of you anything? Something to drink? Cigarettes?"

Charlie found his voice. It was weak and flat. "Water, please, thank you. How long do you think this will take, Randy, is it? Thanks for your help. I'm sure, looking back, this will be one of the nicest things anyone ever did for me, but just now I'm finding it hard to concentrate. I hope you'll forgive me. What more can we possibly tell the police?"

"They'll want to know what Mr....what is your friend's name, I'm sorry. They'll want to know what he was doing here. How he knew Sandal. The usual questions in a situation like this."

"Horner, Lee Horner" Charlie realized that he would have to call Lee's sisters. His older sister was in her eighties. This just might kill her. Poor Lee, he had spent his whole life protecting them from the truth about his life and now everything was about to come out. Charlie hated the world at that moment. The one thing that Lee prized most, his privacy, would be invaded as it had never been before. Charlie felt fury rising in his gut.

"The fucking press. The fucking press." It was the first thing that Luke had said since they left the hotel room. A similar anger seemed to be building in him for the same reasons. One of the things that made him so compatible with Lee was that they both desired privacy and discretion above almost anything else. They would never have fought over that. And if he played it right, Luke could avoid any scandal now. Again, Charlie was grateful to Randy. He had given them time to think. Luke should protect his career. Lee would want that almost as much as his own privacy. Keeping the nature of Luke and Lee's relationship secret is what Lee would have wanted for himself, too. It was the right thing to do all around.

# Chapter 41

In the days and weeks following the baby's funeral, Ben found himself slipping easily back into the mode that had helped him survive after Lynette's death. He worked feverishly at the hospital and spent as little time at home alone as possible. He made a point of checking in with Pam and Brett every day. Brett seemed to be doing all right. He was relying heavily on support from friends at the church and it seemed to sustain him. Pam was another matter. While on the surface she seemed to be calm and quiet, there was something about it that was off. She said all the right things, but it sounded like it had been programmed. Ben often wondered if she was hearing what was said to her. He was reminded of how "tech support" people respond when you call about your computer. You wonder whether they actually listened to what you said or just picked up on a few words and responded to those, giving an answer that is vaguely on target but not really addressing the specific issue. That was the way Pam was reacting to her life.

Ben was having problems with the two most important parts of his life. Brett wanted Pam to stop seeing the psychiatrist. He was convinced that all she needed was the prayer group at the church and the nurturing love of her friends there and he worried that the therapy might make things worse. Ben felt that professional guidance was essential to Pam right now. His own training presented no conflict between psychiatry and his religion, and he tried to help Brett see that both things were good for her. But Brett was becoming increasingly adamant that the only help they needed was the church.

The doctor felt that she was so fragile, he wanted to increase her from one session a week to three. It was a big jump and Ben knew that he would not have recommended it if he had not felt that she needed the extra help. But Brett had prevailed and Pam was continuing her therapy on an even more limited basis than before while increasing her Bible study and prayer group attendance. Ben was silent and respectful of their decision while he continued to hope for the best. He was comforted in the knowledge that this was one time that he and Charlie would have had no conflict of opinion. He had a glimmer of what it might be like if Charlie were really his partner in life. But his life didn't allow him the luxury of those thoughts for long.

The baby's death had taken it's toll on his mother, too. After the funeral, she had been so strong for everyone. As the days went by, she seemed to retreat into a vague fog. When Ben went to her house on the weekend to do her chores, she was listless and not interested in much conversation. Her usual lively demeanor and running, humorous commentary on the oddities in our world were missing. She would sit at the kitchen table with a cup of tea while Ben tried to engage her.

"Mom, so what's with Erica on <u>All My Children</u>?"

"Oh, I don't know Bennie, I haven't seen much television lately. Been too busy with other things." She stared straight ahead, not making eye contact with him.

Busy is a good sign. "What's been keeping you busy this week?" Ben was encouraged if, indeed, that were true.

"Oh you know, Bennie, this and that. I was at the cemetery on Tuesday. Crab grass already growing on that little grave. Can you imagine? It takes time to keep it up. I promised Pam I would. She can't bring herself to go out there, you know. And other things, son. Just other things." She picked at a string on the placemat beneath her cup.

Ben was at a loss. He didn't know how to reach her when she was like this. When Lynette died, it had been Alvah who had kept everyone together. Her tireless energy and effort gave the children a continuity when they had lost their mother and her strength had sustained Ben until he could find it in himself. She had been their rock. Ben longed to help her now that she needed him, but he didn't know what to do.

He sat with her at the table and they sipped their tea.

"I changed the light bulb in the hall. The yard's done for the week and I washed your car for you. Is there anything else you need, Mom? Anything?" Ben was hoping she would open up to him, like she used to.

"No, no, that's all I can think of, honey. Thank you, though." Again, silence and a gaze that drifted off into space. She seemed to be somewhere else.

Ben wanted her to see the doctor who was treating Pam. Maybe he could just prescribe something for Alvah. Ben wasn't sure that his mother would respond to talk therapy all that well, but some of the new antidepressants were quite effective. He would ask Al about it on Monday.

Jacen had come home for a few days, too. The visit was way too short, but it was comforting to have him in the house again. He missed the kids being there. Jacen's friends found out that he was home and the house was again filled with young people. Ben stayed busy in the kitchen with nachos and hamburgers and pizzas and popcorn and soda...like old times. Jacen appeared to be much the same, but there were subtle differences his father could see. His eyes were older, more mature and somewhat guarded. The happy sparkle he had as a kid was gone. Jacen had become a man. War had done that in a way that nothing else can. He spoke lovingly of Catherine and Ben suspected that this was the one. People in their family married early. Alvah had been only sixteen when she married Ben's father. Ben and Lynette were not yet twenty when they married and Pam was eighteen when she married Brett. So Jacen had waited the longest.

Ben realized it was a relief to have another adult male in the family, someone to help shoulder the responsibilities. They found themselves alone late on the evening before Jacen went back to base. It had been a busy day. He spent time with his great grandparents, his grandmother and his sister. And in the evening, his best pals from school came over for old times' sake.

When they left, he wandered into the kitchen and there was the familiar sight of his dad cleaning up after "his kids." Tonight, Jacen felt like he was seeing his dad in a new light. He had always thought of his dad as an "old guy." But here was a different image. Ben moved around the kitchen in a subtle dance step and Jacen realized that he had on a little silver iPod. His dad, who could barely check his email, had an iPod! Where did that come from?

"Holy Cow, dad! Cool! iPod!" he said loudly enough to be heard over the music.

Ben jumped. He had not been aware of Jacen's presence. He removed the tiny earbuds and grinned broadly at his son.

"Hey, dude, yeah, how about that? Pretty cool, huh? It was a present." Ben didn't say who the present was from and Jacen didn't seem too interested.

"Watcha listening to?" Jacen winced.

"Oh, man, You'd hate it. Michael Buble, Il Divo, Katie Melua, Shelby Lynne."

"Dad, that's so weird. Where did you hear about that kind of stuff?"

"A friend of mine has been trying to broaden my tastes. What can I say? I really like it."

"Dad, you're getting very strange without us around. That's for old people."

"That may be true, son, but isn't it time for that? And maybe I like being my own age!"

"Before you go totally over the hill, I wanted to talk to you about Pam and Gramma. They both seem to be in trouble, Dad. Was it the baby's death? What's going on with them?"

Jacen wasn't a child anymore, but a newfound friend and confidante. Ben told him everything that had happened since the funeral including the story of his grandmother's stillborn child. He confided to Jacen his struggle with Brett over Pam's care and his concern that Alvah was showing signs of dementia. Jacen listened quietly and intently.

"Wow, Dad, why didn't you tell me all of this sooner?"

"You had your own war to worry about Jace—that was enough."

"Well, I'm back now and I'll help in any way I can. I can cancel the trip to Catherine's if you want. I don't want you to have to handle this all alone, Dad."

"Oh no, son, you go on. Catherine and her parents are expecting you and you need to do that. I'll be fine. Really. I'm not completely alone. I've got friends, you know."

"Like the one who gave you the iPod?" Ben thought they had cleared that hurdle.

"None of your beeswax, kid. But yes, the friend who gave me the iPod has been a big help."

"OK, I'll back off. It's fine with me, Dad, if you're seeing someone. You're still a young guy and you shouldn't be alone. Mom wouldn't want you to be." Jacen's eyes were filled with love for his dad and tears for his mom.

"Thanks Jacen. You're right. That is how your mom would feel. Maybe there is someone, but I've got so many things to work out on my own yet, OK? I'm all right. Don't worry."

Jacen asked his dad all kinds of questions about how he should act in Maryland. It was obviously very important to him to make a good impression on Catherine's parents. He wanted to know all about etiquette and manners. Lynette had brought up the children well. Jacen was a good boy and now, a good man. His nature would carry him through if he felt uncertain of any rules. He would be fine.

At the airport the next morning, Jacen met his father's eye in a new way. It was the next stage of that complicated business between fathers and sons where barriers are let down, expectations change and two men emerge with love and respect for each other. Ben was proud as he and his mother left the terminal.

Alvah and Ben talked about Jacen on the drive back home. While he was away, he had been very good about writing to his grandmother. Everyone else got email, but she didn't have a computer, so Jacen took the time to write. Most of his letters were about Catherine, so Alvah really knew more about that relationship than Ben did. She too, felt that this was the one.

But all too soon Alvah fell into a vague silence in the car that was not comfortable. She was retreating to that far off place more frequently, Ben noticed. As a way of bringing her back, Ben suggested turning on the radio. "Let's see what's going on in the world." His radio was tuned to one of the local pop stations and they were doing a summary of entertainment news. It wasn't what Ben would have chosen, but it was better than the silence. He heard the word "Dallas" and, thinking of Charlie, he turned up the volume a little.

"Reports coming in from Dallas are still sketchy, but what we have so far is that there has been an apparent murder/suicide at the Edgerton Hotel. One of the victims is playwright Lee Horner. Mr. Horner is best known for a series of Broadway hits in the seventies and eighties including <u>Ashes of Roses</u> that was made into the Oscar winning Julia Roberts movie of the same name. The other victim remains unidentified as of this moment, but we're told that it was a young man of foreign origins. That's all we have for now. Mr. Horner is a native of Texas, but has lived in New York for many years. He was in Dallas working on that musical version of <u>The Last Picture Show</u> that has been getting such great buzz all around. He had been sharing a house with another writer from California and the country superstar Luke Beecham who was penning the music for the show. Mr. Beecham and the other man, whose name we don't yet have, were unavailable to the press for comment. It is uncertain where they are at this time, although we have been told that they were questioned by the police and may have been at the hotel when the bodies were discovered. We'll bring you more on the bizarre story as it unfolds."

Ben wasn't sure he was hearing correctly. He was a simple country boy. He was completely unused to hearing about people he knew on the radio. He hadn't heard a word from Charlie. When did all this happen? The victim was his friend Lee! He had to try to get in touch with Charlie.

He pulled into his mom's driveway and didn't even offer to come in. All he could think about was Charlie. "Hey mom. I gotta go, OK? I've got stuff to do at the house. Do you need anything else?" Ben was eager to leave now.

"No, honey, that's OK. I'm just fine. You run on..." Again, she was listless and seemed to just drift off at the end of a sentence. Ben was definitely going to talk to Al about her tomorrow.

He pulled out of the driveway and called Charlie's cell number. It went immediately to voicemail. He wondered if Charlie had just turned it off. He left a message:

"Hi. It's me. I was just listening to the radio in the car and heard about Lee. They still don't seem to know much. Are you OK? Can I do anything? I don't want to bother you, but just want you to know that I'm here. You've always been so supportive of me. It's time to return the favor if I can. Call me anytime. Charlie, I love you, you know. You're my soulmate." Poor Charlie! What a blow. He and Lee had been family to each other since college. He wished he could go to him in Dallas. He wanted to. But there was so much to do here. He had his own obligations to attend to. He would wait until he talked to Charlie and see what was really happening before he made any decisions.

He thought about what he had said to Charlie on the phone. They really were soulmates. They hadn't known each other all that long and life had not even given them the opportunity to spend that much time together, but they knew what they were to each other. When they were together and looked into each other's eyes, they knew. Some people might find that idea antiquated or corny, but it was the perfect word to describe what they had. It didn't matter what other people thought about that term. That's what they were. Soulmates.

# Chapter 42

The sun was coming up as Luke and Charlie drove back to the house in silence. Both of them needed to absorb what had just happened, what they had just seen. They needed the time alone to do it. It still felt unreal. Charlie thought about seeing Lee's broken body and it was like remembering a film. That couldn't be Lee. It couldn't be.

They got back to the house and it was quiet. No one was around yet, but it wouldn't be long before the press swarmed in. They went into the house, turned off the cell phones, unplugged the land line and sat quietly in the dark for a while, not bothering to turn on lights or open the drapes. Luke was the first to speak. "I'm going to get some sleep. I can't even think anymore. Maybe that will help." He stood and headed for the bedroom. He stopped, turned and looked at Charlie, the hurt and confusion so clear on his face. He couldn't go into the room he had shared with Lee, so he came back into the living room and curled up on the sofa. Charlie went into his room and got an extra blanket and a pillow. He brought them out to Luke, but he was already asleep. Charlie gently slid the pillow under his head and draped the blanket over him. Luke was like Charlie in that respect. In times of stress, sleep was the drug of choice. Then Charlie went to his own room and crawled into bed without undressing. He was asleep as quickly as Luke.

Charlie woke several hours later hearing Luke on the phone. He got up and went into the living room. Luke had made coffee and was talking with his agent in Nashville. Charlie searched for his phone. He needed to hear Ben's voice. He wondered if they had heard anything in California. It began ringing the minute he turned it on. It was Jerry Shallit, one of the producers of the show. Did he know already?

"Charlie, how're you doin'? You OK? How's Luke? Have you boys talked to anyone yet?"

"Jerry, how did you find out about this? No, we haven't seen anyone except the police. The security guard at the hotel was smart enough to get us out of there without seeing any press. What's going on?" Charlie was frightened and didn't know why.

"Turn on the TV, Charlie. It's everywhere. I've talked with our lawyers. Don't say anything yet. We are going to put out a statement in a little while. We're working on it now."

Charlie froze. He had forgotten about Lee's sisters. He had to talk to them immediately. He hoped it wasn't already too late and they hadn't heard about this on some tawdry television program. He would drive down. It was only an hour away. "Jerry, Lee still has family here. I've known them for forty years. I have to go see them, OK? I hope they haven't heard yet. You can get me on my cell. I'm leaving immediately."

Charlie went to tell Luke what was happening and he was still on the phone. Apparently he was getting instructions from lawyers, too. They hadn't even had time to absorb the shock and grief and horror of what they had seen and it felt like they were going to be in the middle of a tornado. It was crazy.

Charlie reached for a pad and pen and wrote Luke a note explaining where he was going. While he was searching for keys and glasses and cell phone, Luke got off the phone. "My agent. Everyone is in a blind panic about this. No one seems to be remembering that two men are dead here. They are all just putting out public relations brush fires. It makes me sick at my stomach." He read the note Charlie had scribbled.

"I'm going with you." It wasn't a request. It was a statement and Charlie was relieved. He hated doing this alone, even though he had known Marilyn and Diane forever. It would just be easier to have someone along for support. He thought of Ben and wished he were here. His sweet, spiritual nature would be just what Charlie needed to help him through this. But he had to get to Valdana. He would call Ben later.

They took the minimum amount of time to get cleaned up and dressed before heading out to the car.

"I'll drive. Get in." Luke was already in the driver's seat and had the car started and in gear by the time Charlie closed the door.

"OK, how do I get there?" They had forgotten that Luke had never been there before.

"Just take the freeway south. There are three exits in Valdana and I'll know which one is the exit to Diane's house when we get there. I can't remember the name right now. Just get on the freeway and we're done."

"I'm on the way. Hang on. Sweet Jesus, I can't believe any of this is happening. Has is sunk in with you yet? I feel like I'm in a bad movie or bad dream."

"I know. Me, too. Hey, since you're driving, do you mind if I try to get Ben on the phone? He turned on his phone again and noticed that he had a voicemail. It was from Ben. He had heard the news on the radio in California. That meant that the sisters had probably seen it, too, unless they don't watch Hollywood gossip shows in the middle of the day. Charlie hoped that was correct. He would never forgive himself if they found out that way. Lee had always been so solicitous of his sisters' feelings. It was odd in a way because Lee loathed Texas and his home town and everything about it. But he had been devoted to his mother and had promised her to look after the girls. He had honored that promise all of his adult life. Charlie silently made a vow to continue that promise in Lee's absence. He would look after Marilyn and Diane. It was the least he could do, for they were his family now.

Ben sounded stunned and concerned on the phone. Charlie thought, with macabre humor, that it was probably a rare occasion for Ben to turn on a radio and hear that someone he knew, even peripherally, had been murdered in a hotel room. Charlie punched Ben's number.

Ben answered on the second ring. "Charlie? Are you OK? Good lord, what happened? Are you OK?" Charlie had never heard Ben sound so anxious.

"I'm all right, I guess, honey. I don't think it has gotten through to me yet. I'm in the car with Luke. We're on our way to Lee's hometown to tell his sisters. I just hope I get there before they see it on television."

"Well, you better hurry. It's all over the news and entertainment shows. Mom and I were in the car coming back from the airport when we heard it. I couldn't quite grasp it at first. I was hearing the words, but my brain kept saying, no, that's not right. You know who Lee Horner is and this isn't happening to him. I came home immediately and called you. I was afraid to stay at mother's. She would have known from my face that something was wrong."

There is was again. Ben's double life. He had to hide this from his family. Poor Ben. He had no one to talk to about this side of his life. Charlie wondered how that lack of support would play out in their future.

"I got your message. It was good to hear your voice. It's a long story. Remember my telling you about that weird kid that Lee met on the internet? They met about the same time that you and I did. That's who it was. That was the other person in the room. We don't know what happened yet. I'm almost certain it was a murder/suicide. I can't imagine another explanation. Have they said anything on TV?"

"No, all the reports are sketchy. They didn't even have the identity of the other man. And they didn't have your name either, but they mentioned Luke by name. You've told me more than they have on television."

"Well, the man had threatened Lee numerous times. Lee broke it off last night and we thought that was the end of it. But the boy called back later and it turns out that he was in Dallas, hysterical and out of control. Lee went to the hotel to try to talk some sense into him and that was the last time we saw him. Luke woke me up around four in the morning and told me that Lee wasn't home yet. We went to the hotel to investigate. The security guard went to check the room and that's when they found the bodies. You know the rest. We had to go up and identify them. I recognized the Spanish boy. Ben, there was so much blood." Charlie stopped. He couldn't go back there right now.

"It's OK Charlie. You don't have to tell me anymore. I know what it was like. How is Luke doing?" Ben was the only one besides Charlie who was in on the Luke and Lee romance. Charlie just had to tell him and it was OK with the guys.

"We're both in shock, I think. Trying to figure out what to do next. He's here with me right now. He's driving me to Valdana to Lee's sisters."

Even though Luke Beecham was a huge star, Ben recognized that they were in much the same place. Luke's life was shattered and he couldn't talk to anyone about it except Charlie. He understood completely and his heart went out to Luke. He understood the need for discretion and Luke's need for friends and sympathy now.

"Is there anything I can do, Charlie, for you or Luke?"

"Could you come to Texas? I really need you right now."

Ben didn't know what to do. He couldn't just leave work without some kind of valid excuse and Charlie wasn't even a part of his life as far as work was concerned. How would he explain that? It would have to be a lie and he had never lied to his colleagues before. He didn't want to start. There were Pam and his mother. Both of them needed him. He knew that he wanted to be with Charlie, but he also knew that his place was here, at home, with his family.

Ben's silence spoke volumes to Charlie. Charlie knew that he was torn. He had not asked for much from Ben. He had always supported his primary allegiance to his family, but this was a pivotal event in Charlie's life. Charlie was essentially alone in the world except for friends like Lee. Losing Lee was like losing his parents or his sister. He felt so deeply alone and he needed Ben to be there for him. It was his turn to come first.

"Charlie, I don't know what to say. I can't just leave. I have a job. I'm not self employed like you are. What do I tell everyone at work if I ask for this time off so suddenly? I can't tell them the truth and I've never lied to them before. Besides, there is going to be a lot of press. You know that. You'll be involved in that. Would you want me to be there? I can't do that, Charlie. I can't get involved on that level. We've talked about this and you know how I feel. Besides, Pam is not doing well at all. I'm afraid to leave her and Mom is getting worse. I'm so sorry, Charlie. I just can't drop my whole life and come to Texas. Please say you understand."

Now it was Charlie's turn to be silent. Luke was concentrating on driving and looking straight ahead. Charlie looked in the distance and all he saw was highway. Endless, Texas highway. Endless, lonely, Texas highway. Finally, he responded to Ben, "I know. You've never lied to me about all this. I just thought that this time, just once, I might come first. I do understand. It's just that I need some understanding right now, too, and you just can't give it. Don't worry, Ben. I'm hurt and I'm disappointed, but this isn't a deal breaker. I'll get through this and we'll talk about it all when I get back to California. Will you stay in touch, at least?" Charlie was going to cry.

"Of course, I will. I love you Charlie. You know I do. I know I'm hurting you and I would give anything not to. It's the last thing I want to do."

"Do you remember what I said to you about that? The offer still holds. Take care. I'll keep you posted about what is happening."

"Remember that I love you Charlie and I'll pray for you. You may not want that, but it'll help. I promise. Call me any time you want to. I'll check in with you, too. You're so strong and good, Charlie. Know your strength."

"Bye, Ben. We'll talk again soon. And, Ben? Everything."

"Ditto, dude." Ben clicked off.

"That didn't sound good, Charlie. He's not coming, is he?" Luke still held his eyes on the road.

"No. It's complicated for him Luke. Just like it is for you. He leads a double life, too. What kind of fucking world to we live in where we can't just be free to love each other without all this goddam bullshit! I'm so sick of it. I'm sick of lying and making excuses and tiptoeing around the world so that we don't upset the fucking heterosexual status quo. We have to pretend to be invisible so they can be comfortable. God forbid that they are uncomfortable! Or worse, we have to pair off and move to the suburbs and adopt Chinese babies and go to the PTA so we can prove to them that we are just as dull and straight and average as they are. Christ, I'm so sick of it.

"I'm sick of a whole lifetime of not having what I want because someone else has decided that it's wrong.

"It doesn't matter how 'out' or liberated you think you are. As long as one of us is still enslaved, terrified of being caught, miserable and sick with longing that has to be hidden—as long as that continues to exist, then we all continue to suffer.

"After all these years of fighting and marching and writing and protesting—it comes down to this—the man I love can't be seen in public with me.

"It's all been for nothing. People are as stupid and gullible and bigoted as they have ever been. Jesus H. Christ on a Styrofoam cross! I'm so sick of the whole bloody thing."

Luke smiled and looked at Charlie for the first time since they had gotten in the car, "Don't hold back, hon."

Charlie laughed. It felt good. Luke sounded exactly like Lee. It was as if he had channeled him. It felt wonderful to laugh and to honor Lee in that way.

"Well, I am sick of it."

"What about me. You're out and single and totally free to do whatever you damn well please. I'm one of those poor schlubs who has to live that lie. It's an awful way to live, Charlie. Not only is it nerve wracking because you have to keep covering your tracks and you never know if you're going to be found out. It's also debilitating to the soul to constantly pretend to be something you aren't. To see it in print and on television. The great big lie that is your life. Back in Tennessee right now there is an army of folks setting about keeping my lie in tact. It makes me sick, too."

"The difference between you and Ben is that Ben's whole existence tells him that they are right. It's even worse for him. Not only is he living a double life, but one of those lives is shameful and sinful to him. I know I'm putting him in a lot of pain. Sometimes it feels like the only way to love him is to let him go. But I can't yet. I'm too selfish. I want him to choose me!"

"I do, too, Charlie. Maybe this will be the turning point for him. I wish Lee were here. He would have something really cynical to add right about now."

"I think we're near the exit. I don't need cynicism, Luke. I need courage and compassion and kindness and love."

"You've got those, Charlie. You've got something else, too. I'm right beside you, OK?" Charlie was grateful to have someone he could lean on right now. Even if it wasn't Ben.

# Chapter 43

For the next two weeks, Ben watched a tabloid and media frenzy build around the bizarre murder/suicide in Dallas. No one in Goldmine knew that he had anything to do with the lurid story, but it was the talk of the town, as it was in every town in America. Move over Anna Nicole, the Horner/Sandal murder case has taken center stage. It was on every patient television in the hospital and Ben was bombarded by images of Charlie looking lost and dazed and hurt and in shock. They were on the phone almost nightly, Charlie pouring out his heart and Ben trying to offer what support he could from a distance. His life had gotten complicated, too, and he couldn't leave his family.

Pam was definitely worse now. She destroyed what had been the nursery. Not long after Brett had remodeled the room, she got hysterical and began a rampage that ended with her in the hospital with a broken wrist and in restraints. Something was broken inside her, too, and needed fixing. Ben was beginning to assess what else they could do to help and they were considering hospitalization on a long-term basis. Brett, who was witness to her violently destructive episode, was no longer objecting to any suggested medical help. He wanted his wife back and he realized that the prayer groups were not enough. Now the task was to find the right place and Ben was spending his little free time researching and visiting facilities in Northern California and Southern Oregon that might be right for Pam.

He was wracked with guilt. Had it been there all along? Had he just not seen it? Could he have helped her sooner? Was he a neglectful parent? He had not been as attentive as he should have after Lynette's death. Did he miss something?

He talked with Jacen about it but he was just as mystified and beating himself up for not being there to help. He was back on base in North Carolina and he and Catherine had announced their engagement. It was going to be a big wedding in Maryland in about a year. It was possible that Jacen would not return to California but decide to build his life closer to Catherine's family. Ben understood that and accepted it. He was just grateful that he didn't have to worry about Jacen, too.

His mother was drifting further away. He had seen this before. It was always hard to diagnose senility or Alzheimer's but Ben had that gut feeling that comes with experience. The listless, dreamy quality that had first shown itself when the baby died had become a semi-permanent state with Alvah. She was functioning. She could drive and she continued to work at the church in various ways. Her friends noticed the change, but just assumed it was sadness and grief over the baby. They didn't notice the differences that Ben did. Already, once, she had called him at work from the grocery store parking lot. She sounded confused and had forgotten why she was there. Not wanting to upset her unnecessarily he soothed her, made light of it and she seemed to be OK. But, it was only a matter of time before the next episode and eventually she would not be able to be left alone. He could hire someone to stay with her or he could do it himself. He was in the house alone now and he could manage that, couldn't he?

He wished that he could be there for Charlie. Ben remembered how important Charlie's presence had been when the baby died. He longed to be able to return that gift, but he couldn't. Too many decisions had already been made that couldn't be unmade by the time he met Charlie. He had kids and responsibilities that he couldn't just toss aside, even if he had wanted to. Of course he thought about what it would be like to be with Charlie, out in the open. It would change everything forever. Pam was certainly in no condition to deal with it. She might not even be aware of anything outside of her own pain. And Jacen would never accept it. He was conservative by nature and by upbringing and his religious beliefs were solid and serious for him. He accepted the church's position on just about everything without question. Ben and Lynette had raised the kids to do that. Ben failed to note the irony of being the victim of his own successful parenting decisions. It was a real possibility that he would lose both of them if he told them about Charlie. That was unthinkable. He wouldn't lose his job at the hospital. They probably couldn't fire him, but his relationships with everyone there would be altered, many of them negatively. He would lose his credibility with the staff, many of whom were fellow church members. He would probably have to find another job.

Being with Charlie would mean giving up everything he had ever known, worked for and loved in his life. Ben just couldn't do that. As much as he loved Charlie, he was too decent, too honorable and too selfless to destroy so much for his own happiness. There were so many other people that would be effected by a decision like that: his family, friends and co-workers. He must honor them, too. He didn't know why this had happened to him, but he did know that he was not the first person to be tested by God and he wouldn't be that last. He only hoped he was strong enough.

The time would come when he would have to let go. He just couldn't do that yet. Charlie needed him and, yes, he needed Charlie too. It couldn't go on indefinitely. It was taking a toll on his health and his peace of mind. For now, he would continue to juggle, trying to live his life as he always had and devote as much secret time as he could to supporting and loving Charlie.

Ben and Charlie had met in the wrong lifetime.

He came home from work, dead tired and intending to call Charlie. He flipped on the television. There was film of Charlie blinking in a storm of flashing cameras and trying to dodge people and noise. Ben knew how much Charlie hated noise and wished he could make things better, quieter at least. Just behind him was Luke Beecham. They were both still in Dallas waiting for the police to finish their investigation and release Lee's body. Charlie had done a good job of shielding Lee's sisters from the glare. The media vampires weren't interested in a couple of old ladies anyway. They didn't add to the lurid side of this story that kept them on the air, but Charlie and Luke did and they pursued the two men relentlessly. Ben knew from talking with Charlie every day that their entire day was planned around dealing with press. The work on the show had stopped almost completely. For now, the Dallas opening had been abandoned and rehearsals were continuing in New York. The producers were waiting to see how the scandal played out. There was even talk of closing down the project completely. Only Luke and Charlie remained in Texas, waiting for Lee. Marilyn and Diane wanted Lee buried next to his mother. Charlie thought that was perfect and Luke agreed. Ben had suggested that Charlie leave all of those arrangements to the sisters and he had done so. It was a good decision. It gave them something to do and allowed them to mourn in a familiar way amidst all the sensational media coverage that they didn't quite understand. Charlie had been grateful for this from Ben. Ben understood the dynamics of family so much better than Charlie.

He turned off the television after only a few minutes. He couldn't stand to see the nightmare that his Charlie was living and he couldn't bear thinking about his inability to do anything to make it better. He was heartsick. He found his cell phone and called Charlie. He answered on the first ring and there was noise in the background.

"Hi. God I'm glad it was you. I haven't talked to anyone but lawyers all day long. Hang on a minute. We're just getting home and pushing through the press outside the house." Suddenly it got much quieter and Ben heard a door slam and someone in the background muttered a profanity.

"That's Luke expressing a sentiment that we both feel at this point. We just got word that we can proceed with the funeral and the burial. I talked to Diane and everything is arranged for day after tomorrow at their church in Valdana. I would have preferred a funeral home and I know Lee would have, but the sisters wanted it at the church. I also know that Lee wouldn't have argued with them about it, so I didn't either. I bit my tongue and went along with everything."

Ben had never heard Charlie be so frank about his views on church. He wondered how many times had had "bitten his tongue" around him. Charlie had always been respectful of Ben. They hadn't talked about religion very much. They both knew that they had very different views about things and their time together was so limited and so precious that neither wanted to waste it in pointless disagreements.

Ben could be generous, too. "It won't hurt anything to agree with them. Lee won't care. Funerals are really for the living anyway, aren't they? Our way of honoring the dead and at the same time attending to our own need to grieve in some public way. It'll be fine."

"You're right, of course. Thanks for reminding me of that. I'm really OK about the whole thing. Luke an I are going to Valdana tomorrow. We've got hotel reservations there under assumed names. We're hoping to keep it quiet."

"I'll be with you in spirit, Charlie, and I wish I could be there with you in person, but my life is crazy. We're still so short handed at the hospital. And I've got to work. Insurance is only covering part of Pam's hospitalization, so Brett and I have to come up with the rest. She doesn't seem any better. I haven't given up hope, but it feels like we're losing her. I'm sorry, Charlie, going on about my stuff when you're the one we should be focusing on. How much longer are you staying in Texas?" Ben wondered what it would be like back in California. The press would not leave him alone here, either.

"No, Ben. Please. I'm glad you told me about Pam and your work. What's happening here doesn't diminish you life or your family's pain. I'm truly sorry about Pam. Time can work wonders. And it's the only real cure for grief. We both know that, don't we?

"I'm coming home right after the funeral. We're all moved out of the house. I've shipped everything back to Sacramento except a small carry-on. Luke is going back to Nashville, too. His management people are frantic that he has stayed here as long as he has. They want him to distance himself from all this as quickly as possible. It's getting harder for them to explain his continued interest in Lee. I'll bet it is. They can't tell the truth. Considering what I know is really happening here and what is getting reported on television, my guess is that ninety per cent of what is reported is pure fiction. The word is infotainment and it is a perfect description. Poor Luke. What kind of world do we live in that denies a man the right to grieve with dignity?"

"I'm sorry for him, too, Charlie. Having to hide his grief in that way. It must be very hard on him and it's very sad." Ben didn't know what to say. It was so clear that they were both talking about him, too, but neither of them would say it. It WAS very sad.

"He's been a good friend, Ben. He's been so supportive of me and absolutely wonderful with Lee's sisters. They've really taken him into the family. Diane wouldn't OK the music with the organist until she had checked with Luke. He seems almost honored to be included. It's very sweet and I'm sorry Lee couldn't be here to see it."

"Well, I'm grateful that you aren't alone during this. I know I've let you down. You'll never know how bad I feel about that. Hurting you is the worst thing about my life right now. You must know that."

"I do, Ben. I do understand your choices and why you have made them. Do I wish it were different? Of course I do. But we live in the real world and I know that world all too well."

"I've got to go. I need to check on Pam tonight before her doctor leaves the hospital. I'll call again tomorrow, OK? Get some rest. I love you Charlie."

"I love you more, Ben. Take care of yourself, please? Try to get more than four hours sleep for a change. I'll be holding only good thoughts about Pam. Give her some time, honey. We'll talk tomorrow."

"Bye. Everything."

Ben sat for a moment. When he was with Charlie or even just talking with him, he was totally engaged and he felt centered and sane, but the minute that connection was broken, he was back in his own reality. He supposed that people who were used to leading a double life felt like this all the time. It was new to him and a bad fit. It was not his nature to be deceitful. And he had been avoiding the spiritual implications of all this. He just wasn't thinking about that at all. He couldn't. Not now. It would have to wait.

He picked up the phone to call Pam's doctor. He was not looking forward to this conversation. He would rather be talking to Charlie. A part of him wanted to go to the airport, get on a plane and be with Charlie at the funeral and afterward. Instead he dialed the number of the hospital.

# Chapter 44

Charlie was thoughtful when the conversation with Ben ended. They had touched on some things that they had been avoiding. How did Charlie really feel about Ben's religion? Well, he certainly didn't agree with any of it, but he had always tried to adopt a "live and let live" attitude. Ben's religion seemed to bring him comfort and structure and add purpose to his life. Those were good things and if Ben needed religion in his life it was OK with Charlie. He didn't see any reason for there to be a conflict. The only conflict he ever saw about religion was when other people didn't accept his point of view and insisted upon proselytizing. Ben wasn't like that and Charlie thought they could live with their differences—if they were ever given the chance, that is.

"What are you thinking about so hard?" Luke was looking at him.

"Oh, Ben and religion and God."

"Oh, all that easy stuff, huh?" Luke smiled wearily. The weeks had taken their toll on his beauty. He looked drawn and tired. Lines creased the sides of his face and he had lost weight. His eyes, always a bit hooded, were even more so and looked dark and sunken. It would be a good thing for him to get out of this environment and get home to Nashville where people would care for him. But Charlie would miss his company greatly.

They decided to just leave the house and head down to Valdana early. They called the hotel and changed the reservation. The press had deserted the front of the house. They were used to the guys not going out again at night, so most of the reporters had taken a dinner break. Charlie and Luke loaded their few belongings into the SUV in the garage. As they left, they mimed to the lone reporter on duty that they were just going out for something to eat. He waved and went back to his solitary vigil. Luke and Lee drove to the rental agency and changed cars. They took a beige four door sedan that blended in so well that neither could remember what make it was. It was perfect.

They were not followed on the drive to Valdana and when they pulled into the hotel driveway were quickly taken to the only suite in the Valdana Inn. The owner of the hotel came by to assure them of complete discretion and privacy. There was no real reason for the visit except that the owner wanted a closer look at Luke Beecham! At least they felt they could trust him to be true to his word and they relaxed for the first time all day. It seemed that they had successfully evaded the press, for a while at least.

The funeral was a blur for Charlie with gospel songs and preaching. There was a sermon that had nothing to do with the funeral at all. Charlie resented the fact that the "preacher" had not even known Lee. He spoke mostly about the sisters. But, he reminded himself, it was for them that this whole thing was happening, so he tried to get his blood pressure down and let go of it.

Luke, on the other hand, was deeply moved by the service. He was brought up in this kind of church and it still got to him. He joined in the singing and he eyes shone with tears during the eulogy. At one point, he discreetly squeezed Charlie's hand so tightly that Charlie checked for broken bones.

After it was over, Luke and Charlie went back to Diane's where the family would be "receiving." By now, of course, the press had caught on and were swarming around the funeral and around the house. Once inside, Charlie and Luke wondered if they would ever be allowed to leave. Everyone seemed thrilled to meet Luke and Charlie enjoyed talking with friends and relatives of Lee's that he had met over the years. The last two times he had been in this house were when Lee's parents died. Charlie had always assumed that they would one day bury the sisters, too. Charlie and Lee would grow old together. It didn't seem possible that he was here for Lee's funeral. He still didn't quite get that Lee was gone and he would grow old without him.

There was no alcohol being served, but Luke had thought to bring a flask for himself and was dosing himself liberally throughout the afternoon. Charlie had a reservation on the red eye back to Sacramento and Luke had the same kind of flight to Nashville. They were using the same airline, so the plan was to drive directly from Valdana to the airport. They would leave Diane's house, drive back to the hotel, leave the beige car there and take a limousine from the back of the hotel that would drop them at the airport. With any luck, they would avoid the press until tomorrow.

As they left Diane's, the press had them literally blocked in. Charlie repeated what he had been told to say, "I have no comment to make. Thank you." Usually, Luke had a similar line, but this afternoon, Luke stopped, cleared his throat and prepared to speak to the press.

"OK, fellas, you want a comment? Here's a comment. Do you know what happened here today? It was a funeral. It wasn't a red carpet event. This isn't Hollywood. We're in a small Texas town where two dear ladies have just buried their last living relative, their only brother. No matter how you want to spin that, these good people deserve the respect and privacy that you would demand if you were in the same place."

Luke paused and swallowed hard. He was just a little drunk, but clear resolve showed on his face and Charlie knew what was coming.

"I just buried the only man I've ever truly loved. You heard me right. I'll repeat it. The only MAN I've ever loved. And we were cheated out of so much time together. You know why? Because of you and the culture of hate that you helped to create and that you certainly feed. Lee and I met several years ago and my handlers thought it was best if we weren't seen together because the press might pick up on something. Well, pick up on this: I loved Lee Horner and he loved me. We were planning to be together for the rest of our lives, living and working and enjoying life. But because of that crazed, sick boy, he was taken from me only a few weeks after we had found each other again. That's pretty terrible all by itself. But then you came along and decided this would sell soap flakes and corn flakes and cars. So you turned it into a nightmare for me and for Charlie here and for the good, decent folks in that house. You have turned our personal pain into entertainment. Are any of you ashamed of what you do? Of course not. It's clear you have no idea what shame is. Goddam you all."

There was absolute silence except for the whirr of the cameras. Luke got in the car, Charlie jumped in and they sped away, nearly hitting a reporter and not caring. They were completely silent in the car on the way back to the hotel. Luke had just set off a nuclear device in Diane Horner's front yard.

Charlie turned sideways in the seat and put his arm on the seat-back. He looked at Luke and said, slowly,

"Don't hold back, hon."

They both started laughing, loudly and deeply. Tears were rolling down their cheeks as they pulled into the hotel and ran in to get their things. However, the thoughtful people at the hotel had already packed everything for them and it was waiting in the limousine, so they just dashed out the back door of the hotel and into the car. They sped off for the airport, still gasping for air and breathless with laughter. Things would get very serious later, but for now the laughter was all that mattered.

# Chapter 45

The firestorm that first erupted after the deaths of Lee Horner and Tadio Sandal was a mere firecracker compared to the mushroom cloud that appeared the morning after Luke Beecham's announcement in Valdana, Texas. The incident that had provided laughter for Luke and Charlie on the way to the airport had turned cataclysmic by the time they deplaned at their respective airports. Obviously, the Nashville airport was the epicenter of this radioactivity, but Charlie was surprised when he arrived home, too. As he came down the escalator there was no indication that anything was going on. He thought that he had outsmarted the media again, but he began to hear the familiar murmurs and clicks and whirrs of the media hive as he got closer to the ground floor lobby. Security guards were keeping them at bay outside the terminal, but it looked as if they threatened to break through at any moment. He ducked into a dark, quiet bar near the baggage claim area to catch his breath and decide what to do next. As his eyes adjusted to the darkness, he noticed that the place was deserted except for one other person, seated in the far corner booth.

"Ben!" Charlie was amazed,"what are you doing here!" Ben stood and Charlie clasped him in his arms in an embrace, leaning in to kiss him.

"Not here, Charlie, for God's sake!" Ben was rigid and unsmiling. Charlie could see that he was terrified. He must have seen the media insanity outside and had come into the bar for much the same reason as Charlie. It was early morning and they had the place to themselves.

Charlie was taken aback. He was tired and edgy and needed someone to take care of him for a change. He had always been the one to make accommodations for Ben and his needs. Now he needed Ben. "I'm sorry, honey. I'm just tired and I was so glad to see you. It means the world to me that you're here. I never expected it." Charlie was looking at Ben closely. Ben was very nervous and backed away from Charlie.

"Let's get out of here, OK? Is there someplace we can go to talk where the reporters can't see us?"

"Look, Ben. Why don't you just go? Leave by yourself and go out to your car and go home. They don't know who you are and won't find out if you aren't with me. Just go. We'll talk later, OK?" The hurt and anger were evident in Charlie's voice. Ben had not felt this from him before and looked as if he had been struck.

"Charlie, I'm sorry. I just can't. I have too much to lose. I wanted to see you. I didn't know the media would be here. Has something else happened?" Ben looked heartbroken and Charlie couldn't stay mad.

" I guess you haven't been watching television. Luke did a very brave and foolish thing yesterday. He made a statement to the press after the funeral that he and Lee had been lovers and lowered the boom on the vultures. It seemed really smart and funny at the time, but we knew he had thrown gasoline on the fire. It was only a matter of time before it blew up and boy, did it. I can imagine what Nashville is like today. Luke flew home last night, too."

"That was a crazy thing to do. His career will be ruined. Everything he's ever worked for will be gone. His fans will turn on him. My mother and all the nurses at the hospital think he's the greatest, but when this gets out, they'll be burning his CD's in the parking lot."

"In the parking lot of your church, Ben? Is that where the fire will be?"

"You don't know how people are, Charlie. You don't have to live in the real world. You are safe in your own little cocoon. Your lifestyle isn't accepted by most people. I'm sorry, Charlie, but that's the truth."

"My lifestyle? It's not a lifestyle, Ben. I thought you would know that. It's my life, my identity. It's who I am in the world. And I do live in the real world, my friend. You better believe I do. Not a day goes by that something doesn't remind me that I'm in what you call the real world. Having this conversation with you for starters. You know me, Ben. You know me better than anyone, or so I thought and yet I'm having the "it's not a lifestyle" conversation with you. That's the real world Ben. You say you love me. You say we are soulmates and you've said I'm the love of your life. Yet you won't even be seen in public with me. That's the real world, Ben. I'm ready to share my life with you. I'm ready to commit to you for real. It's the first time in my life that I've wanted to do that. But the real world? It can't happen because you can't even admit to yourself, much less anyone else, that you want that as much as I do. You play it safe, Ben. You track the status quo. I'm not saying you're wrong to do that, but is that real life for you? Look, you better go. I'll wait here for a few minutes until you've had a chance to get out of the terminal. No one will connect us. We'll talk later, if you want. Think about what I've said. I want you, Ben, more than I've ever wanted anyone else, but we need to make some decisions. Let's think about it and talk later. I'm exhausted and I still have to run the gauntlet."

"Charlie, I'm so sorry. I came here today to surprise you and make you happy and it's only made things worse for you. Is that what we are going to be for each other? I know that most of what you say is true. But you are very wrong about one thing. I do admit to myself that I love you. I love you more than anything, but I have obligations that come before my own personal feelings. I have to honor those. This is heartbreaking for me, too. I'll go. Let's take a couple of days to think and then let's talk again, OK? I know it probably isn't worth much at this point to say this, but you are the love of my life, even more than my wife. There is a connection with you that I've never had with anyone else. My heart is breaking too. Good-bye Charlie."

Ben turned and walked out. Charlie was left alone in the dimly lit bar. He turned and looked at himself in a mirror. He didn't recognize the person looking back at him. It was an old man, sad and tired and beaten down. He rubbed his face as if waking from a long sleep. He ran his fingers through his hair and tried to fluff the silvery mess. It was definitely getting thinner. He straightened his collar and shot his cuffs. He slung his carryon over his shoulder and took one last look. Better—not great, but better.

"Showtime!" Charlie said to the man in the mirror and he walked out the door to face the mob. He would tell them the truth. He was tired of giving lip service to the lawyers. It was time to say something real. This might cost him everything, including Ben, but he was tired of the status quo. He couldn't accuse Ben of playing it safe if he was doing the same thing. He was ready to meet Luke's ante and raise him one. Bring it on.

# Chapter 46

Ben left the airport completely unnoticed. He drove home slowly and without purpose, giving himself time to think. He had never been this sad in his life. On a whim he had just decided to surprise Charlie. He thought they would go back to Charlie's house for some private time. He knew they needed that. They became something else when they were alone together—a whole greater than the sum of it's two very different parts. That connection was getting harder to hold on to, especially now with Charlie in this very public news event. If the media were camped out at Charlie's house, how would they ever be able to see each other?

Ben decided not to go home, but to drive over to Sonoma County to visit Pam. It had been a couple of days and he wanted to talk with her doctor. It was disheartening to see her. Why did she break like that? Yes, losing a child is a terrible tragedy and the loss will always be there, but people learn how to survive. His mother had done so. Ben thought they had given Pam the love and security she needed as a child. Her religious upbringing had been good and true and she was a devoted Christian. They tried to give her everything she would need to get along in the world.

Parents don't have a crystal ball and they can't prepare their children for something they don't even know exists. At least he was here now to help her fix whatever was wrong and he would do whatever it took. He and Brett were both concerned about the cost of hospitalization, but Ben was working extra hours and Brett was prepared to borrow against his business if necessary. They hoped it wouldn't come to that.

Ben knew all the staff at the Riverwood Clinic and they knew that he was "one of them" so he was able to simply wave and go directly to Pam's room without checking in. It was a beautiful facility tucked away in one of those corners of Sonoma County that are hard to find, but worth it once you do. Ben thought it was a good choice for Pam. It was a quiet and restful atmosphere, unlike most hospitals, including the one where Ben worked. He wondered how they kept it so serene. Pam didn't look up when he entered her room. She was seated near the window and looking out, but her eyes were unfocused and the look on her face suggested that she was mentally unfocused as well.

He tried to make small talk. "Hi Pam. How's my girl today? Doing OK? Beautiful view, isn't it?" He spoke softly and tried to sound upbeat, but there was little or no response from her. She continued to stare vacantly. She seemed worse, more remote than the last time he was here.

He left the room, searching for her doctor and ran into one of the nurses he had come to know. He made his inquiry and she gently reminded him that he had not been expected and that the doctor had left after morning rounds. Ben, of course, knew that she was right, he had just hoped to catch Dr. Dutton. He decided to ask the nurse her opinion of Pam's current condition.

"Well, I'm not with her all the time, so I don't know what my observations can tell you. I think you're right, though. She does seem to be more remote, more regressed than she was when she came to us. But the doctor would know more about that than I do. Look, I've been here for a while, Mr. McSwain and I'll tell you this: it just takes time. As a nurse, I'm sure you know that. I've seen real recovery here from all sorts of things. The mind sometimes just needs a quiet place to rediscover itself. Give her some time. The doctor is good. I've watched him work. And this is a good place. You and I know that isn't always true, but from one to another? You can trust Riverwood." Ben fondly thought of Charlie offering him similar solace not long ago.

"Thank you. That does make me feel better. I'm like any other family member when I'm on this side of the bed pan. I understand as a nurse, but as a dad it's much harder to deal with."

"Well, I was speaking to you as both, Mr. McSwain." She smiled gently and Ben felt as if he had an ally.

"It's going to be a long haul. You'd better call me Ben."

"I'm Sheryl, Mr......Ben...you run on home. I'll keep you posted if there is anything you need to know. I'll tell the doctor you were here and have him call you tomorrow, OK? Get some rest, Ben. Frankly, you look like you could use it. We don't need two members of your family here!"

Ben liked her. He was glad that she was keeping an eye on Pam. He knew nurses and he could tell a good one. Sheryl was one of the good ones. Even if he hadn't seen the doctor, he was glad he came today. He felt better about Pam's care than he had a few hours ago.

He started the drive home. Charlie's music filled the car and Ben's thoughts turned to their parting at the airport. He regretted being such a coward. Coward? No, he wasn't a coward. He was just protecting everything he had ever believed in until Charlie Morgan turned his world upside down.

He decided to drive back to Sacramento and make things right with Charlie. He ached to hold him. It had been so long. Ben put his foot to the pedal and drove the way he liked to drive. It didn't take long to round the corner to Charlie's street. It was completely blocked by cars and vans and television equipment. Ben pulled into a parking lot a block away and dialed Charlie's number.

"Hey. I'm so glad it's you. Hang on a minute, I've got to get rid of a producer on the other line." Now that he had Charlie on the line, he didn't know what to say. He couldn't go to the house. "Hi, I'm back. I'm so sorry about earlier. I didn't mean to snap at you. I was tired and anxious from all this."

Ben interrupted him, "Charlie, don't worry about it. It was my fault. I can't seem to stop hurting you no matter what I do. I'm about a block from your house. I was on my way to see you and saw the commotion out front. I can't "run the gauntlet" as you call it. I don't know how, Charlie. It's all so new to me and well, scary. I've got so many people depending on me. The choices I make effect so many different things. I have responsibilities that must be met."

It was Charlie's turn to interrupt. "I know honey. I know. It was selfish of me to confront you like that. It's just that you are a part of my life now and I need you, too. I don't know how we got to this place, do you? I never really thought about choosing to love you. It was just there. I think it happened that day on the train when you got the cinder out of my eye. I think I knew then. And I know you didn't ask for any of this. But it has happened. I think it's wonderful, but I don't know how you feel about it now."

"It's wonderful when I'm with you, Charlie. There don't seem to be any obstacles or problems. But when I leave your house and come back to my world, everything changes. It does become a problem. I was hoping we could talk. Is there any way you can slip out? Any place we could meet?"

"My neighbor, Marie. You could walk to her house. The press wouldn't even notice you. And I can come over through my back yard. It's still private because it's locked, but I can jump the fence to Marie's yard. That would work. I'll call her and call you right back."

It was only a few seconds, "Ben, no one is home. I've tried both of her numbers. I imagine she got out of the chaos. I don't blame her. Anywhere would be better than this."

"I'll just go on home, Charlie. When is this going to be over? How can you stand it? It must be a nightmare for you."

"Well, it's not what I would have chosen, but I had quite a tantrum at the airport after you left. You might catch some of it on tonight's celebutrash news." The lilt in Charlie's voice suggested that he had relished the outburst.

"I couldn't do it. It's just not something I thought I would ever be involved in. I don't mean that the way it sounded. I just mean that I'm a simple, small town boy. I never even gave a thought to celebrities or writers and musicians or anything like that."

"Well, Ben, you should remember that I'm just a small town boy, too. I've had to navigate some treacherous waters over the years, but this has me flummoxed, too. I don't have a clue what I'm doing. I was on a job one minute and the next I'm involved in a murder and the victim is my best friend. I'm not sure I've processed that even now. The press thing seems like something else. It doesn't have anything to do with Lee. It's just a lurid story to them. They forget that Lee was a real person. And that poor sick kid from Spain was real, too. His family and friends must be in shock and suffering, too. I just hope they live in a more civilized environment and can have some peace. That's what I need, some peace and quiet."

"Look, Charlie. This can't go on forever. They will move on eventually, right? I'm here. We can talk on the phone anytime. We'll come up with something, OK? I meant what I said at the airport. I'm not in denial about how I feel about you. I do love you. Don't give up on me yet."

That was just what Charlie wanted to hear, "Ben, when you talk like that, I can put up with anything. I want to find a way to have a relationship with you and for both of us to be OK with it. We just have to figure it out, that's all."

"We will, Charlie. Let's not stop trying."

"I love you, Ben."

"Ditto, dude."

They rang off at the same time.

Ben started up his car and headed back to the freeway and home. It had been a long day with lots of driving, but he felt better than he had in a long time. The driving always helped, but the heart-to-heart talk with the nurse at Riverwood and clearing things up with Charlie made all the difference. Now, he could feel how exhausted he was. He just wanted to go home, take a shower and crawl into bed. He had a long day at work tomorrow that he hadn't even thought about. Life would go on. Was it possible to find a way to honor all of his commitments and keep Charlie in his life, too?

He pulled into his driveway gratefully. It was quiet and no one was watching his house. Was he paranoid? After all, someone could have seen them together at the airport. It seemed secure right now and he was really too tired to give it too much concern. He dropped his keys and jacket in the living room and went into the bedroom to change into shorts and a T-shirt, his uniform no matter what the season. He came back into the living room and turned on the TV on his way to the kitchen. While he was rummaging for something to eat, he heard Charlie's name from the television. He was getting used to that.

"Another of the cast of characters from the Horner/Sandal murder let loose on the press today. After yesterday's stunning Texas tirade from gay country crooner, Luke Beecham, we thought perhaps we had heard it all in this story, but this morning upon arriving back home in Sacramento, California, Charlie Morgan decided to one-up his friend Beecham. Let's roll the film clip of Mr. Morgan's remarks at Sacramento International Airport."

Reporter: "Hey Charlie, with Lee out of the way, are you and Luke the next hot gay item in Hollywood?"

CM: "I beg your pardon? What did you say?"

Reporter: "I asked if you and Luke were an item now that Lee's out of the way."

CM: "Mr. Horner isn't 'out of the way' you cretin. He was murdered. And he was my best friend for over forty years. Do you understand what that means? Do you know what I've lost? And his sisters, whom you harangued to the point of tears, are ages seventy-seven and eighty-three respectively. Are you proud of what you've done to them? And Luke Beecham! How dare you suggest what you've suggested! How dare you! You have no idea what courage that man has shown. Or of the suffering that any of us have endured because of you! All you care about is how much more lurid you can make it appear. It's all about that for you. How it appears! You make these innuendoes and there isn't a shred of truth to them. Yet they get heard and they get repeated and the perception will be that there is something besides friendship and shared grief between Luke Beecham and me. Well, let me be clear: There Is Not! Is that a short enough sound bite for you dimwits?

"And I can't help but wonder if Lee had a girlfriend and I had been by her side through all this, would you have asked the same question? No, this story would have played a lot differently. Stop looking for extra dirt just because the players are gay.

"As for Luke Beecham. He's just an incredibly talented guy who fell in love. What sells laundry soap on your networks is the fact that he fell in love with another man. If Lee had been a woman, this story would have been a footnote the day it happened and been assigned to the memory file along with the other sad Hollywood stories of obsession. But because it involved two men, you've created a melodrama that isn't going to stop delivering for you until you've bled everything you can from it and all the real human beings involved in it.

"My best friend is dead! Do you get that? Have you no decency at all? No restraint? No boundaries or taste or feelings? Who are you people? Were you brought up by trolls under a bridge? You pander to the crassest human curiosity and feed our lowest, basest desires as human beings. You've taken television, what could have been the finest invention of the twentieth century, and turned it into a cesspool of lies and greed and mindless rot. You've tried your best to paint everyone connected to this story as the worst kind of people. You've started making things up because the truth isn't sensational enough for you. Well, we're just good people, that's all. But that doesn't fit the lurid story you've created, does it? So you make it sound like we are all like that poor, sad, sick young man who caused all this grief. Lee was just a quiet, intelligent and very talented writer. He got involved with the wrong person on the internet. It's not the first time that's happened, except this time it was fatal. HE LOST HIS LIFE! Do you people remember that? When you ask me in that smarmy tone if I'm involved with Luke, are you remembering that two men have died? Or do you just want to sell more soap flakes and keep the story alive? I'm going home to my little house where I work in the garden and do laundry and have coffee with my neighbors and live my life just like you do. No, not just like you. I have honor and decency and love for the people who journey with me on this planet. That's something so foreign to you that I'm sure you don't even know what I'm talking about. Now get out of my way."

Ben had not breathed since Charlie began talking. He didn't think Charlie had breathed, either. He didn't know what to think. Deep inside he was so proud of Charlie, but realistically he was terrified for him. He had really put it out there. There was no doubt left who he was and how he felt. It was the line in the sand. Ben didn't know if he had the courage to cross that line and stand with Charlie.

He went to bed, but he couldn't sleep. He kept seeing Charlie's sweet, hurt face as he stood there being so very brave. And alone. Ben should have been with him. He felt that, but he knew that he couldn't. He wondered if he ever could.

# Chapter 47

Charlie felt a lot better after talking with Ben. He had been exhilarated in his moment with the press at the airport, but that soon wore off and the desolation from his argument with Ben set in. It was the first time they had ever had that kind of angry exchange. They were both people who didn't do well with anger and in the past, when they disagreed, they would just smile and move on to something else. Neither was ever anxious for a confrontation. Their time together was so limited, it would have been such a waste to spend that time in anger and discord. They were exactly alike in that. It kept things on an even keel for them, but maybe it would have been better if they had argued more, shook each other up a little. Maybe not. Maybe it wouldn't have made any difference at all.

He peeked out from his living room window at the crowd in his front yard. He was concerned about his neighbors. They were all good friends and he hated to have them inconvenienced like this. He wondered if anyone had called the police. This was crazy. He was a prisoner in his home without privacy or privileges. Clearly, baiting them as he had this morning was a mistake. It had just made things worse. If he had said nothing, they would probably have left by now. He needed to shut up and stop adding to the feeding frenzy.

He went into his back yard and looked over the fence again. He could see Marie in her kitchen now so he hopped over and made his way to her back door.

"Charlie. I didn't know you were back." Marie deadpanned.

"I'm so sorry about all of this. Where were you earlier? I tried to call you. I wanted to get away from all the craziness."

"I was out in the garage. I'm sorry I missed you. This lunacy is getting to all of us, I fear."

"I would give anything to get rid of them. Please let all the neighbors know how sorry I am. What can we do about it?" Charlie gratefully took the cup of coffee that she offered him. Marie was a school teacher and, like the best of her profession, tough on the outside but a softie at heart. She and Charlie had become friends discussing the literature and music that they both loved.

"I'll call Terry and see what he thinks." Marie was already dialing the number of her neighbor on the other side, a gay attorney. Of course! Charlie had completely forgotten about Terry with everything else going on. He was the perfect one to handle all this.

Marie talked to Terry for a while. She "uh-hummed and ah-hahed" into the phone, asking a few pointed questions and tossing Charlie some animated, if mysterious, faces during the conversation. When she hung up, she looked pleased.

Terry's taking care of everything. I began to glaze over when he started talking about complaints and injunctions and all that stuff, but the bottom line is that they will be gone by later today. He started making calls when he got home from work and saw the commotion in front of your house. It's always good to have a lawyer on the block...if he's good enough, he can raise property values!" Marie made Charlie feel better just by being so positive. And he did hope that the paparazzi would be gone soon. He wanted his life back and he wanted to see Ben.

Marie invited him to stay for a while. She had homemade ice cream and Charlie couldn't resist. In a few minutes there was another knock at the back door and Terry came in, barking orders into a cell phone. Marie didn't even say hello, she just prepared a dish of ice cream and set it in front of him. It got him off the phone.

"Hey Charlie, Marie. Thanks. It's all taken care of. The police will be here within the hour and escort everyone away. We'll have our street back. Everybody happy?" Terry took a big bite of ice cream and winced with brain freeze.

"I don't know how to thank you, Terry. You're a doll. I should have married you when I was young and beautiful." Charlie teased.

"You were never beautiful and I can't remember your ever being young either, but you were always entirely too dangerous to marry. Now get over it. What are you going to do now that you have your life back?"

"Well, I'm going to see if I still have a life with Ben. That's the first thing. Then I want to take some time to grieve. I need to do that in a private way now. I might just go away for a while. Ben has worked for a thousand years with no vacation. I'm sure he could get some time off. I thought I might treat us to a few months in Greece or Australia, maybe. Some place very far away. First I have to find out if he's still my guy or not." Charlie knew that Ben would always love him. He just didn't know how that would play out in their real lives.

Charlie enjoyed the normalcy of visiting with his neighbors and the simplicity of a cup of coffee in a friendly kitchen. He felt better than he had in weeks and he thought he could see a glimmer at the end of this dark and harrowing tunnel. He was grateful for that and he was grateful for these friends. And for Ben. Sweet Ben.

By the time Charlie crept over his back fence into his own yard, he could tell that the crowd outside was dispersing. He peeked around the side of his house and saw police cars. Gear was being packed up and reporters were complaining loudly, but they were leaving. That was the important thing. The sound level in his house was almost normal. He looked around for the first time since he came home. It was great to be home. He straightened up, fluffed pillows and brushed his teeth. He crawled into bed with a copy of Vanity Fair, a cup of chamomile tea and a Clif bar. Tomorrow he would see Ben and they would talk. Maybe go away together for a while. For the first time since this horror began, he felt hopeful. He was ready to start his life again with someone he loved so deeply. This would have been the time that he got Lee on the phone to talk for hours and they would laugh at themselves until things weren't quite so serious anymore. He didn't know how to be an adult without Lee. He had never had to before. Could he learn? He guessed he could learn a lot of new things, even at his age. He didn't read for long and was asleep before the tea got cold.

# Chapter 48

Charlie called Ben first thing in the morning to give him the good news about the press. His house and neighborhood remained quiet and undisturbed and he remembered his resolve to keep his mouth shut. He had played into their hands with his outburst and he learned from that. He got Ben's voicemail. He was already at the hospital and he often left his phone in his office when he was on duty. He didn't want it distracting him from his work. Charlie loved that about him. Ben was one of the good guys, that was for sure.

"Hey, dude. Just wanted to let you know that the hordes have left my neighborhood. One of the neighbors is an attorney and he took care of everything. They won't be coming back. I don't think they are camped out anywhere else. I'm not saying another word. Promise. Just wanted to let you know that the coast is clear and I would love to see you. Could you come for dinner tonight? It's a Friday and I know you usually don't have an early call on Saturday mornings, so I thought maybe you could stay over. We'll have a quiet dinner, watch a movie, make popcorn. We haven't done that in ages and it's what I need. Let me know, OK?"

Charlie hung up and started planning what he would do for dinner: steaks, twice-baked potatoes and a caesar salad. Simple. Maybe he would talk Marie out of some of that ice cream. That menu didn't require much prep time, so the rest of his day was free. His house definitely needed some attention and so did his email and the pile of snail-mail that had accumulated. Snail-mail wasn't as important as it used to be, but there was the occasional important piece of the real thing.

He gathered up his laundry to start that process and got out the vacuum cleaner. He thought about how the press had portrayed them in the last couple of weeks. What would they think if they could see him now, doing laundry and running the Dyson? Some evil, glamorous Hollywood faggot he made! The phone rang in the middle of all this and Charlie answered.

"Luke! How great to hear your voice! How are you doing? The Hollywood Troll Brigade still on your tail? "

"It's crazy here. My people are handling most of it. My house has a big fence around it and I've got guards, so the house is secure, but I can't leave without a mob following me everywhere I go."

"We got rid of them here, but I'm not as cool and famous as you are!" Charlie was pleased to hear from Luke. He didn't know if that friendship would hold once he got back to his own world.

"That famous *thang* might be a thing of the past, Charlie. Nashville hasn't exactly rallied to my side since my announcement. My career, if I have one left, will have to take a new turn. I'll no longer be one of the Nashville big, butch, bad boys. Apparently many of the radio stations in the South have been brutal—refusing to play my songs and encouraging people to burn my CD's. Do CD's burn?" Luke's life was coming apart, but he sounded upbeat and unconcerned by what it might mean.

"Oh, Luke. I'm so sorry. You big blabbermouth. You should have kept your trap shut and you would be OK."

"Why you traitor! You sound just like my manager and my agent and my mother! I thought you of all people would get it! I had to take a stand. Finally and forever, to be who I am. Jesus, I was so sick of it all! And Lee is gone, Charlie. What did I have to lose? What did he have to lose? I think he would be proud of me. And I've got enough money saved up to last two lifetimes. If I never make another record, I've done what I wanted to accomplish. So if that chapter is closed, I'll move on to something else. Who knows?"

"I'm sorry Luke. Of course, I support you. You're talking to someone who's been out of the closet for 42 years! I just hate that you have to lose everything you've worked so hard to establish. Your music hasn't changed. YOU haven't changed. All that has really changed is perception. I guess it's all that matters in this country anymore."

"How're you Charlie? Have you heard from Ben? How's he doing with all of this? Are we going to liberate him, too? Should I come out there and work on him?"

Charlie told Luke everything...about the airport and the paparazzi and trying to see each other in secret. Luke had seen Charlie's airport melt down on television. He also told him that he and Ben were having dinner tonight. Charlie expressed his uncertainty about what the future might hold for them.

There was emotion on top of Luke's southern drawl as he responded, "If he's as smart as you say he is, Charlie, he'll make the choice to live his life with you."

"From you mouth to Ben's God's ears. I have no expectations. Ben needs space, but I want him to know where I stand. How're things going with you, my friend?"

"We're still putting out brush fires, but I'm not fooling anyone. The flames are licking the stake! None of that matters now that Lee's gone. I'll be OK, eventually. Lee wouldn't want me to grieve forever and I can't sustain that. My music will come back and I'll have to express that in some way. It probably won't be with a big ole record contract, but that's OK, too! Maybe it's time for my life to get more right-sized. I gotta go. Good luck tonight. Let me know what happens. You've got my cell number, right? Take care, Charlie. I'm glad something good came of all this. We're friends, right?"

"Oh yes, we definitely are, Luke. I wish you would come out for a visit when this dies down. I'll take you over to the Russian River. It's the most beautiful spot in California."

"It's a date. I'll keep my fingers crossed about tonight. Bye, Charlie."

"Hang in there, Luke. I love you."

That made Charlie feel better. He finished the housecleaning and had plenty of time to go to the market, get dinner started, wrap Ben's present and take a nap before he arrived.

Ben showed up about six o'clock. He was later than Charlie had expected him and Charlie began to feel anxious while he was waiting. What was going to happen tonight? He put on a big smile when he opened the door. He was a little shocked when he saw Ben. He was obviously tired and very thin. Charlie hadn't noticed that in the darkened bar at the airport yesterday. All the problems in his life and now in Charlie's life were clearly taking their toll on him. He gave Charlie that million dollar smile anyway. He would always remember Ben standing there on his front steps, looking like that. Moments with Ben were always to be treasured and remembered. He went out to the steps. Ben walked hesitantly at first and then eagerly, as if he had not been sure how he would be received. They held each other in that nonsexual way that people who are truly in love hold each other—that "wow, this is really mine" kind of way.

They stood there for a long time silently. Ben nuzzled his nose into Charlie's neck. Charlie knew that he was getting a good whiff. They loved to smell each other. It may have been the first sense they had of each other. Finally, Ben pulled away, put his hands on Charlie's waist and kissed him— outside, in the daylight in front of the house. Charlie knew what that took for Ben and he appreciated it.

"Come on in. Let's sit a while and talk, then we can eat early, if you want. Poor baby, you look so tired. I always worry about you so. Don't you ever sleep?"

"I'm so used to this Charlie. I've been doing it for years. It's my life. It's what I know. As a kid I picked fruit in the summers. We would get up at four in the morning to get an early start before the day got too hot. It's who I am Charlie. I'm a worker." Ben looked very sad. Charlie hadn't noticed that at first.

Again Charlie realized that the house was so much more alive and purposeful when Ben was there. They sat together on the couch and it was a better couch than when Charlie sat there alone. Later, they would dine in a dining room that only made sense when Ben sat at the table. It was such an odd feeling and Charlie had it every time Ben came into his house. Charlie had been collecting things: furniture, art, other objects that he loved, for years—creating the look that he wanted for his home. Somehow, he had been preparing for the time when Ben would walk in the door; like some part of him knew years ago that Ben McSwain would be a part of his life and was getting ready for that.

"I know that, Ben. I'm sure you know what you are doing. But I love you and that gives me rights and one of those rights is to worry about you. OK? You want a Pepsi?"

"Please, that would be great. Thanks. Just in the can is fine, don't worry about ice." Ben leaned back and put his arm on the back of the sofa and rested his head a minute while Charlie was out of the room. He was not sure he could do this. It was the hardest thing he had ever had to do in his life. He needed to rest first, to enjoy Charlie for a while longer. To make this evening last as long as possible.

"Steaks, potatoes and salad. Homemade pineapple sorbet for dessert drizzled with a little hot Godiva Chocolate sauce. Sound OK?"

"Sounds perfect, Charlie. Everything you do for me is perfect, you know that? No one has ever treated me the way you do. I sometimes feel like I've rubbed a lamp and a genie came out! I don't deserve you, I know that much." Ben was holding Charlie's hand and they were sitting closely together on the couch as they always did. Ben absently caressed Charlie's leg and Charlie felt the bones in Ben's hand, trying to memorize all twenty-seven of them. Ben told him about Pam and about the hospital. He poured out his heart and expressed fears that he couldn't express anywhere else. He had to be so confident and upbeat at home, with Brett and his mother. It was only here, with Charlie, that he could finally let someone share his fears, his insecurities, his humanity.

Dinner was just right. Neither of them were big eaters and the small steaks were perfectly done, Ben's medium well and Charlie's medium rare. The potatoes were a cholesterol nightmare with lots of butter and cheese, but they were Ben's favorite. Charlie had made an extra one, just in case, but Ben didn't ask for more. Charlie loved the salad while Ben pretended to. As Charlie cleared the plates, he reached down and kissed Ben's head, just as he had done that first time Ben came over for dinner. Ben looked up at him. They didn't need to say anything.

Charlie brought out the dessert. It was Marie's homemade sorbet. He suspected that she had made it especially for him. Ben wasn't a big ice cream eater, but Charlie thought he might like this and he did. This time, he did ask for more. When they were finished, they went into the den and climbed onto Charlie's big, doublewide chaise. They both loved this piece of furniture and had figured out how to make it work for them. Ben crawled on first and then Charlie beside him. Ben put his arm around Charlie and they settled in. They had already agreed to watch <u>Brief Encounter</u> again. It was one of Charlie's favorite movies of all time and it was becoming one of Ben's, too. They settled in to enjoy a good film and, perhaps, a good cry.

They sat for a while after the movie was over, not saying anything. The sadness of the film's ending seemed to permeate their mood. Charlie looked at Ben and he saw that he was in agony.

"Which one of us is going to move to South Africa, Charlie? One of us has to. You know that don't you?" Ben made reference to the movie. "I can't do this anymore. I can't do it to you and I can't do it to myself. I'm lying to everyone I know. I can barely look at myself when I shave in the morning. I can't be there for you, either. You had to go through this whole ordeal alone, because I deserted you. You deserve more than that. I love you. You will never know how much. You've changed my life forever, but there are things in my life that are more important, more compelling that my own happiness with you. If I deserted everything I knew to be with you, it would spoil everything. I would learn to resent you and you would resent me. It would be trying to build our happiness on an act of great selfishness. It wouldn't make either of us happy. Oh Charlie. I am so sorry about all of this."

Charlie was shocked. It was not what he was expecting to hear tonight, but a part of him wasn't surprised at all. That part had been expecting something like this from the very beginning. He knew who Ben was and he knew his character. He couldn't do anything else. He felt that odd calmness that comes in a crisis. His voice was clear as he held Ben tightly. "I knew this was coming, baby boy. I knew that you couldn't live like this indefinitely. Oh, part of me hoped that you would just run away from home and play house with me, but I knew that you couldn't do that, not with Pam and your mother. And now

Jacen's getting married and there will be grandchildren. It will go on and on. It's your life. I know that you never meant to hurt me. Neither of us expected any of this. I never expected to love you and I know that it certainly took you by surprise. We're not to blame for this. It just happened and we've both tried to do our best to make it right for ourselves and for each other. But it isn't, is it? Oh, it's right for me. You are the guy I've been waiting all my life for. And I'll always be grateful to you. Now, when people talk about soulmates and true love, I won't be cynical anymore. I'll know exactly what they are talking about, because I finally met mine. So I don't get to keep you forever, but at least I met you and got to know you. That's more than most people get. And Ben, I will always love you and my home will always be your home. I bought a gift for you in Texas that had a different meaning when I bought it, but I want to give it to you anyway."

Charlie got up and brought the gift over to Ben. "There is a local jeweler in Dallas that everyone uses. I had forgotten about it until I got there. Their pieces are so unique and beautiful, so I went to their showroom and had this done for you."

Ben smiled at Charlie as he opened the gift. It was a beautiful silver chain and on it were some charms. There was a small hand signing the ASL symbol for "I Love You." There was a little palm tree, just because Ben and Charlie both loved palm trees and there was a tiny silver key. There was no need to explain any of it. He got it.

Then Charlie said, "That key will always work on my door, no matter where I am. My home will always be your home should you find your way to me someday. I called off the search when I found you."

Ben got up and went to the front door. For a moment Charlie thought that he was going to leave, but he came back. He had just gone to his car to get a small gift-wrapped package. He handed it to Charlie.

"You're not the only one who can do gifts! I got this for you a while back and didn't know when I was going to give it to you and tonight seemed like the right time."

They returned to the den and crawled back onto their chaise. Charlie tore the paper eagerly from the package. "I don't suppose I should get my hopes up for an engagement ring, should I?"

"Gosh, I should have thought of that!"

Charlie opened the hinged box. Inside was a watch, exactly like the one Ben wore and which Charlie had admired on more than one occasion. "Oh Ben, it's perfect. Thank you so much. It will always remind me of you."

"Look on the back. There's an inscription."

It said "For Charlie: Everything, Ben"

It was Charlie's turn to weep. This really was good-bye. He knew that now. There would not be any more phone calls wanting to make it work. This was really going to be it. They sat quietly together for a while. Neither seemed to know what to say. Finally Ben broke the silence.

"I guess I should go, Charlie, under the circumstances." He started gathering up wrapping paper.

"Could I ask something of you, Ben? Stay with me tonight, please? One last time? Let's not end it like this. Let me hold you tonight and wake up in the middle of the night to your warmth. Let me have the joy of smelling the skin on your shoulder first thing in the morning. Please don't go. Let's end this with love the way it began."

"Oh Charlie, I wanted to stay. I just didn't want to make it any harder on you. Of course, I'll stay. I want this as much as you do."

They left the paper and the gifts on the chaise and went to the bedroom. The undressed each other carefully, for the last time. Remembering each touch, each caress. They made love as they always did, softly, quietly and gently. Sex wasn't fireworks for Charlie and Ben; it was candlelight. They held each other tightly after, neither of them really sleeping, too much aware of each other to miss a moment.

Around seven o'clock, Charlie got up to turn on the coffee. As he came back into the room, he looked at his darling Ben in his bed for the last time. He stood there for several minutes. When you love someone, they are just the most beautiful thing in the world.

"You're doing that again, honey." Ben's voice was deep with emotion and he had used the "h" word on purpose.

Charlie climbed back into bed and Ben spooned him. Charlie wanted to remember this feeling forever. It might be the last time he would feel complete. And that is what he felt: completion. Ben made him whole in a way he had never felt before.

Then Ben turned and got out of bed. Charlie didn't turn over and look at him, but got out on his own side. He picked up his jeans from the night before and Ben started dressing, too. Charlie had hoped that they might have breakfast or something, but how much longer could they ignore the inevitable truth? Now was as good a time as any. Ben finished dressing while Charlie made them coffee. They took their cups and went into the living room. Charlie had cleaned up the den and brought their gifts to the coffee table. Ben put on the silver chain.

"Charlie, I'll treasure this all of my life. No matter where I am or what I do. I'll keep this with me to remind me that I have a soulmate out there."

"Ditto, dude" Charlie choked as he said the words, their little in-joke. Ben got up from the sofa, moving toward the front door.

Charlie couldn't believe it was really happening. This was going to be the last time they saw each other. He wanted it to be right. He didn't want to get hysterical and he felt that building inside him. His heart was screaming, "Don't go! Don't leave me! Please choose me! Please choose us!" But Charlie didn't say those things. He walked with Ben to the door and opened it. Ben walked through, stood on the steps and turned back to Charlie. He smiled like the first time and Charlie smiled back. Then he turned down the path and to his car. He stopped as he opened the car door and looked at Charlie again and at the house, as if memorizing that moment. Charlie ran down the path and to the car. He pulled Ben to him and kissed him fiercely. Ben returned the kiss. It was as if they were both drowning and only that kiss could save them. They broke finally and Charlie said,

"Try to forget that, dude!"

And Ben smiled sadly, "I couldn't even if I wanted to, dude."

Charlie walked back to his front porch. Ben pulled out of the driveway. They waved. Ben couldn't see that Charlie was falling apart. But he was.

Charlie didn't see Ben pull over a block away and cry out his broken heart. It was fifteen minutes before he pulled away and headed for home.

# Chapter 49

It was Ben's birthday; he was forty-seven years old. He thought back to this day last year and what a year it had been! His mother, Jacen, Pam's tragic loss—the suffering and heartbreak of his family was his own. And he found the inner strength to shoulder that heartbreak and sustain the people who mattered most to him. And it was this day last year that he had met Charlie. For better or worse, he had found love in the most forbidden place. He could admit that is was love, but he could also acknowledge that it was wrong and end it. Most importantly, he could face himself in the mirror today and know he had done the right thing.

Three months ago, when he left Charlie's house for the last time, he didn't know if this day would ever come again. He had almost turned around several times on the journey home and gone back to Charlie's to take him up on his offer. His heart wanted to live in that little house, work at his job, be happy and love Charlie Morgan. It would have been so easy. All he had to do was walk through Charlie's front door. But he didn't do it. He couldn't do it. All of his training, his upbringing, the world he knew wouldn't let him. These last few months had been agonizing. Everything reminded him of Charlie. He had to avoid certain stores, even certain aisles in the grocery, because they were all about Charlie. People noticed that he wasn't himself. Friends commented that he seemed to be grieving as he did when Lynette died. This was a death, too. It wasn't a breakup that might have involved hard feelings and people who were no longer in love. This wasn't like that. Charlie only wanted what was best for Ben and Ben, of course, felt the same. They still loved each other. Even now, all these months later, Ben knew that Charlie loved him and was probably thinking of him at this very moment—on his birthday. The days went by and no one knew about Charlie, so that didn't confront him. His job and his family kept him busy and occupied.

Pam was improving. She had come home from Riverwood two weeks ago. Although she still had a way to go until she was her old self again, Ben knew that she was coming back to them. He wondered if she would ever be her "old self" again. Does anyone ever return to a self that they once were? Or do they become something new, someone wiser and more mature than before? That's what Ben hoped for Pam. Brett was happy just to have her home. Ben had thought they were too young when they married, but they had proved him wrong. Their marriage thrived and they were closer to each other than ever. Ben hoped they would try for another baby when they were ready. He wanted Pam to have that joy in her life. It had been his greatest joy and the source of his strength.

His mother was not going to get better. That was just the fact of it. You don't recover from Ahlzeimer's. You just slowly and inexorably slip away from everything and everyone. But Alvah was not gone yet and Ben had moved her in with him. He wanted to enjoy her company for as long as he could. She understood what was happening and had agreed to the move, even seemed happy and relieved by it. She and Ben had settled into a loving routine. She fussed and cleaned and cooked and he let her. When he came home from work at night she would feed him impossibly unhealthy meals. Then they would sit together and talk. She knew that it might not be possible to do this much longer and words poured from her. She told Ben about her childhood growing up on a farm near Fresno. She told him about his Irish immigrant great-grandparents that he had never known. She confided in him about the heartbreak of losing a child.

And they finally talked about being abandoned by Ben's father. He walked out the door of their house and never looked back. She had seen him in court for the divorce, but they never really spoke again. Ben had seen him a couple of times as an adult, but he had only said hello, as you would to a stranger or the friend of a friend. He knew he should feel something, even anger, but he didn't. There was just nothing there. He often wondered if it had some kind of influence in his life that he was not aware of. Truthfully, he rarely thought of his father at all. Alvah had made up for his absence and Ben loved her for it.

Jacen was still back east and would be released from the Marine Corps soon. At one time, he had thought of making it a career. Now that he and Catherine were to be married in August, he looked to other options. He had finished his degree while in the service and they would both start graduate school in the fall. Jacen had a job lined up and Catherine's parents were, he felt sure, generously contributing to the kids' welfare. At first Ben was annoyed and alarmed by their help because he thought it was important for Jacen to make his own way in the world. Yet it was a golden opportunity for his son. He seemed to have a splendid future ahead. Jacen was a good man and the love and generosity of his in-laws would not corrupt that. Ben realized that he needed to let go.

Lynette was gone. Ben thought of her now without grief and with a calm affection. He looked back on their life together and realized that their greatest accomplishment was the children. The love he felt for her and not been very romantic, but familial somehow. It had been very special, but it was a naive, young love and not the stuff of great passion. They were virgins when they married. Lovemaking was pleasant enough for them, but neither pressed it ever and they never talked about it. He wondered, if she had lived, what their life would have been like now, with the children gone. What would they have had in common? She was the mother of his children and the sweet companion of his youth. She would always hold those places in his heart.

Ben had learned what real love was somewhere else and he knew that it had not been in his marriage. He had put his family and his beliefs first in his life. He had done the right thing. On this his mind was at peace. But his heart! That was another matter entirely. His heart was wherever Charlie Morgan was at this moment, where he could never be. Around his neck was the silver chain with the three small tokens. He was never without it, even in V-neck scrubs where it showed. No one had ever even mentioned it. His mother and the children didn't even seem to notice. Other things from Charlie, reminders of their time together, were tucked away in a box on a shelf in his closet. Sometimes, at night just before bed, he would take the box down and open it. He would take out the objects, a CD, a little ceramic box, a silver band, ticket stubs from the theatre, the iPod shuffle and a flash drive full of pictures and cards and memories. And there were the things that Charlie had given him that surrounded him every day: the palm tree towels, the colognes, the shirts and a baby blue cashmere sweater. These little treasures reminded Ben that it had been real. Each little memento was perfect in it's own way. Each proved to Ben that Charlie knew him inside and out. He knew all of Ben's senses, the sights, the sounds, the smells that were essential Ben McSwain. He marveled that someone knew him so well, someone so different from him and meant for him. He knew better than to dwell on these talismans. It would lead to dreaming of the possibilities with Charlie and he couldn't do that again. He couldn't allow himself to dream of Charlie.

He was very clear about his path. His family and his religion meant everything to him. He believed in the reality of heaven and hell, of sin and redemption. He knew that what he had done with Charlie was a sin. He also knew that he could be redeemed and spend eternity with those he loved, and to deserve that, to earn that, he had to give up Charlie. It was the hardest thing he had ever done in his life, but the path he had chosen never claimed to be easy. He couldn't live without paradise. So the callous of his faith closed around his tender and hesitant heart, forever denying him the love and life that Charlie had offered.

# Chapter 50

Charlie looked around at all the boxes, some of them already taped and ready for the movers and others still open and wanting to be filled with Charlie's life. He had been thinking about Ben all day. It was his birthday and exactly one year ago they had met on a train. He had thought about sending him a card or a gift of some kind. But to what end? What did he hope to accomplish? Ben knew that he was thinking of him. He knew that Charlie was there. That final kiss, hopefully, forever remembered and burned in his brain. He continued to wrap glassware and place it carefully in a box. He had two more days before the movers would come to take his things to his new home in Portland.

Somewhat ruefully, he referred to it as "Johannesburg" because of the movie <u>Brief Encounter</u>. Moving had been the solution for one of the characters and Charlie understood that completely. He couldn't bear staying here anymore. It was too close to Ben. Many times he had almost gotten in his car and driven to Goldmine, just to be near him. He had Googled a map to Ben's house. He had memorized how to get there, even though he had never been there before. He couldn't go by a restaurant they had shared or a store where they had shopped without reliving the time they had together. His heart stopped every time he saw a dark red car, even if it wasn't a Jaguar. He needed a new start in a new town. Work had taken him to Portland several times in the last few years and he had always found it charming and inviting. He could work anywhere he wanted and Portland offered an environment where his heart could begin to heal. He was looking forward to the change, but it meant really saying good-bye to Ben.

Charlie always held Ben's head when he kissed him. And he looked at him. Hard. Every time. He wanted to memorize the strangeness of his geography. So different from the planet of Charlie. He learned Ben well. The scent of his hair, the colors of his skin, the texture of his unshaven cheek on his lips. And he was glad that he had paid so much attention. For now that it was over, he had Ben in his sense memory forever.

He collapsed inside when Ben left. He walked back into the house and into the bedroom where the bed was still unmade and Ben's presence was everywhere. His knees gave way. He ended up holding onto the edge of the bed like a supplicant in prayer. He put his face into the sheets and breathed Ben into his lungs. He knew it was truly over this time. There had been other times when it had just gotten too hard on Ben to continue and too difficult for Charlie to live with such a small piece of his life, but they had always found each other again, unable to give up what seemed so difficult yet so "miraculous." When Charlie had first used that word to describe their relationship, Ben had looked upset. It occurred to Charlie that their relationship was anything but a "miracle" in Ben's world and according to his rules. But it was a miracle to Charlie. He had waited so long to find him.

He knew he had to honor Ben's wishes now. Something he had said made all the difference in the world. He had mentioned that he "couldn't look himself in the mirror." That brought home so literally to Charlie exactly what this relationship had been doing to Ben. It had been tearing him in two. It was so easy for Charlie. He just loved him and wanted to be with him. To Charlie, it was as simple as Ben putting his shirts next to his in the closet, yet it was anything but easy for Ben. Charlie finally got that. It was the only thing that kept him from using that map and going to Goldmine and begging Ben not to throw it all away.

Charlie knew that one of the things that had attracted them to each other was the recognition that they were both good, decent, moral people. One atheist, one Christian who, together, would have made a good, decent, moral couple. But Ben's religion couldn't acknowledge that morality can exist outside of a religious contruct. If you truly believe that God is love, what purpose does it serve Him to put someone in your life who is perfect for you, who makes you happy and who loves you completely, only to tell you that you must turn your back on him because it's a sin? What Charlie really wanted to ask him was what kind of God would ask you to do this? And why? That isn't love. It's perverse and sadistic. It made no sense to Charlie.

But of course, this wasn't about making sense. This was about faith and faith has nothing to do with logic or sense or personal experience. It has to do with deciding to believe in something and then holding on to that belief no matter what. That's what Ben had done. Charlie didn't believe in religion or God. He believed that Ben would have been the same sweet, wonderful, gentle, moral, good man that he is even if he had never heard of religion.

Charlie believed people are intrinsically moral and good and that is enough of an explanation. We don't have to assign the credit to some mythical power. But he also believed that people have a right to express their spiritual beliefs in any way they choose. Yet sometimes a religious sect decides that they have the one true answer and exerts force to bend others to their beliefs. This is the source of most of the hatred, cruelty, bloodshed and war in the history of the world and Charlie thought that it was time for that to stop.

It was an irony that his "live and let live" attitude was what ultimately led to his letting go of Ben. He had never argued about religion with Ben. He didn't want to argue. He didn't want to change Ben. He just wished that Ben's beliefs hadn't excluded the possibility of their love. But it was Ben's life and his choice to make. And, if Charlie were to remain true to what he believed, he would have to let Ben remain true to himself also.

Charlie continued to wrap dishes. He had been through these arguments a thousand times since Ben drove away from his house. It was always the same. His arguments for their relationship were perfectly logical. They made sense of everything as Ben's presence in Charlie's house had made sense of his furniture. But this wasn't about making sense.

And it wasn't about the furniture anymore, either. Charlie looked around the now-barren living room. He had sold most of his furniture on Craig's List. He had decided that he needed to start over. He would buy new things in his new home in Portland. He was just packing up the personal things he had decided to keep: his mother's crystal, the flatware from his sister and some small appliances. There was the box of his memories of Ben. A medium sized cardboard box was what remained of the great love of his life. He had opened it earlier and tears came to his eyes when he saw the familiar beloved artifacts of life with Ben. He had closed the box, sealed it with tape and marked it for the movers. It was still too early to look through it and certainly too soon to part with it. So it would go to Portland with him. Perhaps there, in his new environment, he would be able to open the box, remember the joy that those things represented and be at peace with his love for Ben.

He had tried going out on a date. It was a disaster and he wouldn't do that again after the move. There were people out there looking for love. He just wasn't one of them. He would concentrate on friendships, work and those artistic passions that brought comfort and rich texture to his life. The connection with Ben was perfect. No, there was no need to look for love again.

He had his "family" and they needed him. He was filling in as best he could with Lee's sisters. He would go back to Texas regularly to care for them. Jim had taken a new job in Oregon not far from where Charlie would be. They were looking forward to being closer than they had been in years. That proximity made the future less fearful for them both. And John and Dru would each offer him a unique sense of home with them that would continue even after the move. Luke Beecham was living in Santa Rosa now, teaching music and writing songs. His audience was certainly much smaller, but he had a loyal following and the music was just as beautiful as ever. He found that he loved teaching. A deep friendship had come from their shared sorrow and Luke found a place at Charlie's family table. Charlie looked at a life that was filled with love and was grateful for it.

And this wasn't about how to stop loving Ben. That wasn't possible. He would always love Ben. That hunger for love he had felt all his life was sated. The pangs in his heart were quieted because Ben had filled it. He had sensed from the beginning that this would be the great love of his life. And it had been life-altering. He had learned that you don't choose love and that it isn't so much a feeling as it is an action. Love requires your energy as well as your heart. And sometimes that action is letting go and sometimes the energy required is for that task.

He wrapped the last of the stemware and placed it carefully in the box marked "Portland." He sealed the box and surveyed the result of his work. Nothing remained of the warm cozy home that seemed so right for him and for Ben. There were bare floors and blank walls and stacks of boxes. It was all the same color now, like a manila envelope. Still hanging from the front window was a small faceted crystal heart that Ben had given him and Charlie had forgotten to take down. It caught the sunlight and, magically, that cardboard colored room was awash with rainbows of light. A sweet kind of sadness filled him. Standing in that rainbow that Ben had given him he knew that he would find peace of mind in his life and joy in his work again. He would accept living the rest of his life without Ben. Charlie would learn to live without paradise, but, oh, for a moment, it had been his!

Lightning Source UK Ltd.
Milton Keynes UK
171546UK00002B/98/P